THE SILVER DOLPHIN

When nineteen-year-old Rachel Devon was left orphaned and inexperienced on a lonely Caribbean island, she was rescued by Niall Herrick, skipper of the yacht *Silver Dolphin*. Niall thought he had found a solution to Rachel's problems — but would it necessarily make her happy?

Books by Anne Weale in the
Ulverscroft Large Print Series:

CASTLE IN CORSICA
THE HOUSE OF SEVEN FOUNTAINS
SOUTH FROM SOUNION
THE MAN IN COMMAND
THE SILVER DOLPHIN

———————◆———————

This Large Print Edition
is published by kind permission of
MILLS & BOON LTD.
London

ANNE WEALE

THE SILVER DOLPHIN

Complete and Unabridged

ULVERSCROFT
Leicester

First published 1963

First Large Print Edition
published February 1975
SBN 85456 315 6

This special large print edition is
made and printed in England for
F. A. Thorpe, Glenfield, Leicestershire

CHAPTER ONE

ON the eighth day after the hurricane, Rachel was returning to the village from one of her solitary, aimless walks when, from the top of the ridge path, she saw that a ship was lying in the lagoon. She was a small trysail-rigged schooner, painted white and with an old-fashioned figurehead above her bowsprit. With a swift upsurge of relief, Rachel recognised the *Silver Dolphin*.

She was waiting on the island's landing-stage when the schooner's dinghy put out and, even at a distance, there was no mistaking the man seated in the stern. Just now, scrambling down from the ridge, she had wondered if the *Dolphin* might have changed hands.

The outboard motor cutting out, the dinghy swung in towards the jetty. But, as the islanders crowded forward to welcome their visitors — the children plunging into the water and splashing excitedly about, like so many boisterous puppies — Rachel hung back. Suddenly her relief at this unforeseen good fortune had given place to shyness and uncertainty.

One of the newcomers was a coloured man, the other a European. The West Indian, a grinning young giant with the physique of his warrior ancestors, was wearing tattered khaki shorts and a rakishly angled yachting cap. His companion, also very tall and with a similar breadth of shoulder, was more formally dressed in a blue cotton shirt and white drill slacks.

Pushing through the crowd to where she stood, he said, "Hello, Rachel. How are you?"

If he had come upon her unexpectedly, Rachel would probably have flung herself into his arms. Now, forewarned, but still unprepared to meet him again, she found herself answering stiffly, "Good afternoon, Captain Herrick. How nice to see you again."

They shook hands and, as his lean brown fingers closed firmly on her own smaller ones, Captain Herrick looked her over with a kind of amused curiosity. It was the way he had looked at her before. Now, as then, she found it oddly disturbing.

2

"So the hurricane hit Anguna?" he remarked, after a moment, with a gesture at the newly built jetty.

Rachel nodded. "Yes . . . We had quite a bad night." She cleared her throat. "Will you come up to the house?"

Like the jetty, the islanders' palmetto-thatched cabins had all been recently rebuilt. On the morning after the hurricane, not one hut or fishing boat had remained intact. It had been as if some monstrous sea beast had risen from the depths of the ocean and tried to trample the island out of existence.

On the way to the Devons' bungalow — all the naked, dripping youngsters now scampering ahead up the slope — Captain Herrick picked up one of the smaller children.

Perching her high on his shoulder, he talked to her in the soft sing-song idiom of the islanders. He had not changed, Rachel saw. Perhaps the lines round his eyes — lines that came from a lifetime spent sailing these glittering Bahamian waters — were a fraction more marked than six months ago. But, otherwise, he was just as she remembered him: his thick dark hair as closely

3

cropped as before, his eyebrows still tilting when he grinned, his eyes as vividly blue in the strong-boned, sea-bronzed face.

Sheltered by a low bluff and built of coral-rock slabs, the Devons' bungalow had survived the onslaught of the hurricane without serious damage. The garden had been laid waste and a storage shed smashed into kindling sticks, but the house itself had stood firm.

The children having been shooed back to the village, Rachel led the way into the simple but pleasant living-room, and called Octavia from the kitchen.

The Devons' big, brown-skinned cook had been dozing in the sun on the veranda. But when she ambled through the door and saw their guest, her yawn changed quickly to a beam.

"Cap'n Herrick! Ah is surely glad to see yo', sah," she exclaimed delightedly. "Youse done come jus' de very time us needs yo'."

"I have? What's your problem, Octavia?" he asked smilingly, as she wrung his hand in her own almost equally powerful one.

Octavia's beam faded as she flickered an anxious glance at Rachel.

4

"De Cap'n . . . he don' know yet?" she asked.

Rachel shook her head. "Octavia, will you make us some tea, please? — Unless you'd prefer a rum punch, Captain Herrick?"

His eyes narrowed slightly. "Tea for me, thanks. Mind if I smoke?"

"Of course not — and do sit down."

As soon as Octavia had left them, he said quietly, "What don't I know yet, Rachel? Is it something to do with your father?"

She swallowed, then turned away so that he should not see her mouth working.

"Father's dead," she explained, very low. "He . . . he was killed in the hurricane."

"Killed? You mean he was at sea when the 'blow' struck?"

Rachel's hands were in the pockets of her salt-stained cotton shorts. She clenched her fists, her nails digging into her palms. She must not let him see her cry.

"No, he wasn't out fishing that night," she said, in a taut voice. "We guessed a 'blow' was coming, so we were all up here in the house. One of the women was having a baby and they put her in my room to be out of the crush. I thought Father was with her. I was busy with the children, you see. They were all terrified, poor mites. There were times when it seemed as if even these walls would give way. When . . . when it was over, we were all so exhausted, we just slept."

Her voice cracked, and it was some moments before she could go on. "I — I didn't wake up till quite late. Everyone had gone back to the village and . . . and the sun was shining. Then Octavia told me what had happened. One of the little boys had been missing, you see, and Father had gone out to search for him. They were found in the scrub behind the village. The boy was alive . . . but my father had been struck on the head by something."

There was silence for some moments while Rachel knuckled her eyes and blew her nose. She was grateful that Captain Herrick did not attempt to comfort her. When Octavia came back with the tea tray, she had recovered herself.

"What about you? Was the *Dolphin* caught in the 'blow'?" she asked steadily.

Captain Herrick took a cigarette from an old tobacco tin and lit it with a battered

6

metal storm lighter. "No, fortunately, we dodged it," he said. Then, when she had poured a cup of tea for him: "Have you thought about the future yet, Rachel?"

"I suppose I shall have to leave here," she said, with a sigh.

"Don't you want to?"

"I've never really thought about it before."

"What were your father's plans?"

She frowned slightly. "I don't think he had any. He never discussed the future — or the past. We were happy here, so we lived from day to day. Isn't that the best way to live?"

"Yes — up to a point, I daresay. But I don't think your father can have intended to remain on Anguna indefinitely, you know. Surely he must have made some reference to *your* future?"

"He did occasionally ask me if I was happy," Rachel agreed reflectively. "I always told him I was, and he accepted it."

"Perhaps in his will — "

"He didn't leave one — at least there's nothing in his deed box. Octavia brought it to me the other day and made me go through it. There are some papers from a

7

bank in Nassau — I don't really understand them — but there's nothing at all to help me decide what to do."

Herrick sat silent for a while. "Look, I don't want to pry . . ." he began.

"Oh, please — ask anything you like. I'll be only too glad of your advice," Rachel put in swiftly. Then, in a wry tone, "But I don't think there's much I can tell you. As I said, after we came to Anguna, my father never talked about the past."

"Do you know why you came here in the first place?"

She shrugged. "Not really. It was such a long time ago — ten years. I do dimly remember living in England before that, but I've no idea why we left."

"Do you know *where* you lived in England?" he asked.

"Oh, yes — in London. It was all very different from Anguna. We had a house with lots of stairs and tall windows. My rooms were right up at the top, and I only went down to the grown-ups' part on special occasions. I hardly ever saw my mother — or father, in those days."

"You had a nurse to take care of you?" he asked keenly.

8

"I think so — when I was small. But after I went to school the maids looked after me."

"What about your mother?"

"Oh, she went away somewhere when I was about seven."

"She died?"

Rachel shook her head. "No, I don't think so. She hadn't been ill. She just . . . went," she said perplexedly.

Captain Herrick lit another cigarette, his expression speculative. "From what you say, it sounds like a fairly prosperous household. Have you any idea what your father was . . . his profession, I mean?"

Once again Rachel had to shake her head. "I know it must sound strange — my knowing so little about him," she said slowly. "But you see I could sense that he didn't want to talk about our other life, so I never questioned him. I have sometimes wondered if he might have been a doctor. The islanders always came to him when they were sick, and he even looked after the women when their babies were born." She hesitated a moment. "I read in a book once about a doctor being struck off the register for doing something illegal. Do you

9

think *that* could have been the reason why Father had to leave England and hide himself away ?"

Captain Herrick reflected for a moment.

"It's possible, I suppose. But having met your father, I don't think it at all probable."

Octavia came back for the tea things, and he rose to his feet. "You look pretty worn out, Rachel. Why don't you try to sleep for a couple of hours ?" he said to her.

"Dat's a soun' suggestion, Cap'n Herrick," Octavia agreed approvingly. "Dis chile ain't slept good since that big blow done come. So yo' go an' do like de Cap'n tells yo', Missy Rachel, and Ah'll make youse gumbo for yo' supper."

"Well, I do feel a bit worn out," Rachel admitted, glad of a pretext to deal with her dusty feet and unkempt hair. She had not bothered to comb it after her morning swim, and it hung down her back in an uncomely salt-sticky tangle.

In her room she shed her crumpled shirt and shorts and stretched out on the bed, intending to relax for a few minutes before starting to tidy herself. But, as Octavia had said, she had had scarcely any sleep since the shock of her father's tragic death. Almost immediately her eyelids began to flicker.

While Rachel slept, Niall Herrick strolled down the path to the beach, his hands thrust into his pockets, a preoccupied expression on his lean dark face.

Presently, relaxing on the sand, his shirt stripped off and draped carelessly over a rock, he lit another cigarette and lay back, one hand cupped under his head. As he lay there, his eyes closed, smoking, a slight smile suddenly twitched at the corners of his firm and rather cynical mouth.

Once before he had stretched out near this post, and on that occasion, half asleep in the sun, he had been roused by a shellful of sea water being trickled over him. He had opened his eyes expecting to find some Angunan imp standing over him, but it had been Rachel.

Rachel holding a large conch, her brown eyes sparkling with mischief, her slender body poised for flight.

He had chased her down to the water, mastered her wild wriggles to escape, and punished her with a ducking. She had come up gasping and laughing, her long hair streaming over her shoulders like a mermaid's, her engaging freckled face glowing with health and happiness as she challenged him to race her out to the reef.

He had regarded her as a child then. She had had none of the precocious awareness of her femininity which was common to much younger girls in the world beyond Anguna. But she had not been wholly a child, he remembered. One evening he had caught her studying him, and had been amused to see a faint blush deepening her tan. Afterwards she had been a little shy with him — except when her buoyant vitality prompted her to another outbreak of youthful tomfoolery.

Poor little devil! She had lost that gay grin now, he thought grimly. And she was as incapable of fending for herself as a kitten in a jungle.

Burying his cigarette end in the sand, he stood up and unbuckled his belt. A few minutes later he was cutting through the water with a powerful racing crawl.

It was more than an hour later when a high-pitched female voice roused Rachel from her sleep. It was not Octavia's voice, nor that of any of the island women. That strident tone and clipped enunciation could only belong to a certain type of English-woman. Fully awake now, Rachel groaned. *Oh, lord !* It must be Miss Finch.

The voice receded into the distance and Rachel swung off the bed, wrapped herself in a large towel and pattered down the passage to the bath house.

Most of the time she and her father had washed in the sea like the islanders, but for the occasional luxury of fresh water bath-ing, Charles Devon had installed a second rain storage tank which piped into an antiquated hip bath.

Fifteen minutes later, in a clean checked shirt and faded jeans — her clothes were all boys' things, and it was nine years since she had last worn a dress — Rachel combed out her tousled wet hair. Then, peering at herself in the mirror, she plaited it into a single sun-bleached blonde braid.

She was now nineteen years old and, until a few weeks earlier, it had never occurred to her that she was different from other white girls.

Lying far to the south of the larger, more

developed Bahamas islands, Anguna rarely saw outsiders. But, not long ago, a luxurious diesel cabin cruiser had called at the quiet little cay. There had been no women on board, but one of the visitors — American businessmen on a marlin-fishing trip — had given Rachel some candies and a pile of magazines. And it had been the illustrations and advertisements in these magazines which had made her realise that she was not only different from other girls, but probably unique.

The girls in the photographs had complexions like pale or faintly flushed flower petals. Rachel's skin was more the colour of a widely advertised breakfast cereal — a deep golden brown, with a dusting of freckles on her nose. The girls in the pictures all had short, silky, curling hair. Not one of them had a long thick pigtail tied round with any odd bit of twine. The girls in the pictures had delicately tinted eyelids, and glistening red lips, and long lacquered fingernails. Rachel's brown eyes were often red-rimmed from prolonged skin-diving along the coral reefs, but even when they were not, they never had the provocative long-lashed gleam of those other girls' eyes.

Her mouth was an untouched healthy pink; her nails short, and sometimes broken from scrambling about among the rocks.

Now, looking at some of the pictures which she had pinned to the bedroom wall and comparing them with the reflection in her mirror, it was all too clear why Captain Herrick had seemed to find her somewhat amusing the first time he had seen her — and again this morning.

When she was ready — her usually bare feet thrust into cheap straw mules — she went to find Octavia.

"Dat Mission Lady done come," Octavia told her sourly, stirring the contents of a big, blackened cooking pot.

"Yes, I know. I heard her. Where's Captain Herrick?"

"He gone down to the village. Don' you worry, he come back soon." Octavia dipped a ladle into the gumbo — a thick okra-based soup flavoured with chicken giblets — tasted it, and threw in some more herbs.

Rachel went through to the front veranda and sat on the steps, hoping Captain Herrick would come back before "dat Mission Lady" descended on her.

However it was Miss Eveline Finch who

returned to the bungalow first, her tall angular figure coming briskly along the path under a bobbing waxed paper parasol.

Miss Finch and her brother, the Reverend Theodore Finch, ran a mission station on one of the larger islands some miles away. Normally, they called at Anguna about twice a year, and it was not long since their last visit. Presumably it was news of the hurricane which had brought them back again so soon.

"Oh, my poor, bereaved child. What can I say to give you solace?" Miss Finch exclaimed dramatically, as Rachel stood up to shake hands with her. "You should have sent us word *immediately*, my dear. Had I known you were here on your own I would have been quite frantic with anxiety. Luckily, the hurricane did not strike Cay Mini."

"But I've often been here alone when Father was away on a fishing trip," Rachel said calmly.

Miss Finch pursed her lips. "Yes, I know, and I must say I most strongly disapprove of your being left without protection. However that is all in the past now, so we need say no more about it. Ah, here

16

comes Theodore. Now, first, let us all go into the house and say a quiet prayer together."

Although she supposed that Miss Finch meant well, after half an hour of her company Rachel was taut with irritation. If she had wanted to share her grief, she would have turned to Octavia. It was sickening hypocrisy for Miss Finch to pretend all this affliction for a man she had always disliked. Even more annoying was her way of referring to the cheerful, placid-natured Angunans as if they were a pack of bloodthirsty savages. It was a relief when Captain Herrick returned.

"Who is that man? Why has he come to Anguna?" Miss Finch hissed suspiciously when, some time later, the two men had moved out on to the veranda.

"Captain Herrick? Oh, he called here about six months ago. I suppose he came back to look us up," Rachel said vaguely.

Miss Finch sniffed. "I don't like the look of him," she said darkly.

Rachel stared at her. "Why not? What do you mean?"

Miss Finch shook a finger at her. "You must try to curb this rather contentious manner of yours, my dear," she said, chidingly. "When your elders express an opinion, it is not at all polite to dispute their views."

"But I want to know what you mean," Rachel persisted.

Miss Finch pursed her thin lips. "Let it suffice to say that Captain Herrick is *not* the type of person whose acquaintance I would wish to cultivate," she said in a repressive tone.

And, before Rachel could press for a more explicit explanation, Octavia announced that their supper was ready.

As soon as her brother had said grace — and after she had discreetly assured herself that the cutlery was clean — Miss Finch began briskly, "I think, Theodore, that as soon as you have performed the proper funeral office at poor Mr. Devon's grave tomorrow, we will return directly to the Mission. I am sure poor Rachel cannot wish to stay in this unhappy place a moment longer than is necessary."

"But, Miss Finch — " Rachel began protestingly.

"Ah, you are thinking that you must not be a burden to us," the missioner's sister said understandingly. "Well, you need have no qualms on *that* score, my dear. After a few weeks' training in the work of our Mission clinic, you will be a most useful addition to our busy little community. Don't you agree with me, Theodore?"

"Why, yes, indeed — most certainly," her brother assented, rather jumpily. He had been lost in enjoyment of Octavia's rich, spicy gumbo, and the question had startled him. However as he always did agree with Eveline's opinions, it did not really matter that he had missed whatever she had been saying.

"Then it's all settled," Miss Finch said decisively. "We'll return to Cay Mini immediately after lunch." She looked across the table. "And when do you plan to leave Anguna, Captain Herrick?" she enquired, with a disapproving glance at the tall glass or rum and ginger ale which Octavia had brought in for him.

Herrick lifted the glass and extended it towards her, bowing slightly. "Your very good health, Miss Finch," he said gallantly. Then, as her cheeks flushed red with annoyance, "I'm sailing on the midnight tide."

"So soon?" Rachel asked in dismay. Last time, he had spent two nights on the island.

"Why, yes, I think so," he said casually. "I only came here to see you and your father. If you're going off with Miss Finch tomorrow. . . ." He finished the sentence with a gesture.

Rachel watched Octavia clear away the plates, a feeling of panic rising in her. Oh, confound the Finches! Why had they had to turn up today, before she had made any plans? Anyway she certainly wasn't going back to the Mission with them: her life would be made utterly miserable there. Miss Finch would probably expect her to wear the same prim long-sleeved dresses that she wore herself — perhaps white cotton stockings as well. And, once in their debt, how would she ever get away? Oh no — the idea was quite unthinkable.

"Captain Herrick, do you ever carry passengers?" she burst out abruptly.

"Why, yes — if they're prepared to rough it with us."

"Could you — would you take me?" Rachel asked imploringly.

Miss Finch gasped. "*Rachel*! What a

ridiculous question. Of course Captain Herrick cannot take you anywhere. You are coming to the Mission with us."

"But I don't *want* to go with you," Rachel said bluntly. "Oh, I appreciate the kindness of your offer, but — "

"It is not a question of kindness. It is our duty," Miss Finch said firmly.

"Perhaps that's why she doesn't want to go with you," Captain Herrick suggested flippantly.

Miss Finch's sallow complexion took on a curiously mottled purple hue. "There is no need to be rude, Captain."

"That wasn't my intention," he said evenly. "But since Rachel doesn't wish to go to the Mission — "

"Rachel must do as we think best for her," the missioner's sister cut in sharply. "As I have already told her, she is far too young and inexperienced to be cast adrift outside, Anguna. Later, when she is of age — "

"But, Miss Finch, if anyone has to look after me, surely it ought to be my own relatives," Rachel broke in, rather desperately.

"I wasn't aware that you had any rela-

21

tives," the older woman answered tartly.

"Well . . . I must have some somewhere," Rachel said reasonably. "If Captain Herrick could take me back to Bermuda with him, I might be able to trace them."

"And I have already told you that to undertake such a voyage is quite out of the question," Miss Finch snapped back, with glacial finality. "Don't you agree, Theodore?"

The missioner flushed and cleared his throat. "Er . . . yes — yes, indeed," he murmured uncomfortably. "But perhaps the Captain shares that view, my dear Eveline. He has already told us that his living conditions are a trifle on the rough and ready side. To have a young lady aboard would be somewhat of an embarrassment, no doubt."

"But I'm not a 'young lady'!" Rachel exclaimed, in desperation.

Captain Herrick laughed. For a moment, she thought he was on her side. But, after studying her face for some seconds, he shook his head.

"I agree. You're not precisely what I would call a 'young lady', Rachel," he said teasingly. "All the same I think perhaps you should be guided by Miss Finch's feelings on this matter. A stay at the Mission will give you time to get your bearings, you know."

"You mean . . . you refuse to take me?" she asked shakily.

He frowned suddenly, his dark face hardening, his mouth grim. "No, I won't take you," he said curtly.

Soon afterwards, he took his leave of them. Still shattered by his abandonment of her, Rachel could scarcely bring herself to shake hands with him.

"Goodbye," she said stiltedly. "I don't expect we shall meet again."

"Don't you think so?" His grip on her fingers seemed to tighten. There was something in his face she could not read.

Then, after civil farewells to the Finches, he was gone.

Half an hour later, Miss Finch said bracingly, "Now it's really silly of you to sulk, my dear. You cannot seriously have thought that Captain Herrick would agree to that wild scheme of yours?"

Rachel bit her lip. "I still don't see why not," she answered brusquely.

The missioner had gone out for his evening stroll, so they were alone in the lamp-lit living-room. Miss Finch had produced her needlework, a shapeless calico undergarment. Watching her as she sat at the table, busily stitching — rimless spectacles pinching the bridge of her nose, her shoulders rigidly straight — Rachel shivered at the prospect ahead of her.

There would be no long days of swimming and skin-diving with Miss Finch as her mentor. From morning till night she would be instructed and supervised and criticised. All the careless freedom of Anguna would be lost to her — perhaps never to be regained. It was like facing a long prison sentence.

Miss Finch looked up from her sewing. "To be frank with you Rachel, I think it is high time that you had a little more discipline in your life," she said. "Far be it from me to express any ill of the departed, but I have always deplored your father's casual views on your upbringing."

But Rachel was not listening to her. Leaning out over the window ledge, she was watching the ship in the lagoon.

If only she could understand why —

after seeming so friendly and anxious to help at first — Captain Herrick had let her down so shatteringly.

"Why wouldn't he take me? *Why?*" she puzzled wretchedly.

Forgetful of her companion, she must have spoken the thought aloud.

"Because he is evidently a man of higher principles than one would expect of someone of his calling," Miss Finch remarked austerely. "Oh, good gracious, girl — surely you must see the extreme impropriety of travelling alone with a comparative stranger."

"But we wouldn't have been alone. Captain Herrick has a mate on board."

"A Negro seaman can scarcely be regarded as a suitable chaperon for a young and innocent girl — and innocence is *not* always its own protection, I fear," said Miss Finch. "Surely your father must have warned you about such things? No . . . perhaps not. It would be difficult for a man to discuss such a delicate subject."

"What delicate subject?" Rachel asked blankly. "Oh, you mean washing and going to the privy? I don't call *that* such a terribly delicate — "

25

"No, I did *not* mean those things," Miss Finch cut in. "Although they would certainly cause some embarrassment to any modest and sensitive person," she added distastefully. "What I did mean, however — and it seems I must put it quite bluntly — is that, had you been so unwise as to travel with this Herrick person, you might subsequently have found yourself in a . . . *a most unpleasant predicament!*" At this point, the missioner returned, and Miss Finch suggested that Rachel might pack some of her belongings before going to bed.

"No doubt there are various mementoes which you will want to bring with you," she said. "In future, of course, your clothes will be made by my sewing girls. We do not approve of trousers, do we, Theodore?"

So Rachel said good-night. But, instead of going to her room, she slipped along the veranda to find the cook.

"Oh, Octavia, what *am* I going to do?" she asked distractedly, when she had told the Negress what had happened. "I was so sure Captain Herrick would help me. Now I may be stuck at the Mission for years."

Octavia was smoking a large cigar. "Ah

26

never did take to dat ole Mission Lady," she said, scowling. "Tellin' me Ah don't done keep my kitchen clean! Now yo' knows dat ain't de troof, Missy Rachel."

"Oh, Miss Finch has faults to find in everything," Rachel said dismally. "Father couldn't stand her. Octavia — what if I refuse to go with her? They can't *force* me to go on the Mission launch. I could come and live with you in the village."

But Octavia shook her head. "Yo' knows dat ain't so, Missy Rachel. Dat Mission Lady, she'd fly in such a fret she'd make bad trouble. 'Sides, dere ain't nuffin' here for yo' since de good Lawd done took Marse Devon. Youse not a li'l gel no more, chile. Dat's time yo' find yo'self a husban'."

"I'm not likely to find one on Cay Mini," Rachel said bitterly.

Octavia reflected for some moments. "Yo' knows what Ah tink?" she asked, at length. "Ah tink dere's only one ting yo' can do — an' dat's to git yo'self hid on dat ole *Dolphin* boat."

"You mean . . . get on board secretly? But how could I?"

"Yo' can swim, cain't yo'?" Octavia enquired calmly.

"But Captain Herrick would be furious," Rachel objected.

"Yo' keeps yo'self hid till de mornin', an' dere ain't nuffin' he can do 'bout it, honey."

"If only I dared," Rachel murmured. "Oh, no, Octavia — it's impossible."

The cook shrugged her shoulders. "Okay, if'n yo' tink so. But de way Ah sees de matter, dat's no worse den yo' livin' with dat Mission Lady."

One hour later, at a few minutes past eleven, Rachel sat up in bed and pushed back the single light blanket. The missioner was spending the night in her father's room: his sister lay on a camp bed a few feet from Rachel's.

After waiting a moment to be sure that Miss Finch was soundly asleep, Rachel slid quietly off the bed and climbed through the nearby window. At the far end of the veranda she could see Octavia waiting for her.

"Now dere's no call to fret, Missy Rachel. De Cap'n he ain't a-goin' to beat yo'," the cook said reassuringly, passing over the small oilskin-wrapped bundle which contained all that Rachel was able to take away with her.

"Oh, Octavia, I'm going to miss you dreadfully," Rachel whispered huskily.

"An' Ah'll miss yo, too, mah honey. Youse bin lak yo' was mah own chile," Octavia whispered back, wiping away the tears that trickled down her fat cheeks. "Ah'll be prayin' dat de Lawd keep His eye on yo'."

A few moments later, after one last loving hug had been exchanged, Rachel was on her way.

Down in the settlement, the villagers were still dancing and singing round the driftwood fire they had built. Some of the bravest seamen in the world, they were childishly frightened of the dark and of the "haunts" that roamed abroad after sunset. Normally, nightfall found them securely shut up in their cabins. But the arrival of the *Dolphin* made a special occasion, calling for suitable festivities and the singing of favourite calypsos.

As Rachel hurried down the path to the lagoon, she could hear them chanting their latest composition — a description of the recent "big blow".

She was barefoot, and wearing nothing but the yard of gaudy cotton stuff which, bound round her body from armpit to thigh, was her only form of night-clothing. But it was a warm night, and not physical cold, but nerves, which made her shiver.

Reaching the water's edge and keeping well out of sight of the village, she peered at the moonlit anchored schooner. No, the dinghy was not alongside, so Captain Herrick and the mate must still be with the Angunans. With any luck it would be another half hour or so before they returned on board and prepared to put to sea again.

Fastening her bundle to the end of her pigtail and hoping that Octavia had made it watertight, Rachel waded into the sea. With noiseless breast strokes instead of her powerful crawl, she headed for the schooner Ten minutes later she was dripping salt water on deck.

The last time the *Dolphin* had called at Anguna, Rachel and her father had been invited on board. As far as she could remember, the only possible hiding-place would be down in one of the sheet lockers beyond the saloon. There were holds in the stern and in the bows, but the hatches were probably padlocked. Even if they were not, she did not fancy spending the night with the inevitable fruit spiders.

Before going below, she wrung out her soaking night-wrap, opened her bundle and dried herself carefully on a shirt. She could be discovered at once if Captain Herrick came back on board to find puddles all over the place. Unfortunately Octavia had not packed a second shirt, so she had to put the damp one on, but at least her shorts were dry.

It was approaching midnight when she heard the dinghy coming back. She could tell the time by the luminous hands on her father's wrist watch. Already it seemed hours since she had crawled into hiding behind a stack of musty sail canvas.

Soon after the two men came aboard, she heard the mate shout suddenly. For a moment, she thought he must have spotted the wet patch on the deck. But nothing happened and after a while she relaxed again — as far she could relax in such a confined space and with only a keyhole for ventilation.

For the following half hour, she crouched in the darkness, listening to the footfalls overhead and wishing she had brought something to eat. She had been too upset at supper to have any appetite for Octavia's gumbo, but now she felt hollow with hunger. Presently, startled by a sudden rumbling and creaking immediately overhead, she realised they were winching up the anchor chain.

But it was not until the schooner had glided through the passage between the coral heads and was well out into Anguna Sound — the wide deep channel between the reef and a treacherous stretch of shoal water — that Rachel suddenly realised just how recklessly she had acted. And, as the creaking of the sails grew louder and the ship began to heave slightly, her misgivings increased.

They had been at sea for more than an hour when, at last, someone came below. Rachel could hear him moving about the galley and whistling softly. But whether it was the Captain or the mate she had no means of telling.

After some minutes a delicious aroma of chocolate began to permeate the atmosphere. Her hunger — and the tension of lying low — were more than Rachel could bear. Easing her cramped legs, she felt for the unlatched door and pushed it open an inch.

The saloon was still dark, but in the lighted galley the mate was stirring the pan of hot chocolate. As she watched, he poured the thick sugary liquid into two tin mugs. Then, coming out of the galley, he put the lamp and one of the mugs on the saloon table, and disappeared on deck with the other mug. A few minutes later, Captain Herrick came down. Rachel waited until he had sat at the table, lit a cigarette and drunk some of the chocolate. Then she climbed out of the cupboard and moved hesitantly towards him.

Of all the reactions she had anticipated — astonishment, anger, perhaps even some unrestrained cursing — she had never expected that he would accept her appearance without comment.

Yet, after staring at her for some seconds — with no sign of surprise or indignation — he went into the galley to fetch a third mug. Pouring most of his own chocolate into it, he pushed it across to her.

"Want something to eat?" he asked evenly.

Rachel shook her head, then nodded. Her hands were so unsteady that, when she grasped the mug, some chocolate splashed over the table.

"I'm — I'm sorry," she stammered hoarsely.

The Captain's eyes narrowed as he saw how her hands were shaking. Moving to a wall locker, he produced a small metal spirits flask.

"Cognac," he told her succinctly. "You may not like it, but it will pull you together."

The brandy both warmed and steadied her. By the time he had fetched some biscuits, a tin of American butter and some sliced salami, she was able to thank him more composedly. Nevertheless, it was an unnerving experience to have him watch her eating, his own expression quite unreadable.

"Are . . . are you very angry?" she asked, at last.

"Did you think I would be?"

"Well, yes . . . of course I did. But I had to risk that. I — I was desperate."

"So it would appear," he said drily. "What would you like me to do with you? Clap you in irons? Or give you a taste of keel-hauling?"

"I suppose that means you're going to take me back?" Rachel said miserably.

"Not at all. Why should I? You took the chance — you must also take the consequences."

"You mean I can stay? You really mean that?" she asked breathlessly.

"Don't look so pleased. You may come to wish you'd gone to the Mission."

"With Miss Finch? Never!" Rachel said vehemently. "You don't seem to realise what she's like."

"She'll certainly be extremely distressed when she finds you missing in the morning," Herrick said gravely.

"Oh, yes — horrified! She'll visualise me in that 'most unpleasant predicament'," Rachel answered unguardedly. "But I don't think she'll worry for long," she added hastily. "She never liked my father, you know. She'll say it was only to be expected of me."

"So she told you what you would have

risked if I had agreed to take you with me, did she?"

Rachel flushed slightly. "Oh, she's one of those who thinks the worst of everybody," she said uncomfortably.

"But you hope for the best, I gather?" he said, in an odd tone.

But Rachel was not sure what he meant by this remark, so she passed it over, and said, "Why wouldn't you take me in the first place?"

He shrugged. "I had my reasons. Come on, you'd better get to bed. Brought any gear with you?"

"Not much. Just these clothes and some oddments. But I have a little money — I can pay for my passage."

He smiled suddenly. "Oh, in that case we must try to make you comfortable. I was going to let you sleep in the galley, but if you're paying your way, you'd better have a first-class berth. You can clear away those things while I make up a bunk."

Since it was now nearly two in the morning and she had just experienced one of the most taxing days of her life, Rachel was longing for some sleep. But weary as she was, she could not help being interested in the neatness and compactness of the cooking quarters. Everything was so spotlessly clean that even Miss Finch could not have faulted it.

It was not long before she heard Captain Herrick call to her. He was in a small cabin adjoining the long narrow saloon, and was searching in a locker under the bunks. The lower of the bunks was neatly made up with clean but un-ironed sheets and a bright Dutch blanket.

"If you're cold in the night there are some more blankets in here," he told her, straightening. "And I've put out some gear you will need. A toothbrush . . . soap and towel . . . and a nightdress."

"A nightdress?" Rachel repeated, astonished.

"Well, it may be a little on the long side, but it should serve for the time being," he said casually. "Now I'd better get up on deck again."

It was not until after he had left her that Rachel realised that this must be his own cabin. There was a razor and other shaving tackle on the shelf above the hand basin, and a thick grey wool sweater on a peg behind the door. On the chest of drawers

— securely bolted to the deck, she noticed — there was a man's black-backed hairbrush and a rolled-up leather belt. Two prints of old sailing barques were clipped to the varnished bulkheads.

Having washed her face and hands and brushed her teeth, Rachel examined the nightdress. It was made of some fragile material which she had never seen before and was the colour of an early morning sky. When she took off her clothes and slipped it carefully over her head, the folds of delicate fabric felt lighter than a handful of sea-foam. But it *was* much too long for her. She wondered who it had belonged to.

She had climbed into the bunk, and was on the point of turning out the lamp when a tap at the door made her jump.

Hurriedly sitting up again, and drawing the sheet up to her chin, she called, "Come in."

It was Captain Herrick. Stepping over the coaming, a glass in his hand, he said, "I think we're running into a slight squall. You'd better drink this to help you sleep soundly."

"What is it?" Rachel asked.

"Only a mild sedative. It won't hurt

you." Waiting for her to finish it, he said, "Oh, by the way, don't forget you haven't got too much headroom when you wake up tomorrow. I've known people to almost split their skulls if they aren't used to sleeping in a berth."

Rachel handed back the glass. "I wish you hadn't put me in your cabin," she said shyly. "Isn't there anywhere else I could sleep? I don't want to be more of a nuisance than I need."

"I expect we'll survive it," he said coolly. Then, bending down towards her, he put out his hand.

Instinctively, Rachel shrank back and drew in her breath.

The Captain's mouth hardened slightly. Then, feeling the end of her pigtail, he said crisply, "Your hair is still wet. Oughtn't you to dry it?"

It was useless to pretend that she had not involuntarily recoiled from him. She had jerked away as sharply as if there had been a scorpion rearing at her.

Scarlet with confusion, she stammered, "It — it won't hurt me. I'm used to it."

Captain Herrick straightened, made an adjustment to the port and turned towards the door. Then, taking down the oilskins that had hung behind it on a hook, he turned to look at her again.

"So Miss Finch's warning about me has carried some weight after all," he said derisively. "I'm afraid you flatter yourself, Miss Devon. I may not be a pillar of moral rectitude, but I do draw the line at making advances to unusually gauche adolescents. However, if you remain unconvinced, let me point out that there's a most efficient bolt on the door. Good-night."

A second later she was alone again.

CHAPTER TWO

AT first, opening her eyes in a dazzle of reflected, wavering sunbeams, Rachel could not think where she was. After sitting up and getting a crack on the head that made her ears ring, she was even more confused. Then, slowly, rubbing her scalp, she remembered.

In spite of the agony of embarrassment in which Captain Herrick had left her, she had slept almost at once, and without stirring. The sedative he had given her must have been quite a strong one.

Now, climbing out of the bunk — careful not to bang her head a second time — she found that the schooner was at anchor again. And, if there had been a squall in the night, there was no sign of rough weather now. The sea was as calm as a rock pool, with brilliant sunshine glancing and glinting on the surface and gilding the sand under the shallows. Where the water was deep, as round the *Dolphin*, it was even more blue than the sky — and the sky was an infinity of azure. It was going to be one

of those golden Bahamian days which —
so her father had often said — made the
climate of these islands one of the best in
the world. Twenty minutes later, after
making up the bunk and folding the
flimsy nightgown, Rachel ventured on deck.

There was no sign of Captain Herrick,
but the mate was frying gammon over a
sand-boxed charcoal burner on the foredeck. The smell of the sizzling rashers
made Rachel's mouth water.

"Mornin', Missy Rachel. Mah name
Teaboy. You sleep good?" he asked,
beaming.

"Yes, very well, thank you."

"De Cap'n he swimmin'," Teaboy said.
"Mebbe you like swim too, Missy?"

"I think I'd rather have some breakfast,
if you can spare some."

"Surely, Missy. Ah cooks you a nice big
egg, eh?"

In spite of his height and powerful
physique, he was probably not much older
than herself. And, while his features were
blunt and negroid, his eyes were a clear
light grey. Perhaps his forebears included
one of Morgan's buccaneers, or an English
colonist.

The eggs had been expertly basted and were crisping at the edges when there was a splashing sound from below the starboard rails. A moment later, tanned, and glistening from the sea, Captain Herrick came aboard.

"Morning, Rachel. I didn't think you'd be up yet," he said easily. "Want a quick dip, or are you hungry?"

Relieved that he seemed to have forgotten what had happened last night, Rachel managed to say cheerfully, "Good-morning, Captain. Well, Teaboy has just cooked me an egg and I am a bit ravenous."

Herrick reached for a towel and gave himself a cursory rub down. Then, taking the mug of black coffee which Teaboy had already poured for him, he relaxed into an ancient, splitting basket chair and lit a cigarette.

"Did you have a good night?" he asked lazily.

"Fine, thanks. Oh, wouldn't you like to have this as you've been up longer than I have?" — this, as Teaboy passed her the plate of gammon and fried eggs.

"I had breakfast at sun-up." The Captain strapped on a wrist watch and settled more comfortably in the chair. In navy cotton boxer shorts and with his hair wet and ruffled, he looked younger, but no less authoritative. Rachel could not be sure how old he was as she was not used to judging the age of Europeans. She thought he was probably about thirty. Watching him as he drew on the cigarette, his eyes on the southern horizon, she noticed that he had shaved. Had he come into the cabin while she was still sleeping, or had he borrowed Teaboy's razor? And did they always shave so early — or had they felt obliged to because she was with them?

"Do you always stop for a bathe in the morning?" she asked presently.

"Not always. It depends on our schedule. We're on a short run today so we can spare a couple of hours," Herrick told her.

By the time Rachel had finished her breakfast, Teaboy had disappeared aft.

Pouring herself a second mug of coffee and adding the thick condensed milk, she wondered how best to broach the subject of her foolishness last night. Even if Captain Herrick did not wish to refer to it, she would not feel comfortable until she had attempted an apology.

"Captain Herrick . . . about last night — " she began diffidently.

Stretched out in the chair, his feet propped up on a tea-crate, the Captain had closed his eyes. As he did not open them when she spoke, she thought he must be dozing. But after a moment, he said drowsily, "Mm . . . I'm listening."

She had not expected it to be easy but, with only half his attention, it was even more difficult than she had anticipated.

"I — I just wanted to say that I think you misunderstood me," she blurted out nervously.

Again, it was several seconds before he made any response. Then, opening his eyes and turning his head to look at her, he said sceptically, "Do you think so? I don't believe I did."

Rachel's cheeks flamed, and she wished she had never begun this. Instead of helping her out, he was obviously going to make it as embarrassing as possible.

"But do go on," he continued blandly. "What exactly did I misunderstand?"

"Oh, if you're going to be sarcastic — " she began hotly, jumping to her feet and intending to march off and leave him.

45

His hand clamped firmly on her wrist, and she had to subside on to her box again.

"There's no need to rush off in a tantrum," he said negligently.

"I am *not* in a tantrum!"

"You seem very cross about something."

Rachel glared at him. "Well, wouldn't anyone be cross when . . . when they're trying to apologise, and you just lounge there and *goad* them?" she retorted.

"But if it's I who misunderstood, surely I should be making the apology?" he suggested mildly. "Now, suppose we start at the beginning again. What did I misunderstand, d'you feel?"

"Oh, nothing . . . it doesn't matter," she said vexedly. "If you don't mind, I'd like to go back to the cabin."

"But it was you who raised the subject, my dear girl."

"And now I've dropped it again — and I'm not 'your dear girl' — and please let go of my arm."

"Yes, by all means — when I've set you straight on certain points." He relaxed his grip slightly, but not enough for her to pull free.

"What points?" she asked coldly.

46

"In the first place, you know perfectly well that I didn't misunderstand anything. The facts of the case are that you were tired and pretty jumpy, and I was a more or less strange man, and Miss Finch had been at pains to impress on you that men — all men — were lecherous brutes. In view of all that it would have been fairly surprising if you hadn't been afraid of me," he told her reasonably. "And your shudder of repugnance didn't cut me to the quick, you know."

"I didn't think it had," she said, in a low voice.

"The second point," he went on, "and it's a very sound rule at all times, is never to start anything which you aren't prepared to finish — whether it's an explanation or an apology or merely sending someone to blazes. Now I've said my piece, so you can either flounce off in a huff or hit me with the frying-pan. Which is it to be?"

He had let go of her wrist now, and she knew he was silently laughing at her. Last night he had called her "an unusually gauche adolescent". At the moment he made her feel like a silly, bad-tempered ten-year-old. And yet all she had wanted to do was make some amends for, briefly, mistrusting him.

At last, unwilling to accept his hurtful mockery, but knowing there was nothing she could do about it, Rachel mustered a smile. "One can't 'flounce off' in shorts," she said wryly.

His mouth quirked. "Good girl," he said approvingly.

Then Teaboy called to him from below, and he left her to finish her coffee.

Later in the morning, after Rachel had had a swim and they were under sail again, she said, "Captain Herrick, isn't there anything I can do — to make myself useful, I mean ?"

He considered the question for a moment. "Well, you could mend a shirt I've torn, if you like. It's in the top drawer of the chest in the cabin. Teaboy has a 'housewife' he will lend you. Oh, Rachel, just a minute" — as she turned to climb down the companion-way.

"Yes ?" she asked, pausing, expecting a second task.

" 'Captain Herrick' is rather formal, don't you think ?" he said, over his shoulder. "Try calling me Niall, will you ?"

In the days that followed, Rachel was surprised to discover how little she missed Anguna. Although the sea had been an integral part of her life for so long — the pounding of the breakers on the reef an unceasing *leitmotif* at every season of the year — she had never before experienced the delights, and the hazards, of living under sail. She found it strangely exhilarating.

When Niall Herrick had found that she had only one set of clothes, he insisted that she should borrow some of his shirts and shorts. Then, after she had washed out her own things, Teaboy had shown her how to make use of his laundry line in spite of a lack of clothes pegs. What she must do, he explained, was to underlay a piece of the line with the point of his marlin-spike, and then tuck the hem of her shirt through the opening. By this method, the sharpest gust of wind could never blow away her clothes. And, although it was soon obvious that both men could cook, and sew, and clean as well, if not better, than most women, the mate also allowed her to share some of the galley chores so that she should not feel too idle and useless.

Every day, after that first morning, she would wake to find the *Dolphin* lying at anchor near some nameless and uninhabited little cay. Then a rap on the door would make her scramble out of her bunk to join Niall for a swim before breakfast.

The "schedule" that Niall had mentioned seemed to be a very leisurely one, as often the whole day was spent at anchor — all three of them diving for clams to make into a chowder, or swimming ashore to explore the islets. Then, towards evening, Niall would sleep for a couple of hours before spending most of the night at the helm. And below, lying in his cabin — which soon seemed as familiar as the bedroom at the bungalow — Rachel would listen to the creaking of the sails, and feel the slow soothing undulation of the schooner moving northwards before the wind.

On the fourth night out, Niall let her take a turn at the wheel. It was bright moonlight and they were in an area free from dangerous coral-heads and tricky sand bars.

"Don't worry, you aren't likely to sink us. Just hold her steady," he instructed.

So Rachel gripped the helm and held it steady — which was not nearly as easy as it looked, she found. And then she began to understand why Niall never seemed particularly fatigued after one of his long night watches. Because — whatever it might be like when the weather was squally — on a night like this, the helmsman could feel like a god.

"Enjoying yourself?" Niall asked, from close behind her.

Rachel braced herself more firmly and drew a deep breath. "It's wonderful!" she exclaimed, and heard him laugh.

But it *was* a wonderful sensation: the wind so tangy with sea-spray and the wheel holding steady under her hands and, up at the bows, the silver-painted dolphin figurehead rising and dipping like a live thing.

And then, just as she was feeling that she could go on like this for ever — never growing tired as long as the wind held — something unexpected happened. She must have slackened her hold slightly as, with a sudden strong tug, the wheel wrenched out of her hands and began to spin. With a shout of alarm she felt the deck lurch, throwing her off balance.

"Don't panic." Niall's voice was steady and untroubled. With one swift step forward he had saved her from falling over and also righted the helm again.

"What happened?" Rachel asked breathlessly, caught between him and the wheel.

It was Teaboy who answered her. He must have finished washing up their supper things and come up to join them for a while.

"Dis ole gal *Dolphin*, she ain't 'customed to bein' handled by a lady," he said, chuckling. "Ah reckon she don' like dat, Missy Rachel. You best watch out how she treat you now. Mebbe de ole gal jealous, eh, Cap'n?"

Niall had a couple of aqua-lungs on board, and the following morning he gave Rachel a lesson in using them. During the night they had anchored off a string of cays which were guarded by a particularly fine reef. So, as soon as the sun was up, Teaboy took them over to it in the dinghy and kept watch on the surface while they were both under the water. While Rachel had so often explored the labyrinth of corals around Anguna, she had never been able to dive below a certain depth, or to stay down longer than the span of one deep lungful of air. But, although Niall warned that she must still not go down too far until she was used to a greater pressure of water, the aqua-lung did free her from the need to surface so frequently.

After half an hour of roaming through the forest of brilliant-coloured coral — watching the combers burst into a million shimmering bubbles as they dashed on the top of the reef — they left their equipment in the boat and swam in to the beach.

Rachel had lost the piece of string which fastened her braid, and her hair was coming loose. While she plaited it together again, Niall lay beside her and sifted sand idly through his fingers.

"I should think it was on a cay like this that old Morgan buried his treasure," he said presently.

"Do you think there is a treasure?" Rachel asked. Long ago, Octavia had told her what most of the islanders believed — that somewhere, on some undiscovered cay, the famous English pirate had hidden his loot.

"Why not? We might even be sitting on

it," Niall said, smiling. He yawned and stretched out on his back, clasping his hands beneath his head and narrowing his eyes against the sun. "I'd like to have met Sir Henry. He must have been quite a character."

"You were born in the wrong age. You could have been one of his captains. I should think you'd have liked that sort of life," Rachel said thoughtfully, looping her braid into a knot so that it would not work loose again.

"What — roving the Spanish Main? You are complimentary."

"Oh, I didn't mean the plundering and . . . and the orgies. But I'm sure you would have enjoyed sailing a galleon, and fighting sea-battles."

"Well, thank you for absolving me from the orgies," he said drily. "Though, as far as plundering goes, shipwrecking used to be quite a respectable livelihood in Bermuda before we cashed in on the tourist trade."

"You mean wrecking them deliberately? Why, I think that's much worse than piracy."

"I'm inclined to agree — but our great-

great-grandfathers didn't. There's a story about a ship being lured on to the reefs one day while everyone was at church. Someone went to tell the parson, and he announced it from the pulpit. 'But the congregation will remain seated until I have taken off my surplice,' he told them. 'And then, lads, we'll all start fair.'"

"He must have been a very peculiar clergyman," Rachel said with a shiver. "Were you born in Bermuda, Niall?"

"Yes, I was. But by the time you arrived in the world, I was blowing on my chilblains in a draughty Hampshire prep school."

"Were you?" she asked, in astonishment. From what little she knew about such places, the regimented world of an English boy's preparatory school was the very last background she would have ascribed to him. "Didn't you hate it?" she asked. "I mean the cold, and all the rules, and being so far away from home."

"I wasn't exactly keen," he admitted wryly. "If it hadn't been for the war, I should probably have tried to make a getaway."

"But weren't your parents terribly

anxious about you, with the bombing and everything?"

"They were drowned in a sailing accident when I was a baby. I was brought up by my grandmother."

"Well, wasn't she worried?"

"I doubt it," he said carelessly. "She had her own troubles. Besides, once the Nazis' U-boats were dodging about the north Atlantic, getting home would have been more of a risk than sitting tight."

"So what happened when the war ended?"

"I finished my schooling and then I had a spell in the Navy. After that I had a look round the Pacific for a couple of years and then I came back to settle down."

"If you can call it 'settling down'," she said, smiling. "How often do you get back to Bermuda?"

"Oh . . . often enough," he said vaguely.

"And is this how you're going to spend the rest of your life — sailing the *Dolphin* round the islands?"

"I hope so. Why? Do you disapprove?"

"No, of course I don't. I think it must be an ideal life — for a man," she tacked on.

"But not for a woman, hm?"

"Well, not for your wife. She'd scarcely ever see you."

"I could have her on board with me," he pointed out. "Or don't you feel that a woman could be happy living on the *Dolphin*?"

"Not knowing any women except Miss Finch — no white women, I mean — I can't really say."

He arched one eyebrow at her. "You're a woman yourself, aren't you?"

"But I'm not like other girls," she said, frowning. "How I feel about things is probably quite different from how most of them would feel."

"Very likely — but how would you feel?"

Rachel shifted her position, drawing up her legs and clasping her arms round her knees. "I love living on the *Dolphin*," she answered slowly. "If only I were a boy, I could earn my living at sea. Niall, do you think I shall ever be able to fit in — when we get to Bermuda, I mean?"

"Certainly you will. Why not?"

Rachel sighed. "I suppose I feel rather like a nun who's been thrown out of the convent," she said anxiously. "It's been so long since I lived in the outside world that

I've really forgotten what it's like — even from a child's point of view. Apart from you and the Finches and one or two American yachtsmen, I haven't had anything to do with white people."

"Oh, you'll soon get the hang of it," he said bracingly.

"Will I? How do you know?"

Niall sat up and dusted the sand off his legs. "Of course you will, little juggins. Six weeks from now you'll be taking it all in your stride. You may feel like a nun, honey, but you weren't intended to be one. Convents and coral islands are for people with a special kind of temperament. You're a perfectly normal young woman — and you ought to be doing all the things that normal women enjoy. Tell me, were you never bored with your life on Anguna?"

"Bored? No — never. There was always plenty to do."

"But didn't you ever want to do other things? Buy a pretty dress? Go to a party?"

Rachel did not answer for a moment. She was playing with the end of her braid, a habit she had whenever she was troubled or deep in thought.

58

"I've never done those things," she said, at length. "Isn't there a saying — 'what you never have, you never miss'?"

"There is . . . but it isn't strictly true," Niall said, in an amused tone. "There are some things we all have a yen for — with or without experience of them. Take . . . kissing, for example. You've never been kissed, but I expect you've wanted to be. Even if you'd never read about it in books — and if Anguna had been uninhabited — you'd still have known you were missing something."

"But I have been kissed," Rachel told him. "I wish I hadn't," she added, grimacingly.

Niall frowned. "What do you mean?"

"Oh, it was ages ago. I'd practically forgotten about it."

"Well . . . go on."

Rachel shrugged, surprised that the incident should interest him.

"Oh, I was about sixteen, I suppose. Some boys came to Anguna . . . American students. They were doing some kind of marine research. There was a professor with them and he and Father used to talk for hours. Anyway, one afternoon I was alone with one of the boys and he suddenly grabbed me."

"But you didn't much care for it, I gather?"

"Nor did he! I pushed him backwards into a rock pool and he fell on a sea-urchin — and you know what agony their spines are," she said, with remembered satisfaction.

Niall laughed. "I do indeed. Did you prise them out for him, or leave him?"

"Oh, I had to squeeze them out or they might have gone septic. But he must have had a very sore foot for several days."

"Callous little creature! Still, don't let the episode sour you. Sudden grabbing is never the best approach."

There was a shout from Teaboy, who had been fishing from the dinghy. Niall got to his feet and held out a hand to pull her up.

"Come on, let's see what's for lunch."

Later in the day, the *Dolphin* had to negotiate a perilously narrow passage between two twisting barricades of coral. Teaboy said this would save them twelve hours' sailing time, but to Rachel, leaning

60

over the rails, it looked an impossible feat of helmsmanship. As they approached the mouth of the channel, she could see the jagged outcrops of coral beneath the surface and the alarmingly limited clearance on either side. If Niall made one error of judgement, the schooner's bows would ram straight on to the rock.

"Youse no call to look so scared, Missy Rachel," said Teaboy, seeing her anxiety. "De Cap'n and old lady *Dolphin*, dey closer dan brother an' sister. Ah's nebber done seen him take no chances with her."

And although it seemed to Rachel that to take such a hazardous short-cut was a chance of the utmost recklessness, yet ten minutes later they were safely beyond the last outcrop.

Just before sunset, Teaboy lit up his charcoal burner and began to prepare a favourite Bermudian supper known as Hop'n John. This, Rachel discovered, was much the same as Octavia's peas and rice recipe, except that Teaboy added bacon to the mixture. Chopping the onions for him, she saw that Niall was standing up in the bows, admiring the lovely pearl-streaked skyscape. Something in the way he stood there, his hands resting lightly on the rails, reminded her of what the mate had said earlier — that Niall and his schooner were as close as a brother to his sister. Or was the bond even stronger, perhaps? Like that between a husband and wife?

Niall had asked her if a woman could be happy on the *Dolphin*. But if he was already in his thirties and had not yet thought of marriage, perhaps his life held no place for a woman.

After supper, the mate went to fetch his drum — an empty lard keg with a goatskin stretched over the top. And, while Niall and Rachel relaxed in the creaking old basket chairs, Teaboy beat out goombay and calypsos.

Tonight, however, the pulsing rhythms failed to start Rachel's feet tapping. She felt tired and curiously depressed. And when Teaboy began "Hold 'Im, Joe" — a song about a donkey which had been one of the favourites on Anguna — a rush of homesickness welled up in her.

Later, while the men were drinking canned beer, she said briefly that she was sleepy, and went below.

She had been lying on her bunk for about

half an hour, still dressed and wide awake, when Niall knocked.

"Can I come in a moment, Rachel?"

She opened the door to him. "Is anything wrong?"

"Oh, you aren't in bed yet. No, everything's fine. I just want to get some gear out of the locker."

As he lit the lamp, Rachel turned away. She did not want him to see her face.

"Well, this time tomorrow, you'll be seeing the sights of Nassau," he said, presently, straightening from the locker.

She swung round. "Tomorrow? So soon?"

Niall put the clothes he had wanted on her bunk. Then, his hands on her shoulders, he said quietly, "You've been crying. I thought you were very quiet tonight."

"It's nothing. I was just . . . a bit depressed," she said huskily, wishing she had had the presence of mind to whip under the blanket and pretend to be asleep.

"Thinking about your father?" Niall asked gently.

Rachel nodded. "But I'm all right now. What — what time shall we get to Nassau?"

63

"About noon, or soon after. Want something to help you get to sleep?"

His hands were still resting on her shoulders and, when his fingers tightened a fraction, Rachel felt a strange thrust of excitement, a kind of tingling sensation down her spine.

She shook her head. "Oh, no — I'll sleep all right."

"Perhaps this will help." He bent his head.

Before she had grasped his intention, his lips had brushed lightly over her cheek — almost, but not quite, to her mouth. She was still frozen with stupefaction when, picking up his things, he reached the door.

"Good-night, Rachel. I hope that was better than the other time," he said quizzically.

When Rachel saw Niall the next morning, a deep flush of colour ran up under her tan. But he was busy at the map table and did not seem to notice her confusion.

As Niall had forecast, the *Dolphin* put in to Nassau a little after midday. An hour later, all three of them went ashore.

To Rachel, that first afternoon in the busy, traffic-crowded shopping centre of the Bahamas' capital city was like entering an entirely new world. Almost everything was strange to her — the big, shiny American limousines, the horse-drawn surreys, the awning-shaded pavement cafés, and the department stores and office buildings.

Walking along Bay Street, with Niall and Teaboy strolling a few paces behind her, she was like a wide-eyed three-year-old seeing her first Christmas toy fair, an Alice in a modern Wonderland.

"Oh, Niall . . . Teaboy . . . look!"

Every few minutes she would swing round to draw their attention to a fascinating display in a shop window, or to one of the elegantly dressed women tourists.

Presently Teaboy left them to visit some cronies. After Rachel had stepped off the pavement at a crossing, and had almost been knocked down by a bus, Niall took her hand.

"I think I had better hang on to you. That driver almost had heart failure," he said, smiling.

About four o'clock he took her into a

café, ordering coffee for himself and an elaborate fruit sundae for her.

"Well, what do you make of it all?" he asked, lighting a cigarette.

"It's . . . heavenly," Rachel said breathlessly, her eyes growing wider with delight when the sundae was set in front of her.

"Yes, I suppose it would seem so to you," Niall remarked drily.

"Don't *you* think so?" she queried, puzzled. Then, before he could answer, "Oh, Niall, do look at that girl coming in. Isn't she beautiful — and that dress!"

Niall shifted his position slightly. "Yes, she's pretty enough," he agreed, but without much enthusiasm.

"I think she's lovely," Rachel murmured, taking in every detail of the girl's appearance. "I wish I looked like that."

"I don't think you ever will."

Rachel flinched slightly, then quickly got on with the sundae. He had spoken without thinking, of course. He hadn't intended to crush her. So it was silly to feel hurt because, in a moment of involuntary candour, he had said what she knew to be the truth.

But, later, as they walked through

66

Rawson Square to the open-air straw market, and then on to the Prince George Wharf to see a cruise liner, her interest and excitement were tempered by a lingering sense of inadequacy. It was no use trying to blind herself to the facts. She was an alien, a misfit. However hard she tried to adapt herself to these new surroundings, she would never be able to acquire the poise and finish of girls like the one in the café.

The following morning Niall took her to see the trained flamingoes parading in the Ardastra Gardens, and in the afternoon they climbed up the steep Queen's Stairway to Fort Fincastle. Among the other people looking over the ramparts was an elderly American with two youngsters, doubtless his grandchildren. Watching the three of them for a moment, and then listening to Niall explaining when the fortress had been built and for what purpose, Rachel felt that his attitude to her was very much that of a man who was temporarily in charge of some friends' schoolgirl daughter, and who was putting himself out to keep her suitably entertained.

Her glance strayed to another couple —

a boy and a girl who were leaning against one of the old cannons and exchanging a look which made it clear that, as soon as they were alone, they would be in each other's arms.

And suddenly Rachel knew that she did not want Niall's kindness if it was prompted by nothing but an innate chivalry towards anyone as unfledged and alone in the world as she was. She wanted him to look at her as that boy was looking at that girl.

That night they went to a cinema where Rachel saw her first Western — but not her first movie, because she dimly remembered being taken to see some children's films in London. Afterwards, they had supper in a restaurant.

The place was already crowded when they arrived and they had to wait until a table was free.

"Like to try a cocktail?" Niall asked, as he helped her to perch on one of the high leather-topped stools along the counter.

"Won't it make me drunk?" she asked doubtfully.

His mouth twitched. "Only mildly hilarious," he assured her. "A blackstrap and a Bacardi, please." — This to the grinning Bahamian barman.

"What's a blackstrap?" Rachel asked, when the man had moved away to get their order.

Niall explained that it was a fermented rum, darker and more potent than the distilled kind. Her Bacardi would be a blend of freshly squeezed lime-juice, light rum and a dash of grenadine syrup. A few moments later, taking a cautious sip of the mixture, Rachel had to agree that it was the most delicious drink she had ever tasted.

It was not long before a table was ready for them and while Niall considered the menu, Rachel looked round at the other diners. A few of the women were in short evening dresses with sparkling ear-rings and bracelets, and satin or fur stoles draped over their chairs. However, most of them wore cotten sun-dresses or sleeveless jersey tops and tapered silk trousers. They were all very animated, she noticed, and most of those who had finished eating were smoking cigarettes in elegant holders.

She was so interested in everything about them that it was several minutes before she began to realise that, while she was gazing at them, quite a number of people were openly staring at her.

"What's the matter?" Niall asked, after he had chosen their meal and noticed her heightened colour.

"Oh . . . nothing," Rachel said evasively.

"My dear child, you're as fidgety as a puppy. There must be something wrong. Do you want to go to the powder-room, or whatever it's called here?"

"No, of course I don't. I'm not a six-year-old, you know," Rachel flashed at him indignantly.

"Well, what is it, then?"

She bit her lip. "I don't think you should have brought me here. I'm not dressed properly . . . people keep staring."

"Certainly they're staring," he said evenly. "Most of them live in this rarefied atmosphere all the time. They don't often see a girl like you."

"If you knew they were going to gape, I think it was unkind of you to bring me," she said, in a tight voice. "It's not my fault if I look . . . peculiar."

"You don't look at all peculiar. You're a very attractive girl."

70

His tone was so matter-of-fact that, at first, Rachel could not believe she had heard him correctly. Then, for one heart-stopping moment, she almost believed he meant it. Finally she saw the truth of the matter.

He must have realised that he had hurt her feelings in the café yesterday, and so he was trying to make amends — and to boost her confidence in herself. What a guileless little ninny he must think her!

She smiled suddenly. "I'm sorry," she said brightly. "It was silly of me to fuss. Could I have another Bacardi, do you think?"

For the rest of the evening she was unflaggingly cheerful and talkative.

Next day, after breakfast, Niall went off to order provisions. He asked Rachel if she wanted to accompany him, but she made the excuse that she had some clothes to wash. As soon as he was out of sight along the waterfront, she told Teaboy that she was going up to Bay Street for half an hour.

"You be okay by yo'self, Missy Rachel?" the mate asked anxiously.

"Yes, of course I will, Teaboy. I just want to have my hair cut."

"Maybe Ah go with you — sees you don't git yo'self knocked down," he suggested.

"No, I want to go by myself," Rachel said firmly. "Don't worry: I'll be careful."

There was a beauty parlour on the corner of Bay Street which she had noticed the day before. When she reached it, she paused in front of the window for a moment, studying the display of scent bottles and plucking up her courage to go inside.

The girl at the reception desk was a pretty Bahamian in a primrose nylon overall. "May I help you, miss?" she asked pleasantly, as Rachel hovered uncertainly inside the door.

"I'd like to have my hair cut, please."

"And a shampoo and set?"

"No, just a cut."

The girl consulted her appointment book. "I'm afraid we can't take you right away. Can you wait fifteen minutes?"

Rachel nodded. "How much will it cost?" she asked diffidently.

"A trim is twelve shillings, miss."

"Oh, I see. Well, I'll wait, then," Rachel said, relieved.

The receptionist ushered her to a couch and gave her some magazines to read.

Actually it was almost half an hour before another assistant came to take Rachel through to the salon. There were a number of women under drying-hoods, but they were all deep in periodicals or having their nails manicured and only glanced at her briefly.

The assistant helped her into a gown, drew out a thickly padded chair, and said that their stylist would be with her in a moment.

To Rachel's surprise, the stylist was a short, rotund Frenchman with a little pointed beard and an enormous carnation in his buttonhole.

"*Bonjour, mademoiselle.* You wish for a trim, I understand? Ah, but what magnificent treesses! You seriously desire me to sever this so luxuriant peeg-tail? You would not prefer a chignon, perhaps?"

"No, I want it all cut off, please," Rachel said firmly.

The hairdresser shrugged his padded shoulders. "*Mais certainement* — if you

73

insist, *mademoiselle*. It is merely that one so rarely sees hair of such length nowadays — and of such an exquisite natural blonde also. Perhaps, if I were to demonstrate how it would look if — "

"Mademoiselle's hair will remain exactly as it is," said a cold voice.

The hairdresser started in surprise. "Oh, I beg your pardon, *monsieur*. I did not see you there. You wish to speak to my client?"

"I do — but not here," Niall said grimly, looking at Rachel through the mirror with an expression that made her quake.

"But, Niall — " she began.

"I'll wait for you outside. If you aren't with me in three minutes flat . . ." He shrugged slightly, leaving her to draw her own conclusions as to what the consequence would be. Then with a nod to the bewildered Frenchman, and ignoring the now interested regard of the other customers, he went back through the waiting lounge.

Suddenly, Rachel was so furious that she almost had the rashness to defy him. What right had he to burst in here and make a fool of her? What she did with her hair was her own business.

74

But, on the point of telling the hair-dresser to proceed, she felt her courage ebbing. Niall was not a man whose ulti-matums were bluffs. If she wasn't outside in three minutes, he would undoubtedly come in and fetch her — by force, if he had to.

"I am sorry, *monsieur*. I'm afraid I haven't time to have a trim now. Perhaps another day," she said constrainedly, slip-ping out of the folds of the pale pink wrapper.

"Of course, *mademoiselle* — whenever you wish." The hairdresser was still too perplexed to be annoyed.

Niall was standing a little way up the street, lighting a cigarette.

"Very sensible," he said tersely, when she reached him. "No" — as Rachel drew in a breath — "we won't fight here, my little termagant. If you want to spit fire at me, you can do it where we won't have an audience."

And, with his fingers gripping her arm above the elbow, Rachel was marched back to the quayside.

When they reached the *Dolphin*'s berth, Teaboy, who had been lounging on a bollard, sprang down on to the schooner's deck to help Rachel jump. But, ignoring his hand and with one furious glare, she made the descent unaided and went down to the saloon.

Between Niall and the mate, she was as assiduously supervised as she would have been by old Miss Finch, she thought wrathfully.

"Now, what have you got to say for yourself?" Niall enquired coolly, when he had followed her down the companion-ladder.

"What have *I* got to say?" Rachel almost choked with indignation. "I think it's you who should do the explaining."

"Teaboy told me you had sneaked off somewhere. I thought it best to come and find you," he said negligently.

"I did *not* sneak off — I merely went."

"Choosing the moment my unsuspecting back was turned." Niall's tone was like a lash. "Oh, come now, Rachel, don't take me for a fool. You knew I wouldn't approve, so you went on the sly."

"I did no such thing! If you must know, I wanted to surprise you," Rachel flared hotly. "How could I know you wouldn't approve? I can't see what business it is of yours if I wanted to have my head shaved."

His expression was grim again. "As long as you're in my charge, *everything* you do is my concern," he said emphatically. "I prefer your hair the way it is."

"*You* prefer — what about my feelings? I may have been brought up on Anguna, but I'm not feeble-minded, you know. You haven't any right to dictate to me."

"The captain of a ship — even of this size — has absolute rights where the well-being of his passengers is concerned."

"Oh, has he!" Rachel exclaimed. "Well, in that case, *Captain* Herrick, I'll pay you whatever I owe and get off your ship." She turned to slam into the cabin.

The next instant, she was pinned against the bulkhead and Niall was having the hatefulness to laugh at her.

"Let me go!" she flamed, struggling violently.

But he was much too strong for her. And when, knowing her efforts were futile but determined not to submit, she jerked her head back and got a painful crack as it knocked against the bulkhead, he became

77

even more detestable. Instead of keeping her trapped by the elbows, he shot both his arms round her waist and held her hard against his chest. The final humiliation was that, as soon as he had done this, Rachel felt all her resentment and fury ebbing away. Instead, she was filled with a shaming but uncontrollable excitement.

"Having second thoughts?" Niall asked mockingly, when she had given up twisting and wriggling and was standing quiescent against him.

"Please, Niall, let me go now," she said hoarsely. It would be the end of everything if he felt how wildly her heart was beating.

"In a minute . . . I want to tell you something."

His hold was more gentle now, although still too firm to let her escape. The pressure of his hands against her back seemed to burn through her thin cotton shirt. His mouth was only inches from her forehead. She was beginning to tremble . . . to want to stay in his arms for ever.

"Tell me what?" she asked faintly, when he did not go on.

"Perhaps I was a shade too rough on you," he said quietly. "But as I said, I like your hair the way it is. That pigtail is very appealing . . . very feminine. If you have it chopped off, you'll lose something."

Her hands were resting against his shoulders, and it took all her will power not to slip them upwards, round his neck.

"But it looks so old-fashioned," she said lamely. "All the other girls have short hair, Niall."

"Is it so terribly important to be like the other girls?"

"I — I wouldn't feel quite such a freak."

He let her go. One moment he was holding her: the next, he was several feet away.

"Being different doesn't make you a freak, honey. Look, wait till we get to Bermuda, will you? If you still want to have your braid cut then — well, fair enough. But I think you may change your mind."

"Very well — if you think so," she said doubtfully. "I — I'm sorry I said what I did, Niall. I don't really want to leave the *Dolphin*. Unless" — in a low voice — "you're getting sick of me."

He smiled slightly. "Not entirely — when you're tractable. Now you'd better go and make your peace with Teaboy. I have some work to do."

Niall had said that they would probably stay in Nassau until the end of the week. Two days later, he hired a boat and took Rachel water-skiing along the coast.

Ever since she had seen the younger tourists skimming over the water behind speedboats, Rachel had longed to try the sport, but whether Niall had guessed this she could not tell. Perhaps he was only staying in Nassau to give her a chance to acclimatise herself to civilisation. Perhaps inwardly, he was impatient to get to sea again, and the idea of water-skiing was not intended for her pleasure but to work off his own restlessness.

To balance on the two long blades looked quite easy, but first she had to learn how to take off — and that was not easy at all, Rachel discovered. However, Niall was an expert and very patient, and after five or six failures she mastered the starting technique. Once she was upright on the water, with her knees straight and the tow-line stretching tautly to the speedboat, it was only a matter of keeping balanced.

"Oh, Niall, that was marvellous. I felt like a flying fish," she said happily when, two hours later, they sat on the beach, resting.

The boat had been secured to a mooring-post, and Teaboy had gone off to have a swim.

Niall opened a packet of sandwiches and uncorked the vacuum flask which was full of chilled Cuba Libre.

"You've done very well for a beginner. A few more runs and you'll be ready to go on to mono-skiing."

Rachel munched a sandwich, and sampled the refreshingly cold blend of rum and Coca-Cola.

"This is almost like Anguna," she said absently, looking along the deserted stretch of beach, with its pale pink sand and backdrop of tall leaning palm trees.

They were some miles from the city, well beyond the elaborately landscaped gardens of the millionaires' villas and the luxury hotels.

Presently, when Niall seemed to have fallen asleep, she was able to lie on her elbow and watch him. Most of the time, she hardly dared to glance at him for fear he would guess what had happened to her.

She had fallen in love with him — she knew that now. Perhaps, in a way, it had begun the first time she had met him. But then she had felt only a kind of restlessness. Now, it was something much more powerful — a longing, a hunger, a heartache.

Niall opened his eyes and caught her watching him. Rachel sat up in a hurry.

Terrified that her expression might have betrayed her, she said rapidly, "I've been thinking, Niall — about how to earn my living when we get to Bermuda. I doubt if I'd be suitable as a shop assistant, and I couldn't work in an office without training. Do you think they would take me in a hospital — as a nurse, I mean?"

"Probably." Niall rolled on to his stomach, and reached for his cigarette case. "Do you think you'd like nursing?"

"I don't know — I think so. Anyway I haven't much choice in the matter. I must find work as soon as possible, so I'll just have to take what I can get."

Niall was silent for some moments. Then he said slowly, "Yes, nursing would be one answer, I suppose. But I think I have a better idea."

"Oh? What is it?"

He drew on his cigarette. Without looking round, he said casually, "How would you like to be a wife, Rachel?"

"A wife?" she repeated blankly.

"Yes — my wife."

CHAPTER THREE

HE was joking, Rachel realised, with anguish. He could not be serious — no, of course not! Yet, just for one second, she had thought . . .

"Oh, you fool — you idiot!" she cried silently.

But it was herself she apostrophised, not Niall. He had only meant to tease, not to torment her. But if he knew . . . if he had any idea how cruelly the joke had hurt her. Well, thank heaven, he didn't know. He almost certainly would have done if he had been facing her; and he might guess even yet if she didn't give a light-hearted answer.

She was still trying to think up some flippant piece of repartee when Niall swung over on to his back again. Sitting up beside her, he said, "You look quite scandalised. Is the very idea so repugnant?"

Rachel managed a laugh, or rather a sound which she hoped would pass for one. "My situation isn't quite as desperate as all that, is it?" she asked, in a brittle tone.

To her surprise, Niall did not grin or

feint a cuff at her. "I'm sorry." His voice was clipped. "I sometimes forget there's a gulf of ten years between us. No doubt thirty seems almost senile to you." With one swift, supple movement, he got to his feet and walked off.

For some moments she stared blankly after him. Then, shedding some — but not all — her caution, she sprang from the sand and ran after him.

"Oh, really, Niall — you aren't trying to fox me that you *meant* it?" she said, reaching him.

His cigarette was only half smoked, but he flung it away with a curious violence.

"Yes, I did, as it happens," he said crisply.

"But . . . but I thought you were joking," she stammered.

He lifted an eyebrow at her. "Oh, I'm a devil for merry quips and amusing hoaxes. Anything for a good guffaw, you know."

"Oh, please — you needn't be sarcastic," she said quickly.

Glancing down at her, his expression softened a little. "Don't fuss, Rachel. You haven't broken my heart, you know. All the same, a ripple of girlish laughter *is* rather an ungracious reaction when someone has just proposed to you. You might try to be a little less candid the next time it happens."

"But, Niall — you don't understand," she began anxiously.

"Let's forget the whole subject, shall we?"

"I don't want to forget it. I want to explain. Oh, *please*, won't you listen a minute?"

He had begun to walk down towards the water, but, at her imploring tone, he shrugged and stood still again.

"I didn't mean to sound rude and ungracious. I — I just couldn't believe that you were serious," Rachel blurted. "I still can't believe it — not really. Why should you want me to marry you?"

His eyes narrowed. "You mean you might consider the suggestion?"

"Well, of course — if you swear it isn't a joke."

"Jokes of that nature could be dangerous," he said drily. Then, taking her hands, "Very well, I'll ask you again. How would you like to marry me, Rachel Devon?"

Before she could answer him, there was a hail from Teaboy. He was wading out of the sea, less than twenty yards away from them.

"Oh, damn the boy," Niall said softly. Then, with reluctant amusement, "I'm afraid we shall have to discuss this later on. Hello, Teaboy. Found something for the pot?"

The mate was carrying a large oilskin bag. Like Niall, he always wore a sharp hunting knife when he went into the water, and a pair of rubber diving goggles were slung round his neck.

Shaking himself like a dog, he said cheerfully, "Ah's done catched some pusfellers, Cap'n. Ah's plannin' to fry dem fo' youse supper."

Plunging his arm into the bag, he brought out an armful of squirming octopi.

They were only the smallest of their species but, as they wrapped their tentacles round Taboy's forearm, Rachel gave a cry of dismay.

"Oh, can't you put them back, poor little creatures? I hate seeing them cooked," she exclaimed.

"Are you fond of them?" Niall asked curiously.

"Why, yes, I am — aren't you?" she

asked, in surprise. Reaching into Teaboy's bag, she found one still writhing at the bottom. Lifting it out, she let it cling round her wrist and examined it. "They remind me of my pet one, Mister Pod. I kept him in a rock pool at home, but he needed such a terrible lot of crabs to eat that I could hardly keep him going. Anyway, he was washed out one night in a storm. He's probably quite a giant by now."

Niall grinned. "It's not only your pigtail that distinguishes you, Rachel. There aren't many women who find something endearing about cephalopods. Heave 'em back, Teaboy. We can't fry some of Miss Rachel's best friends."

"But, Cap'n, you's always done relish dem," Teaboy protested.

"That's all in the past, my lad. From now our motto must be 'kindness to cuttlefish'."

Watching them wade into the water, Teaboy scratched his curly head. "Now, if dat ain't de craziest notion — throwin' away mah fine catch of pus-fellers," he muttered, mystified.

It was about nine o'clock in the evening when Teaboy asked Niall if he could go "over the hill" for an hour or two.

"Where's over the hill?" Rachel enquired, after the mate had swaggered off in a dazzling Palm Beach shirt, immaculate white trousers and his treasured pair of pea-green suede shoes.

"It's the coloured people's quarter. Most of the best goombay clubs are there," Niall explained. Then, "Like to go for a stroll, or shall we stay here?"

"I — I think I'd rather stay here tonight. My legs are a bit tired from all that skiing," Rachel said nervously.

For the past four hours — ever since they had left that quiet beach — she had been waiting for this moment, for being alone with him. Now it had arrived — but she was no nearer knowing what to say to him.

"Yes, you're bound to feel a certain amount of muscle strain," Niall said easily, pushing the old basket chairs together. "Here, prop your feet up on this box."

"And not only muscle strain," thought Rachel. She wondered how long it would be before he broached the subject which must surely be uppermost in both their minds.

But it seemed that Niall was less on edge. After settling beside her in his chair, he lit

89

one of his evening cheroots and sat placidly smoking for ten minutes.

"You're very silent. What are you brooding about?" he asked at last.

"Oh, for goodness' sake — what an inane question," thought Rachel, with a spasm of irritation. "What *else* would I be thinking about?"

"About whether to marry me, I suppose?" he went on, before she could answer. "Has the shock worn off a little now?"

"Yes . . . a little," she said tensely.

"But you still haven't made up your mind?"

"Oh, Niall, how could I have? We — we've scarcely discussed it yet. It isn't exactly a trivial matter, you know."

"Not trivial — but fairly simple," he said mildly. "I need a wife; you need a place in the world." Then, after a pause, "You like me, don't you?"

"Yes, of course I like you — but that has nothing to do with it."

"I should have thought it had everything to do with it. You can't marry someone who's repulsive to you."

"I shouldn't think you would be repulsive to any girl," she said, in a low tone.

"You flatter me," he said drily. "But, in spite of my overwhelming charm, you still seem very dubious about marrying me."

Rachel nibbled her lower lip for some moments. "Niall . . . you say you need a wife," she began hesitantly. "But it seems to me that you have everything you need as you are. You're not a domesticated person. A wife would be a curb on your freedom."

"Perhaps: I'm prepared to accept that. Even gypsies have families, you know."

"But why me? Why choose me?" she asked perplexedly.

Niall flipped his cheroot into the water. "You said the other day that you were not like other girls," he reminded her. "That's exactly why I think we ought to suit each other. I don't want to change my way of life, and you are one of the few girls who could fit into it. Unless you're beginning to feel that you'd like all the luxuries you've seen recently?" he added questioningly.

"I just want to be happy," she said simply.

"Don't you think I could make you happy?"

"I'm sure you could. But could I make *you* happy, Niall?"

"Why not? I'm not difficult to please." He reached out his hand to touch her arm. "Look, sleep on it, Rachel. Think it over. You don't *have* to marry me — as you said, your position isn't desperate — but I think you'd find it suited you pretty well. Anyway, have an early night and we'll talk about it again in the morning."

But, although she did as he suggested and went down to the cabin and to bed, it was several hours before Rachel finally slept. The course of her entire future life was in the balance.

Towards midnight, she heard Teaboy come back on board. Evidently, Niall too, was still awake. She heard the mate speak to him and his low-voiced reply. Perhaps he was still sitting where she had left him, listening to the strumming of a guitar from one of the fishing sloops, and watching the night life of the harbour.

By one, everywhere was still, except for the occasional creak of a mooring line and the soft plashing of water. Rachel sat up, thumped her pillow, drank some lime-juice and lay down again. If only she could make up her mind!

Perhaps, feeling about Niall as she did, it was foolish of her to hesitate. Perhaps she ought to have said 'yes' immediately — grasping the offer with both hands, not wondering and worrying half the night.

And so she would have done — if Niall had said anything about loving her.

But he didn't love her, that was obvious. He must like her, he might even be quite fond of her. But if he loved her, he would have said so — surely he would?

The more she thought about this, the less she succeeded in convincing herself that Niall was a man who shied from any emotional declarations. No, if she faced the facts squarely, he had most likely asked her to marry him because, from time to time, he missed the companionship of someone of his own race. And also, perhaps, because he wanted a son to take over the *Dolphin* one day.

At the thought of bearing Niall's child, she shivered suddenly. How could she marry him and live with him if he didn't love her? Yet, if she refused him and they parted in Bermuda, she might never — or scarcely ever — see him again. Which prospect was worse? To share his life, and to accept that he could give her nothing more than kindness and a certain limited affection? Or at the finish of this voyage to say good-bye, and then to fend for herself in an alien environment?

At two in the morning, still racked by uncertainty and doubt, she drifted wearily to sleep.

"Where's the Captain, Teaboy?"

Rachel had overslept, and it was past nine o'clock when she appeared on deck next morning.

"He gone shoppin', Missy Rachel. He somewhere in Bay Street, Ah reckon. Don't know 'zactly wheres," the mate told her.

"Do you think he'll be long? I — I want to speak to him."

"No more'n half an hour, Ah don't reckon. Ah'll git yo' breakfast while you's waitin'."

"Oh, just coffee will do. I'm not very hungry." Rachel began to pace restlessly about. Now that she had made up her mind, she wanted to tell Niall and get it over.

He was back within ten minutes. Catching sight of his tall figure striding along the next wharf, she felt a last moment pang of indecision. Then her resolution hardened again. Scrambling up on to the quay, she went to meet him.

"Hello — what's up? Something wrong?" he asked quickly.

Rachel shook her head, at the same time drawing a deep breath.

"Niall, I've thought it over. I will marry you," she said bluntly.

For one instant he looked at her so strangely she wondered if he could have changed his mind. Then he smiled.

"Well, that's good, because I've just bought a bottle of champagne."

"Champagne? But isn't that very expensive?" she asked, startled.

"It is — but we can stand it once in a while." He linked his free arm through hers, and started to walk back to the schooner.

"But why today? Is it your birthday?" Rachel queried.

"You are dull this morning," he said

95

teasingly. "The champagne is for drinking to our future, little addlepate."

Rachel stopped short and freed her arm from his. "You mean you *counted* on my accepting you?" she asked frostily.

"I would have been surprised if you hadn't," he said equably.

"Oh, that really is the limit!" Rachel exploded. "When I think what a wretched night I spent — and now you calmly tell me that you *knew* I was going to agree. Oh, of all the arrogant, conceited, utterly infuriating — "

But Niall cut short this unflattering assessment of his character. "Are you breaking it off again? So soon?" he asked her mockingly.

At this point the appearance of a large loading cart forced them to step apart. By the time it had rumbled past, Rachel's indignation had cooled slightly.

"Shall I sling this in the harbour?" Niall asked wickedly, brandishing the paper-wrapped champagne bottle as they moved towards each other again.

Unwillingly, Rachel found herself laughing. "Have you ever *not* got your own way?" she asked resignedly.

"Unfortunately, yes — many times." His tone was light, he grinned at her.

So perhaps it was only her fancy that his eyes held a momentary bleakness.

Back on the *Dolphin*, Niall told Teaboy to put the champagne in the ice-box.

"Miss Rachel is going to stay with us permanently, Teaboy," he explained. "We've decided to get married."

The mate seemed delighted by this news. He would go to the market and buy a green turtle, he said, beaming. The occasion called for a special *pièce de résistance* for lunch.

"Dat's if'n yo' ain't had no turtles in de family, missy?" he added as an afterthought, remembering her distaste for fried octopi. "But de Cap'n, he mighty partial to turtle meat."

After he had gone, Niall said, "Do you mind not having an engagement ring, Rachel? At least, not until the end of this trip?"

"Oh, Niall, of course I don't mind. I — I don't expect anything like that."

"Well, I thought this might appeal to you." He produced a small packet from his pocket.

"You needn't have bothered to buy anything. I don't want to be a lot of expense to you. Oh, Niall, it's beautiful!"

The packet, she had found, contained a tiny chased silver dolphin. It hung from a thread-fine silver chain and was meant to be worn round the neck. It was the first piece of jewellery Rachel had ever possessed, and she had never seen anything so exquisite.

"Let me fix the catch for you," said Niall, moving round behind her.

As his fingers brushed against her nape, Rachel said shakily, "I would much rather have this than an ordinary ring, Niall. But what with this, and the champagne, and now a turtle, I seem to be costing you a fortune. Please don't spend any more on me."

"Why not? You're my fiancée now, remember. And I'm not exactly a pauper, you know."

"No . . . but it isn't as if we were a normal couple," she said, flushing.

He had come round in front of her again. "The necklet will look better when you have some dresses," he said, studying her. Then, "We're not so abnormal that I can't even give you a present, are we?"

"Well . . . you know what I mean," she said awkwardly.

"I'm not sure that I do. Are you under the impression that our future relationship is going to be in a completely different footing from a 'normal' marriage?"

Divining what he must mean, Rachel grew scarlet, "No . . . no, of course it won't," she said rapidly. "I just meant that I didn't expect you to be . . . extravagant."

"Oh, I see," he said drily. "Well, you can leave me to deal with our finances. I shan't be so indulgent with you that we run up vast debts and have to bolt for it. You may even find out I have a mean streak."

"If you had, you wouldn't have given me this," she said shyly, touching the chain round her throat. "I — I haven't thanked you properly yet."

With a quick step forward, she put one hand on his forearm and reached up to quickly kiss his cheek. Then, swiftly, she retreated again.

For a moment, Niall's face was unreadable. Then he said briskly, "Thanks — and now we'd better discuss the actual wedding. Have you any objection to getting married right away?"

"You mean, here — in Nassau? Oh, but I thought we'd be married in Bermuda."

"There are reasons why I'd prefer to do it here," Niall said casually. "Oh, there's nothing wrong or shady, I promise you. I haven't got a wife in every port — I'm not a notorious bigamist."

"But won't your people want to be there?" she asked, troubled. "Your grandmother . . . all your friends."

"I shouldn't think so. It won't be a grand social function — just a short ten-minute affair at the registry office. You don't mind that, do you? You weren't expecting all the trimmings . . . a veil . . . orange blossom?"

"Oh, no," she said hastily. "Not at all." But she had not even known that there were such places as registry offices. It was yet another example of her ignorance. So their marriage would be a contract, not a sacrament. She found the idea oddly chilling.

"Right — then I'll attend to it today," said Niall, his tone very practical and businesslike. "Can I have your birth certificate and so forth?"

Rachel nodded. "I'll get them from the cabin."

But, when she was alone for a few moments, she sank down on the bunk and closed her eyes. At this time yesterday the future had still been irresolute. Now she had not only committed herself, but was being given no chance for revocation. It was like being swept into a whirlpool . . . dizzying, frightening. All she could cling to was a dream — a dream that, if she could be a good wife to him, Niall might one day discover that he loved her.

In spite of Rachel being under age, in view of her curious circumstances, Niall was able to obtain a special licence. They would be married in two days' time, he told her briefly, returning from his interview with the authorities concerned with such matters.

Next morning, without saying where they were going, he took her to a dress shop in Bay Street.

"I've told Mrs. Conway what you need, Rachel," he said, after introducing her to the proprietress. "She'll show you several dresses that are suitable, and you can choose whichever you like best. Then you can wait for me in the café across the road. I'll be away about half an hour."

After he had gone, Mrs. Conway took Rachel into a fitting-room. She was a tall, handsome woman in her fifties, beautifully dressed and groomed, but not in the least supercilious.

"Well, first, let's see what size you'll need, my dear," she said, finding a tape measure. "Hm, Mr. Herrick was right. You're a stock size ten. Most men have no idea of women's dress sizes. Now if you'll slip off your beach clothes and put on this foundation and these stockings, I'll go and fetch some dresses that should suit you."

The "foundation" she had indicated was lying in a box on the chair. Rachel lifted it out of the tissue-paper and examined it. It was a feather-light white lace basque with long satin suspenders. Fortunately, Mrs. Conway was away some time, because Rachel had difficulty in fastening all the hooks down the back. Then, terrified she might spoil their gossamer texture, she put on the sheer nylon stockings.

"Can you manage, my dear? Oh, yes — good." Mrs. Conway had swept back through the pale green velvet curtains and was hanging several dresses on a rail.

"There, you see what it does for you?" she asked, as Rachel fixed the back suspender buttons and straightened to study her reflection. "You are lucky — you have an excellent figure. But even a perfect figure needs a light foundation. See how it pulls your waist in and streamlines your hips?"

To Rachel, all the dresses seemed so pretty that she asked Mrs. Conway to choose for her.

The older woman pursed her lips and considered. "Well, the blue is very effective," she said slowly. "But perhaps — for a wedding — not quite formal enough. If I were you, I think I should have the primrose wild silk. Then, without the little jacket, you can wear it at parties and even dances."

"There isn't a white dress that would fit me?" Rachel asked hesitantly.

"Oh, not white, my dear — not for a wedding," Mrs. Conway said, surprisingly. "I agree it would look lovely against your tan, but the bride will be in white, you must remember? I never recommend white for the guests' dresses."

"No . . . I suppose not," Rachel said awkwardly. Evidently Niall had not mentioned that she was the bride and this her wedding gown. What *had* he told her?

"Now that hem will have to be altered — but that won't take long — and you'll need a petticoat, some gloves and suitable shoes," Mrs. Conway went on. "I can do the petticoat and the gloves, but the shoes you will have to get elsewhere. Oh, and what about a hat, I wonder? No, I expect when you put your hair up, a hat looks wrong. I'll show you some flower sprays I have. They came in from France just this week. They're attached to little combs, so you just fix them on your hair wherever you like."

Fifteen minutes later, after the petticoat and gloves had been selected — and a diadem of tiny yellow buds and green velvet leaves — Rachel crossed the street to the café. Mrs. Conway had promised to send everything round to the schooner as soon as the dress was ready. But, when Rachel had asked what she owed her — hoping her nest-egg of not quite nine pounds would be enough — the modiste had said Niall was paying the bill. And before Rachel could insist on paying it herself — as soon as she had fetched her money from the *Dolphin* — some other customers arrived.

"Niall, I can't let you pay for all those things," she objected, as soon as he joined her in the café.

"Certainly you can, and I already have," he said firmly. "Mrs. Conway tells me you need some shoes now. We'll go along and get them as soon as we've had our coffee."

"I'm going to pay for those — or I won't wear any," Rachel informed him determinedly.

The plain ivory court shoes — which, with their almond-shaped toes and spindle heels, looked absurdly incongruous below the rolled-up bottoms of her jeans — cost nearly four pounds. Rachel was appalled. If shoes were so expensive, the price of her dress must have been ruinous.

As soon as they returned to the schooner, she insisted on giving him the money for them.

That night — her last night as Rachel Devon — Niall took her out to supper again. But this time Rachel was not troubled by self-consciousness. She was too preoccupied. All she could think about was that, at noon tomorrow, she would become Mrs. Niall Herrick.

"Oh, by the way, I had a word with Monsieur Antoine this afternoon," Niall said suddenly, after they had finished the meal and were lingering over coffee.

"Who is Monsieur Antoine?" she said blankly.

"Your hairdresser friend — although I doubt if that's his real name. I seem to detect a note of Cockney somewhere," Niall said, in an amused tone. "Anyway, whether he's from Paris or Pimlico, he'll be waiting to transform you at ten o'clock."

"You've made an appointment for me?"

Niall nodded. "Mrs. Conway said something about a French headdress and your needing a professional hair-do."

"What exactly did you tell her about me?" Rachel asked curiously.

Niall grinned. "I said you were fresh from a convent school in Europe, and had no women relatives to advise you."

"Why didn't you tell her the truth?"

He seemed to hesitate for a moment before answering. "She might have passed

106

it on to the local press," he said, shrugging. "It would make quite a story, you know. A mysterious English hermit being killed in a hurricane . . . his daughter left stranded . . . a whirlwind marriage."

"Do they print things like that?" she asked, surprised.

"Indeed they do — and a piece in the *Nassau Daily Tribune* could lead to the agencies getting hold of it. Before we knew it, we might well be making world headlines. I don't want to spend my honeymoon being pursued by indefatigable press hounds."

Later, walking back to the ship, he said suddenly, "You know that you can still change your mind, Rachel? It isn't too late to back out."

"Do *you* want to do that?" she asked anxiously.

"I don't — but you might, honey. It's not so easy to tell what you're thinking now. An acquaintance with civilisation seems to be making you less transparent."

"Is it? I don't feel any different."

"Yesterday morning — when you were so annoyed about the champagne — you said you'd spent a wretched night," he reminded her. "Why 'wretched', may I ask."

"I . . . I was exaggerating," Rachel said awkwardly. "I think most people do when they're angry."

"But you had some trouble coming to the big decision, I gather?"

"Well . . . didn't you think about it before you suggested the idea?"

"Yes, I did — but not to the extent of sleepless nights. Which reminds me — you ought to get to bed soon. I don't want a bride with bleary eyes."

They parted at the head of the companion ladder, as Niall said he would smoke for a while before turning in himself. Since they had been in harbour, he had been sleeping in a hammock slung in the saloon.

Rachel had wondered if, tonight, he would kiss her again. But, although he touched her cheek with his forefinger, his 'Good-night' was as casual as always.

Next morning, Rachel kept her appointment with the hairdresser. And, whatever his real nationality — and his pronounced French accent did seem to slip in moments of stress — Monsieur Antoine was certainly a master of his craft. Although Rachel had always swum without a bathing cap and had spent long hours in hot sunlight, her hair had not suffered from neglect. Whenever there had been sufficient to spare, Octavia had washed it in rainwater and, every night, she had insisted on brushing it for Rachel, often rubbing in a palmful of coconut oil.

Secretly impatient of these nightly ministrations, Rachel had only put up with them because she knew they gave pleasure to the cook. Now, listening to Monsieur Antoine, she realised that she ought to have been grateful to Octavia. Because, according to the hair stylist, both sun and salt water could have lamentable effects on women's hair.

"I tell you, *mademoiselle*, if you were to see some of my clients it would amaze you," he said sadly. "Their condition is pitiful — but pitiful! Scalps that have been grilled like fillet steaks. Hair that is as dry and brittle as straw. No lustre, no body, no life. And then they expect a perfect *coiffure*. I ask you, how can an artist like myself be expected to create a masterpiece with such hair? Another larger roller, *s'il vous plaît*" — this to the assistant at his elbow.

"It must be very difficult," Rachel agreed. She was glad that he talked all the time. It helped to calm her nerves.

"*Difficile?* it is not merely that — it is impossible!" he exclaimed vehemently. "Frankly, *mademoiselle*, it is a matter of astonishment to me that, having acquired so deep a sun-tan, your hair remains a pleasure for me to dress. Now, Marie will conduct you to the dryer."

It was a quarter past eleven before he finally completed his handiwork and stepped back to await her reaction.

"You like it, *mademoiselle*? You are satisfied?" He brandished a mirror to show her the back view.

"Like it? I can't believe it's me," Rachel exclaimed, with shining eyes.

And, although she had watched her reflection while he worked, the finished effect was still something to take her breath away. How glad she was, now, that Niall had prevented her from having her pigtail shorn. Smoothed back from her temples and swept up from the nape of her long slim neck, her hair was dressed in a crown of smooth, gleaming coils.

"You see, I have designed it so that your headdress will fit just so. Now, a light spray of lacquer and . . . *c'est fini!*'

After she had thanked him, paid the bill, and bought herself the pale rose lipstick recommended by the receptionist, Rachel hurried out into the street. Before she dashed back to the *Dolphin*, she had something very important to do.

There was a gift shop at the corner of the block and, luckily, an assistant was free to serve her.

"Good-morning. I want to buy a present," she said hurriedly. "Something for a man."

The salesgirl made several suggestions, but all were far beyond Rachel's means. At last she produced a cigarette case.

"Oh, yes, that would be perfect," Rachel said, remembering the battered old tin which served Niall for this purpose at present. "But how much is it?" — eyeing the shop's clock which now showed twenty minutes to twelve.

To her relief, she found that it cost sixpence less than the money she had left.

As soon as the girl had wrapped it, she dashed out of the shop and back to the waterfront.

Neither of the men were on the deck when, panting, she reached the *Dolphin*. She had almost finished dressing before she heard their voices above her on the quay.

A few minutes later, Niall tapped at the cabin door.

"Are you there, Rachel?" he called. "Want some help with a zip or anything?"

"Oh, please — don't come in. I won't be a minute." She didn't want him to see her until she was ready.

It was three minutes to twelve by her father's watch when she drew on the supple white kid gloves. There was no long mirror in the cabin but, as far as she could tell, everything was in place. The seams of her stockings were straight, her petticoat was not showing, the diadem was secure on her high-piled hair.

With her cheeks as pink as the new lipstick and her heart thudding, she opened the cabin door. "I'm ready now, Niall."

"Ah . . . just in time for a shot of Dutch courage — if you need it. Teaboy's gone to get a cab," said Niall, from inside the galley. A second later, coming into the saloon with a bottle in one hand and a couple of glasses in the other, he stopped short.

"D-do you like the dress? Will I do?" Rachel asked, at last, when it seemed he might stand like that indefinitely.

Niall set down the bottle and the glasses and moved towards her. Taking both her hands, he said softly, "And you're the girl who wondered why people stared at her. You look . . . enchanting, Rachel."

"Hey, Cap'n — de cab's waitin'," Teaboy shouted down the companionway.

"No time for Dutch courage after all." Niall let go of her hands and hurriedly shrugged into his jacket. "Mind you don't catch your heels on the rungs, honey."

Half an hour later, it was all over. The irrevocable step had been taken. "I should think you must be hungry, Mrs. Herrick," Niall said teasingly, helping her down the companionway to the saloon again. "You didn't have much for breakfast. Come on, Teaboy — the bride is wilting from under-nourishment."

Teaboy followed them down the ladder

and dived into the galley. A moment later he reappeared with a large napkin-shrouded tray and set it carefully on the table.

"Dere yo' is, Mis' Herrick, ma'am" — he swept off the covering with a flourish — "Dat's what de Cap'n ordered special," he announced.

"But, Niall, where did it come from?" Rachel asked, never having seen anything like the array of *vol-au-vents* and *bouchées* which were set out on the tray.

"From a local catering firm. This is more or less what people eat at wedding receptions in England."

Rachel sat still holding the posy of pale yellow rosebuds which Teaboy had handed to her when she climbed into the taxi to drive to the register office. Looking down at them, she said quietly, "You've thought of everything, haven't you? Thank you, Niall."

It was not until some time later — Teaboy had discreetly disappeared again — that she remembered the cigarette case.

"I forgot — I have a present for you, too." Fetching it from the cabin, she gave it to him.

"Why, Rachel, this is just what I've

always wanted," he said, smiling. And, taking her hand in his, he kissed her fingers.

In the hours that followed, Rachel began to wonder why she had ever doubted that their marriage could be a success. When he asked how she would like to spend the afternoon, she suggested swimming. But Niall said that she must not spoil her hair yet — he had a surprise in store for her — so they went for a drive along the coast in a hired car.

Before they set out, Rachel changed back into her jeans and took off the circlet of flowers. But Niall did not change and, as they drove out of the city, she thought that he, too, looked very different from usual.

He was wearing a pale grey tropic-weight lounge suit, with an immaculate white shirt and a dark silk tie. A stranger would never have guessed that he was a sailor. Today, he looked more like a distinguished man of affairs.

In the evening, he took her to one of the grandest of the big hotels.

"I thought you would like to show off your dress and your hair," he explained, when they were sitting at a table on the terrace.

Below them was the moon-spangled sea, and all along the terrace hung Chinese lanterns. This was the Nassau of the millionaires and the famous. Everything about it — from the thick damask napery to the crystal vases of carnations on every table — was of the finest and most expensive quality. It was a world of soft carpets and attentive waiters, of rich and rare dishes and vintage wines.

Even the atmosphere was redolent of the finest Havana cigars and elusive French scents.

On a dais in the indoor part of the dining-room, a band was playing selections from Broadway musicals. After they had dined, Niall asked Rachel if she would like to dance.

"But I don't know how," she objected.

"Don't be nervous, it isn't difficult." He took her by the hand and she had to go with him.

The floor was small and crowded. The music was a quickstep. With Niall holding her close, and having a natural sense of rhythm, Rachel soon found that she could follow his steps quite easily. By the time the music ended she was relaxed and even enjoyed herself.

"Would you like to be spending your honeymoon here?" he asked her suddenly, when they were dancing again, this time to a slow dreamy waltz.

"No, I don't think so — not really," Rachel said thoughtfully.

Now that she was less dazzled by the women's fashionable clothes, she was beginning to notice how hard and dissatisfied many of them looked. Even the girls of her own age had blasé manners and mouths that seemed to hint at spoiled petulance. They even danced in a languid, bored way — but then none had an escort like Niall. What few younger men there were present were somewhat fatuous-looking, Rachel thought. Most of the men were of her father's generation or even older. But they were not fit and vigorous, as Charles Devon had been. Their bodies were overweight and flaccid. She could not imagine any of them going out into the fury of a hurricane to rescue a lost Bahamian child, as her father had done — and Niall would. It was their wealth and not their own force of character that gave them their authority.

"No," she said decidedly, after a pause. "No, I feel more at home on the *Dolphin*. This is lovely for one evening — but not for always."

Niall drew her closer, his left hand tightening. She was glad that his fingers were not soft and too carefully manicured. His hands were always clean, but they were a sailor's hands, lean and hard, the palms calloused.

It was barely ten o'clock when he said, "It's been a long day for you, honey. Let's get out of here, shall we ?" He beckoned the waiter to their table.

And it was soon afterwards, as they left the dining-rooms and passed into the opulently-appointed entrance lounge, that something happened to spoil everything.

The doors of a lift had just slid open, and among the people stepping out was a woman with dyed ash-blonde hair and a face that looked curiously like a mask. She was in full evening dress with white fox furs, and accompanied by a sleek, olive-skinned young man who was carrying a poodle.

"Why, Niall Herrick . . . of all people!"

she exclaimed, sweeping towards them. "I had no idea you were staying here, Niall. But we only flew in this morning. I've been in New York, you know."

"Good-evening, Mrs. Lancaster," he said stiffly.

"Oh, I forgot — you haven't met Ramon," she said, glancing at the young man at her elbow. "Mr. Herrick is an old friend from Bermuda, Ramon darling. And this . . . ? looking enquiringly at Rachel.

"This is Miss Devon," Niall said curtly. "Miss Devon . . . Senhor Salvador."

"*Senhor . . . Senhorita.*" The young man bowed from the hips, his dark eyes kindling with admiration as he took in Rachel's sun-gold hair and bare brown shoulders.

But Rachel was not flattered by the look. It was obvious that Niall did not like these people, and she did not much care for them herself. In a girlish strapless crinoline of pale rose tulle — lavishly embroidered with pearl drops, rose-coloured sequins and crystal beading — and with her face so heavily made up that the skin beneath the maquillage was quite invisible, Mrs. Lancaster could still not conceal that she was fifty-ish. A vivid cupid's bow was painted

over her own thin lipline, and her eyelids
were spiked with fake black lashes. Admit-
tedly, her figure was superb, but a three-
strand pearl choker did not hide the signs
of sagging at her throat, and her hands,
heavily jewelled, were beginning to mottle.
As for the bold-eyed South American, with
his thin dark moustache, and frilled voile
dress shirt under a white tuxedo, he was
too sleek, too suave.

"You live in Nassau, Miss Devon?"
Mrs. Lancaster enquired, her eyes flicker-
ing over Rachel with undisguised curiosity.

Rachel nodded. It was true, for the
moment.

"If you're out for the evening, why don't
you join us?" Mrs. Lancaster suggested.
"It's always more amusing to make up a
party. Ramon darling, do put Coco down.
She wants to run about, I expect. Now,
where do you suggest we ought to go,
Niall?"

"Thanks, but we're on our way home,"
Niall said, unsmiling. "Some other time
perhaps."

"But the night has barely begun, my
dearest boy," Mrs. Lancaster said, flutter-

ing her eyelashes. "Nobody goes home before midnight."

"Miss Devon is tired and has a head-ache."

"You mean you want her to yourself — naughty boy! And of course you don't care for night life, do you? That was why I was so surprised to see you *here*."

"If you'll excuse us . . ." he began, taking Rachel's arm and beginning to move away.

"Oh, Niall, you've heard the good news . . . about Nadine?"

Niall stood still again, and Rachel thought he tensed slightly. But his face remained expressionless.

"No, I can't say I have. What news?"

Glancing at the older woman, Rachel saw a look that could have been malice on her face. But whatever it was, it was only perceptible for an instant. Then pursing her artificial mouth, she said wryly: "Well, I suppose I shouldn't call it *good* news, in the circumstances. You see, Sir James had a heart attack last month. He and Nadine were staying in Monte Carlo, and he collapsed in the Casino one night. Such a frightful shock for her, poor darling —

although he was not a young man, one must remember."

"He's dead?" Niall asked tersely.

"Yes . . . and Nadine is a widow, poor sweet. But not for very long, I imagine. She arrived back in Bermuda last week, and I can't say she seemed overwhelmed with grief. But then it wasn't exactly a love-match, I imagine." Mrs. Lancaster gave a brittle, tinkling laugh. "You'll find she's even lovelier than she was. Running round Europe — no doubt it was all that hectic social life that caused Sir James's heart trouble — seemed to have given her added charm, I thought. And she was never lacking in charm, was she, Niall?"

He did not answer her, and there was no doubting the grimness about his mouth now.

"I hope you enjoy your stay in Nassau, Mrs. Lancaster," he said formally. "Good-night — good-night, Senhor Salvador."

A few moments later, he was handing Rachel into the back of a taxi-cab.

It was a ten-minute drive back to the waterfront, but all the time they were in the taxi Niall sat in silence, not even smoking. Although it was too dark to see his face clearly, the glow of the street lamps showed that his hands were clenched into fists. Absorbed in some fierce, private anger, he seemed to have forgotten her existence. Rachel shivered, but not with any physical chill. She had a sickening premonition that, in the space of those few minutes in the hotel lounge, all the promise of the day had been destroyed.

At the end of the quay where the *Dolphin* was berthed, Niall helped her out and thrust a handful of coins at the cab driver. Then, without taking her arm or even glancing at her, he strode towards the schooner. He did remember to help her down on to the deck, but it was the briefest of contacts.

In the saloon, Rachel said in a low voice, "Shall I make some cocoa . . . or tea, perhaps ?"

"What ? Oh . . . yes, if you like." He was still almost totally preoccupied.

Rachel went into the galley and found a tea towel to protect her dress. She lit the burner, put a pan of milk on to heat and slid back the hatch over the china shelves.

After she had blended the milk and cocoa powder, she glanced into the saloon.

Niall was standing where she had left him, staring at nothing, his jaw set hard.

He was still lost in thought when she carried in the steaming mugs of cocoa. But, as she set them on the table, he suddenly put his hand on her arm. The abruptness of the movement startled her. She gasped and moved back a step.

"Oh, Niall, please don't — "

Before she could finish — and she had been about to beg him not to spoil their happy day by being so angry about the encounter with Mrs. Lancaster — there was a groan and a thud from overhead.

Niall's reflexes were much swifter than Rachel's. While she was still registering the thump, he was halfway up the companionway. By the time she put her head above deck, he was kneeling by a man's inert body.

"It's Teaboy," he said sharply, over his shoulder. "He's either dead drunk or unconscious. You'll have to help me get him below."

By the time Niall had turned the mate over and got his hands under his armpits, Rachel recovered the presence of mind to kick off her high-heeled ivory slippers.

Gripping Teaboy's legs, she helped to haul him to the head of the companionway.

But it was no easy task to manoeuvre the seaman's slack body down the narrow stairway. He weighed at least thirteen stone and it was all big bones and hard muscle. Niall took nearly all the weight, and even he — as tall and as powerful as Teaboy — was sweating with exertion when they had done it.

They laid him on the floor of the saloon, and then Rachel gave a stifled cry of horror. There were bright smears of blood all over the skirt of her dress.

"He isn't dead. I felt his pulse." Niall was unscrewing the lamp from the gimbals that kept it in position when the schooner was ploughing through rough seas. But when he set it on the floor by Teaboy's head, he too had to bite back an expletive.

The whole of Teaboy's right trouser leg was sodden with blood, one shirt sleeve was soaked, and there was blood on his coarse crinkly hair.

"A knife fight," Niall said tersely. "Get some water and cloths. It may not be as bad as it looks."

When Rachel came back with a bowl of

cold water and all the clean tea towels she could find, Niall had cut away the sticky, blood-drenched trouser leg.

Without looking up, he said, "You'll find a first aid case in the bottom right-hand locker over there. And fetch a couple of blankets, will you?"

Having carried out these orders, Rachel filled a kettle and lit the burner again. Then she returned to the saloon.

"Better not watch this — it isn't very pretty," Niall said brusquely. He was examining a deep jagged wound on the mate's thigh.

"Don't be silly. I'm not afraid of blood." Taking his knife, Rachel carefully slit the sleeve of Teaboy's shirt.

The injury to his arm was not as serious. After she had cleaned and dressed the gash, Rachel had a look at his head. The blood here had oozed from a swelling on the crown of his skull.

"Someone has given him a terrific bash on the head, Niall," she said anxiously. "The swelling is as big as a turtle's egg. What on earth can have happened to him?"

"A brawl in some bar, I should imagine. He's certainly been drinking — you can smell it. But I've never known him fight unless he was forced to — he's tough, but he isn't the pugnacious type," Niall said, frowning. "Ah, I think he's coming round. I'll move the lamp."

But though Teaboy did recover consciousness, he was too dazed and incoherent to tell them much.

"He'll have to go to hospital for an X-ray. There could be some internal bleeding. He's certainly quite badly concussed," Niall said presently. "Stay with him while I telephone for an ambulance, will you?"

He was not away long, but before he came back Teaboy seemed to grasp where he was. Peering up at Rachel, who was kneeling at his side, holding his hand, he muttered, "Ah's sorry Ah's messed up yo' weddin' day, Missy Rachel. De Cap'n, he sack me for sho'."

"The Captain isn't angry with you, Teaboy. You just lie quiet while we fix you up. Don't worry about anything."

The mate screwed up his eyes and gave a grunt. Clearly, any movement of his head gave him hell.

"Dat sho' was de Cap'n's lucky day

when he done call Anguna an' find you, missy," he murmured thickly.

The ambulance arrived soon after Niall. The two white-coated attendants strapped Teaboy to a stretcher and hauled him on deck again.

"Can I come with you?" Rachel asked Niall.

"Better not — this may take some hours. Try and get some sleep. You needn't be scared of being alone here. There's a watchman along the wharf who will see that no one tries to come aboard."

"But, Niall — "

"There isn't time to argue. You get to bed."

After the ambulance had driven off, Rachel closed the companion hatch and climbed wearily down to the saloon again. It was barely eleven o'clock, yet now that the emergency was over, she felt leaden with fatigue and disappointment.

The two mugs of cocoa she had made had long since grown cold. She poured the stuff away, washed the mugs and made herself a drink of hot milk. Then she took off her ruined wedding dress — the petticoat was also badly stained — and rolled them both into a bundle. Perhaps the dress could be cleaned — she didn't know. At the moment she never wanted to see it again. It was a symbol of this whole disastrous climax — or, more accurately, anti-climax. Poor Teaboy didn't know it, but her wedding day had been spoiled long before he came reeling back. It had been ruined by that horrible Lancaster woman.

Dejectedly drinking the milk, Rachel wondered how Niall had come to know such a person. The woman was obviously not of his world, yet she had greeted him and conversed as if they were closely acquainted. And who was the girl called Nadine who had lost an elderly husband in Monte Carlo? Niall must know her, too — and she also sounded like a rich Society person. What was it Mrs. Lancaster had said to him in that sly voice? *She was never lacking in charm, was she, Niall?*

Had Niall once been a victim of that charm? Had Nadine rebuffed him, or made a fool of him, because he was only the master of a trading schooner? And was he still deeply in love with the memory of her, and had married her, Rachel, to quench his longing?

But if that was the truth, and Nadine was free now . . . *Oh, dear God, how could he do it!* Rachel thought, anguished. *And why did I ever agree to this crazy marriage?*

CHAPTER FOUR

IT was the early hours of the morning when Rachel was roused by several voices. Dressed in her jeans and one of Niall's thick oiled-wool sweaters, she had been lying on the bunk in a restless doze. Now, jerking up in alarm, she heard car doors slam and a motor starting.

Niall was coming out of Teaboy's cabin when she hurried into the saloon. He made a gesture cautioning her not to speak too loudly, then went into the galley and took down a frying pan.

"Teaboy's all right now. You get back to bed," he said, finding the bacon and the egg box.

But Rachel was wide awake now and — before she had lain down on the bunk — she had made several important resolutions. The most difficult of these was to show no sign that there was anything at fault between them. She had undertaken to make Niall a good wife. Hard as it might be — perhaps impossible — she was going to try to keep that pledge.

"I'll do that for you," she said firmly,

taking hold of the bacon. "You sit down and have a smoke. What happened at the hospital?"

If Niall was taken aback by this newly purposeful manner, he did not contest it. Perhaps he was too tired even to notice. Pulling down the spring-back wall seat, he did as she suggested and took out his cigarette tin.

"What did the X-ray show?" Rachel asked, snipping along the edges of the bacon rashers and arranging them neatly in the pan.

"There's no fracture — just concussion. He seems to have an exceptionally thick skull. They had to put some stitches in the leg wound, but if he stays in bed for a day or two and then takes things easily for a while, he should be as good as new. I'll make sure he goes for a check as soon as we get home."

"Wouldn't it have been best for him to stay in hospital, as we'll have to wait here until he's better?" Rachel asked, cutting thick slices of bread.

"We aren't staying here," Niall said tersely. "We're leaving first thing in the morning."

"You mean you'll hire a man to take Teaboy's place?"

"No, I'll manage single-handed. I've done it before."

"But, Niall, what's the point? We aren't in any rush, are we?"

"I just want to get back, that's all." His tone was quiet but adamant.

Rachel turned the bacon and broke in two eggs. "Because Nadine is there now," she thought heavily.

When he had eaten, Niall went back to see Teaboy. He was still in the mate's cabin after Rachel had washed the dishes and put everything neatly away.

She decided to go back to bed.

There was a strong breeze blowing and a good deal of cloud about when the *Dolphin* sailed away from Nassau and headed for the North-east Province Channel and, beyond that, the vastness of the Atlantic.

Niall told Rachel that there was nothing she could do to help, so she spent most of the morning keeping an eye on Teaboy and cleaning out the saloon. While she was doing this she had a look at some of Niall's maps and hydrographic charts. As far as she could make out, Bermuda lay at least six hundred miles north-east of the Bahamas, with nothing but ocean in between. She had no idea of what speed the *Dolphin* was capable, but it seemed a very long run for a man to undertake unaided.

Niall came below for his lunch. But after eating some cold turtle pie and gulping down a mug of black coffee, he looked in on Teaboy and went on deck again.

By tea-time a strong swell had risen, although the sky was still blue between the cloud banks, Niall said unemotionally that the wind was swinging round to the northern quadrant and they could expect a big sea to build up.

"You'd better strap Teaboy in his berth — and take a couple of the sea-sickness pills in the first aid box. You may start feeling queasy later on," he said.

An hour later he came down to fetch his oilskins. On no account was she to come on deck again.

"But can you manage alone in this weather?" she asked, really worried now. "Can't I do something to help you? I don't think I'll be sick."

"The only way you can help is by staying where I know you're safe and dry," he said hurriedly. "It's slippery on deck, and we're beginning to roll. Now make sure nothing is lying about loose, and if you do feel ill, for Pete's sake lie down on the bunk. Then you'll still feel pretty rough, but you probably won't get to the stage of vomiting."

"Well, that's a great comfort," Rachel responded, rather tartly. He must have known this morning that this weather was in the offing. Why couldn't he have delayed for twenty-four hours? Even if he wasn't concerned about *her* feelings, he should have had some consideration for Teaboy. The mate felt miserable enough without being lashed into a rocking bunk and half deafened by the waves and the buffeting wind.

"Don't look so scared. We aren't in any danger, I promise you." In heavy sea-boots and the shiny black oilskins, Niall disappeared on deck again.

After he had gone, Rachel followed out his instructions about making everything fast. But when she went back to see Teaboy, he was trying to unfasten the webbing bunk-belt. He kept insisting that he must get up and give Niall a hand — although every time he raised his head an inch, he winced at the excruciating pain it caused him.

"Don't you dare attempt to get up," Rachel told him sharply. "If you do, the Captain really *will* sack you. Now I'll give you another of these capsules, and you must promise me to lie still and be sensible."

Since it would be impossible for him to sleep with all the noise that was going on, Rachel stayed with him and tried not to show how anxious she was.

But it was an unnerving experience, being forced to stay down there in the cabin while, above them, all hell seemed to be let loose. Supposing Niall slipped just as a wave broke over them? Supposing they ran aground in shoal water — or were they over the deep ocean now? now? Supposing a sail broke loose? Supposing . . .

Controlling a shudder, she made herself shut her mind to all these disastrous possibilities. At least she was not feeling sea-sick yet.

The first pale grey light of dawn was out-lining the shape of the porthole when Rachel was woken by a hand on her shoulder. Her brain fuddled, her legs and arms cramped from her crouching position, she found Niall standing above her.

"Teaboy's asleep. Come and have some tea and something to eat," he said.

The tea was already made and, as she hobbled into the galley, rubbing her arms to rid them of pins and needles, Niall took a pan from the stove and spooned six or seven scrambled eggs on to thick wedges of buttered bread.

"This probably makes you feel green, but you must try to eat some," he ordered. "The best cure for sickness is a full stomach."

"I haven't been sick. It was Teaboy. I could eat the whole lot," Rachel said hungrily.

His eyebrows went up. "Teaboy was sick?" he asked, astonished.

Rachel was already tucking in to her share of the creamy yellow eggs. "I suppose it was because of his head, and having had nothing to eat since yesterday's supper. After the gale died down, I cleared the place up as much as I could, and then I just couldn't keep my eyes open. What happened on deck? Is there much damage?"

He shrugged, pouring the tea. "Nothing serious. We're some way off course, I'm afraid, but the rest of the trip should be quite smooth."

After they had eaten, Niall advised her to join him on deck for half an hour to clear her lungs of the stuffiness in the cabin. The mate, exhausted, was snoring gently.

"What's that, Niall?" Rachel asked, pointing over the rails as they stood on the foredeck a little later.

The sea was a dark indigo colouring — fathoms deeper than the waters surrounding Anguna.

Niall glanced over the side. "Oh, that's sargassum weed. Don't you know about the Sargasso Sea?"

Rachel shook her head, wondering if she would be able to persuade him to sleep for a couple of hours. She felt tired herself, but Niall looked gaunt with fatigue. Normally so clean and spruce, this morning he had a heavy growth of stubble and his eyes were red-rimmed and bloodshot.

"In the old days people used to believe that ships were often lost in the Sargasso. It was supposed to be a graveyard of hulks — ships that had been trapped in masses of seaweed."

"Are we near it now?" Rachel asked anxiously.

"We're heading that way, but it won't harm us. It covers a pretty vast area to the south of Bermuda, and most of the weed is in the central zone. The rest of it is just exceptionally salty. That's why, when you swim in Bermuda, you'll find yourself much more buoyant than usual."

"In the sea perhaps, but not in myself," she thought wryly. Aloud she said, "Can't you get some sleep now. You must be so tired."

"I may take an hour after lunch. At the moment I've got some repairs to do." Lighting a cigarette, he walked off along the deck and left her.

Thirty-six hours later, in the splendour of a crimson and gold sunset, they reached Bermuda. Reflecting the colours of the skyscape, the waters of Great Sound were like an expanse of rich Venetian-red silk.

As they passed below the dark grey bulk of a Royal Navy cruiser there was a piercing whistle. Rachel looked up to see a sailor waving to her. Further on, the tall mast and cross-spars of an old-fashioned full-rigger were sharply outlined against pink clouds. And, past the Sound islands, nearing Hamilton Harbour, there were vessels of every size and kind . . . one of the great Furness Line luxury liners, long low-lying oil tankers, shabby tramp steamers and dozens of large and small pleasure yachts.

Dusk had fallen before they were ready to disembark. Rachel wondered how she would be received by Niall's grandmother. Would she be kind and homely, a white-skinned counterpart of Octavia? Or would she be shocked by and resentful of her grandson's precipitate marriage and treat his strange unwelcome bride with marked antagonism?

But before going to the old lady's home, which Rachel visualised as a small pin-neat cottage close to the harbour, they had to take Teaboy to hospital. He seemed to be almost completely recovered, but his leg wound needed attention.

Niall left Rachel in their taxi while he took Teaboy into the hospital building. He was away about twenty minutes and came back alone. Teaboy would follow them later after he had had various checks, he told her.

After driving for about another five minutes — the roads seemed very narrow and tortuous — the cab turned through a tall gateway. As they rounded a bend in the drive, Rachel saw that they were approaching a large mansion with many brightly lit windows and an elegant pillared portico. "What now?" she wondered tiredly. She was longing to have something to eat and flop into bed. Whatever urgent business Niall had here, she hoped it would not take him long.

But when the taxi drew up under the portico, Niall paid the driver their fare and asked him to unload their belongings.

"Out you get. We're home," he said to Rachel.

"Here?" she exclaimed, climbing out. But Niall was already pressing a bell and did not hear her.

Almost at once the door was opened by an elderly coloured manservant in a white linen jacket and black trousers. He looked something like old Sam on Anguna, amiable and wise, and with a tonsure of grizzled curly hair. But his deep voice was almost like that of an Englishman's except for a slight softening of consonants.

"Why, Mister Niall, we weren't expecting you home so soon. There's nothing wrong, I hope, sir?" he exclaimed.

"No, nothing wrong, Joseph — just a change of plan. How is everyone?"

"Miss Julie's very well, sir, but Mrs. Herrick — " He stopped short, catching sight of Rachel, who had been hovering uncertainly in the background. "Oh, I beg your pardon, missy. I was so surprised at seeing Mister Niall, I didn't notice he had company."

"This is Joseph Barker, Rachel," Niall told her. "He's been part of this household since before I was born. Nearly fifty years now, isn't it, Joseph?"

"That's correct, Mister Niall. I wasn't above eleven years old when your father brought me to Moongates."

Rachel held out her hand to him. "How do you do, Mr. Barker," she said shyly.

"Look, Joe, we've had a pretty gruelling run. Call one of the girls to look after

Rachel, will you? We both need a bath and a change."

The butler nodded understandingly and pressed a bell in the wall. Then he went outside to fetch the baggage which the cab-driver had left on the steps.

A few moments later, a pretty coffee-coloured maid came hurrying through a door at the back of the hall. She was wearing a pale blue uniform dress with an organdie collar and cuffs, and a stiff bow of matching blue ribbon was perched on the top of her head.

"Good-evenin', Marse Niall. Good-evenin', missy." Her smile exposed two rows of milk-white teeth.

"Hello, Rietta — how are you? I want you to show Miss Rachel up to the bathroom. Find her some night gear and see she has anything else she needs, please."

"Surely, Marse Niall." The girl looked at Rachel with interest. "You come this way, missy, if you please?"

She turned towards the broad curving staircase and Rachel moved to follow. But, before she had reached the first stair, a door to their left suddenly opened and out

143

came a number of men and women. They were all in evening dress, and chatting and laughing. But when they saw Niall and Rachel their voices stilled.

"Why, Niall, sweetie — I didn't expect you back yet."

The last person to come into the hall was a tall, willowy brunette in vivid flame chiffon. Reaching Niall's side, she gave him an affectionate hug and kiss.

"I suppose you're too tired to come out with us ? We're just off to Melanie Allen's birthday ball," she explained, stepping back again. Then, seeing Rachel, "Oh, I'm sorry. I didn't realise you had someone with you."

There was a momentary pause while she waited for Niall to introduce them, her expression faintly puzzled but politely welcoming. Her guests were also eyeing Rachel curiously: the women with raised eyebrows, the men less critically.

"This is my sister Juliet, Rachel," Niall said. He was obviously annoyed by this development.

Juliet Herrick smiled and put out her hand. "Welcome to Moongates, Miss . . . ?"

"Rachel is my wife," Niall said curtly.

There was a moment of absolute silence after this announcement. No one moved. But their faces, Rachel noticed, were all incredulous.

Juliet was the first to recover. "W-why, Niall, what a lovely surprise! Why ever didn't you warn us? We . . . we could have had everything ready for you," she exclaimed. Then, before he could answer, she had stepped across to Rachel and seized her hands. "Forgive me, I'm a little taken aback," she said unsteadily. "We've always thought of Niall as a confirmed bachelor, you see. But I couldn't be more pleased that he isn't. Oh, I shall have to ring the Allens and say I can't come now. They'll understand, in the circumstances."

"No, that won't be necessary, Julie," Niall said shortly. "It would be better if you went ahead as planned."

"But, Niall, don't be so absurd, I can't — "

Her brother cut her short.

"We're both pretty whacked — especially Rachel. I want her to go straight to bed. You can talk tomorrow."

Juliet started to object, then changed her

mind. "Yes, you do look rather ragged," she admitted. "Perhaps you're right, Niall. And, as you say," — smiling at Rachel again — "there'll be plenty of time to talk when you've had a good rest. Not that *I* shall get much sleep tonight, I fear. I'm much too excited . . . and delighted." With a warmth that seemed quite spontaneous — but could have been assumed for the benefit of their audience — she pressed Rachel's hand and kissed her cheek. "You can meet all our friends another time. I'm sure they understand how tired you are. Good-night . . . sister-in-law."

"Excuse us, will you? Good-night." Niall nodded coolly to his sister's guests, then took Rachel's arm and led her upstairs.

In the hall, the visitors started to talk again. Rachel heard someone say, "How exciting for you, Julie — and your grandmother will be pleased." Someone else, a man, said, "Striking little thing — reminds me of a Lorelei — that hair, y'know."

Then, a woman's voice said, sharp with malice: "I wonder how Nadine will take this when she hears?"

It was precisely at that moment that

Rachel stumbled. Not looking where she was going, she tripped on a stair. So she had no means of knowing whether Niall's fingers tightened to steady her balance, or if he, too, had heard that particular remark. On the landing, he said, "I'll go and clean up and see you later. Rietta will take care of you." Then he disappeared down a long corridor.

"This way, Mis' Herrick, if you please." The maid led her away in the other direction.

When Rachel saw the bathroom, she gasped. Not only was it twice as large as her bedroom at the bungalow on Anguna, but both the walls and the ceiling were faced with large squares of white-veined sapphire marble. The floor was laid with a softer blue thick-pile carpet — protected near the bath by a fluffy saffron rug — and there was an armchair loose-covered with saffron terry-cloth. The bath itself was sunk into the floor, and had lustrous oiled-silk shower curtains, the colour of conch-pearl, and a battery of mysterious taps and knobs.

Rietta ran hot water and threw in some crystals from a large gilt-spiralled china jar. Then she slid back the door of a closet and took down a yellow towelling robe.

"This here is the ladies' bathroom, ma'am. The gentlemen uses another one," she explained, waiting for Rachel to take off her crumpled clothes. "Now, if you'll 'scuse me, I'll go and find you a nightgown."

When she had gone, Rachel turned off the central faucet and climbed into the deliciously scented water. There were tablets of pale blue soap and others shaped and coloured like real lemons, in an amber glass bowl. Tucking her hair into the frilly plastic shower-cap Rietta had given her, she lay down and gave a sigh of physical pleasure.

Then she frowned and sat up again, beginning to lather herself. Why had Niall deceived her about his background? Well, perhaps he had not actually deceived her — because he had never said anything much about it. But even that, in the circumstances, could be called dishonest. Surely he must have realised what a shock it would be when she found that his home was so palatial? And, if he had a mansion and servants and every luxury, why did he pass for a freighter captain?

Rietta was not away long and, when Rachel had finished bathing, she held out the robe and helped her into it.

"My, you surely spoiled your hands on that old schooner, ma'am. You'd best sit down and let me see to them. Your room ain't quite ready for you yet."

So Rachel sat back in the armchair, and Rietta produced a box of various instruments and began to manicure the white girl's unkempt hands. And, having softened and smoothed back the hard cuticles and snipped away some hang-nails and filed the tips, she completed the treatment with a coat of clear shell-pink varnish, and then turned her attention to Rachel's toes. Finally, she massaged both her hands and feet with a fragrant white cream.

"I glad to see you don't do no smokin', ma'am," she said, smiling. "Miss Julie, she smoke like a cookin' stove, and I have a ter'ble time with that old nicotine stain. I'm Miss Julie's personal maid, you understand. But I'll look after both you ladies now."

Having put away her manicure equipment, she then produced two brushes for Rachel's hair. This she brushed vigorously for several minutes, and then wound it in a chignon and pinned it up.

"This sure is most beautiful hair, ma'am," she said admiringly. Then, "You don't have no perfume with you, I expect?"

"No, I'm afraid not, Rietta," Rachel said wryly.

The maid opened a drawer which seemed to be full of small bottles, phials and sprays. "That don't matter — Miss Julie, she have enough for ten ladies," she said, over her shoulder. "Now I reckon this 'Fidelwood' should suit you. It ain't made nowhere else but in Bermuda, and I know Marse Niall likes the smell of it. He always gave her a big bottle of that for her birthday."

Presently, wrapped in the flowing bathrobe and moving in an aura of expensive scent, Rachel was led back along the passage.

The bedroom which had been prepared for her was at the back of the house, with glass doors leading on to a balcony.

"This called the Coral Suite, ma'am, on account of them tapestries," Rietta explained, indicating two long silk panels, embroidered with coral-fronds, which ornamented one wall. "While Marse Niall a bachelor, he sleep in room over the landing. Now his room right next to this, through that dressing-lobby." She pointed out a closed door beyond the bed.

The bed was the largest Rachel had ever seen — probably eight feet across and set on a low dais. It had a high headboard padded with coral-red silk, and the matching silk bedspread had been turned back to show lace-edged linen pillowcases and hand-embroidered sheets.

"Now, you put on this nightgown and the wrapper, and I'll go see if Cookie done made your supper ready," said Rietta. "Miss Julie, she never wear this 'ticular gown. She prefer pyjamas."

Rachel had thought that the nightdress Niall had given her on the *Dolphin* was lovely, but it could not be compared with the one Rietta held now. A cascade of palest apricot chiffon, it flowed in a myriad of tiny pleats from a puff-sleeved Empire bodice of matching lace. Motifs from the lace were appliquéd all over the voluminous double-chiffon négligé and this had long full sleeves and a high neckline fastened with fifteen or twenty miniature buttons.

But although both garments were so beautiful, Rachel hesitated to put them on.

"I don't think I ought to borrow Miss Juliet's clothes, Rietta. I have a nightdress of my own, if you could find where my duffel-bag has been put. It's one Mister Niall lent me — a grey canvas thing."

"I'se already unpacked that for you, ma'am. I put that blue nightgown in the laundry basket. You cain't wear that till I washed it, and Miss Julie won't take no offence. She left word with Joseph as I was to loan you anything of hers you might be needing."

So Rachel put on the apricot chiffon nightdress and the négligé, and Rietta made her use one of Juliet's lipsticks, and insisted on brushing her eyebrows with a tiny brush and applying some dark paste to her eyelashes.

"Now you look just the way a bride should, ma'am," she said, satisfied.

A few moments later, there was a tap at the door and another younger manservant wheeled a trolley into the room. There was a small log fire burning on the wide stone hearth, and placing a folding table on the large white fur hearthrug, he covered it with a snowy damask cloth and began to set out the things on the trolley.

There was a serving bowl of soup on a hot-plate, a whole cold chicken surrounded by salad, another bowl of trifle topped with meringue, a platter of various cheeses and a basket of rolls. There was also a bottle of champagne in an ice bucket, the impedimenta for coffee-making on a separate tray, and a dish of rich cream pastries and éclairs.

"There! Now we leave you to rest yourself, ma'am," said Rietta, when everything was arranged. "Marse Niall, he join you in a moment. Good-night, Mis' Herrick. Hopes you sleeps sound." And, switching off the ceiling lights so that the room was lit by firelight and one table lamp, she smilingly withdrew.

But it was more than a moment before Niall came in by way of the balcony. And, after ten minutes of waiting for him, Rachel was so jumpy that she helped herself to some of the rich-smelling lobster *bisque*. Perhaps the soup would steady her nerves, she thought hopefully. But when the glass doors opened suddenly, she was still so tense that she almost spilled soup on the filmy négligé.

153

Niall closed the doors behind him. He was wearing a navy silk dressing-gown over plain blue poplin pyjamas, and had shaved off his rough growth of beard. But he still looked grey with fatigue, and in a mood of controlled irritation.

"Are they making you comfortable?" he asked coolly. Then, noticing what she was wearing, "Good lord! Where on earth did Rietta find that fancy-dress outfit?"

His tone was so scathing that Rachel flinched.

"It belongs to your sister. I — I didn't want to wear it, but I had to . . . Rietta insisted."

"Well, it's totally unsuitable for you. Tomorrow you must buy some things of your own," Niall said briskly. Then, eyeing her more closely, "And you can tell Rietta I don't care for war-paint either."

"I—I'm sorry, Niall. She was only trying to . . . improve me," Rachel said, in a crushed voice.

"I prefer you as you are. Would you care for some chicken?"

"No, thank you — I'm not very hungry."

When he had carved some for himself, Niall attended to the coffee percolator.

After one sardonic glance at the champagne, he ignored it.

Although he had completely killed her appetite, Rachel forced herself to take a little fruit salad. Presently, when he was pouring two cups of coffee and she thought he might be slightly mellowed by the food he had eaten, she said nervously, "Niall, why didn't you tell me about all this?"

He put the coffee at her elbow, placed the cream jug and sugar bowl beside it, and went back to his own seat. "All this what?" he asked unhelpfully.

"This house . . . your being so rich . . . your sister."

"Why didn't I tell you about Juliet? Oh, because I think it's a mistake to try to describe people. It might have put you off her," he said negligently.

"Did you think it would put me off *you* if I had known how you really lived?" she asked flatly.

"It might have done. But I didn't think 'all this' was particularly important. Does Moongates displease you in some way?"

It was impossible to talk to him while he was in this mood, Rachel thought hopelessly. Aloud, she said quietly, "I wish you wouldn't treat me like a child, Niall."

He swallowed the rest of his coffee, stood up and reached to press a bell.

"And I wish you would take life as it comes, Rachel. You're too much inclined to question everything. Try to relax and not worry over trifles. Now George will come up and clear these things in a moment. As soon as he's done so, your best plan is to go straight to bed. You look thoroughly washed out."

As he turned towards the balcony doors, Rachel could not stop herself exclaiming: "Why *did* you marry me, Niall?"

His expression was completely unreadable. "I thought we had already discussed that," he said evenly. "Good-night."

When Rachel woke up the next morning, Rietta was drawing back the curtains from a second large window opposite the bed. Rachel, who had always slept with the night breeze blowing in on her, had opened the balcony doors before climbing into bed.

"Morning, Mis' Herrick. You like to take your shower before breakfast, or wait till you has eaten?" the maid enquired. "We don't usually serve breakfast in the dining-room, you understand. I bring you a tray when it suits you."

"Oh, then I'll have a shower first, please, Rietta."

"What you like to eat, ma'am?"

"Oh . . . anything will do. Whatever there is."

"You ain't on no diet like Miss Julie?"

"A diet — what's that?" Rachel asked.

"That's to keep your figure right, Mis' Herrick. Miss Julie, she has a very strict diet. No sugar, no nice cakes, never no bread. All she has in the morning is one of them diet rolls and a cup of black coffee."

"But she's so slim already."

"That's what Marse Niall tells her, ma'am. He ain't at all partial to scrawny women, I don't think."

"Well, I'm certainly not going to start starving myself," Rachel said decidedly. "I'm always very hungry in the morning."

"Then I'll tell Cook you eat whatever pleases you," Rietta said approvingly.

"Oh, Rietta — just a minute."

"Yes, ma'am?"

Rachel hesitated, wondering how best to express herself. "Rietta . . . if I seem rather slow-witted about some things, it's because

I've always lived in a small village," she explained slowly. "I'm not used to big houses like this — or to places like Bermuda, for that matter. So if you see me making any silly mistakes, I wish you'd tell me."

"Why, surely, Mis' Herrick. But you don't need trouble 'bout that. No one ain't going to care what you do, so's you make Marse Niall feel good. And there ain't no doubt on that subject, I'm sure."

After she had showered and cleaned her teeth, Rachel returned to the bedroom and plaited her hair. Then, still wearing the towelling bathrobe because she had nothing else to put on, she went out on to the balcony.

Below her was a sloping stretch of lawn and, beyond it, a little sandy cove. Everywhere she looked there seemed to be flowers. Sweet-scented honeysuckle climbing up the columns supporting the balcony, hedges of hibiscus and oleander, a profusion of morning glories and bougainvillea.

"Good-morning. How did you sleep?"

Rachel swung round to face her husband as he came quietly along the sunlit balcony. It ran the full length of the house, and there were other glass doors like her own.

"Oh . . . excellently, thank you. And you?" What sort of mood was he in this morning? she wondered.

"I was too tired *not* to sleep soundly. Had your breakfast yet?"

"No, Rietta is bringing me a tray soon."

"I'll share it with you. Ah, that's her now." Niall moved to the bedroom door. "We'll have that out here, Rietta, please. Is there enough for two, d'you think?"

"If there ain't I can soon fetch some more," Rietta said cheerfully, setting the tray on a low cane table. All the furniture along the balcony — several tables and various chairs and full-length loungers — was made of shaped and polished cane, and the chairs were upholstered with vivid linen squabs.

The breakfast was as lavish as their supper had been. There were two covered dishes containing bacon and eggs, and a foam of wahoo kedgeree; there were home-baked cheese and currant breads, four different bowls of sweet preserves and a napkin-lined basket of fresh fruit.

Rachel tried a little of everything. Helping herself to some more of the peach preserve, she found Niall was watching her, looking amused.

It was such a relief to see him smiling that she smiled warmly back, and said gaily, "Rietta asked me if I had a diet. I think I may have to have one soon. All these delicious sugary things . . . I shall get as fat as Octavia!"

Niall laughed, and Juliet, coming out on to the balcony, must have seen them as a completely normal honeymoon couple.

"Good-morning, you two. You sound very cheerful," she said, yawning. She was wearing a vivid emerald kimono embroidered with dragons, and her hair was brushed back under a bandeau. "Niall, have you got a ciggy on you, sweetie? That dance at the Allens' went on till four. I feel like a zombie this morning."

Niall passed her a cigarette from the case which Rachel had given him, and his sister sank, groaning, on to a lounger.

"Can I have some coffee? I can drink out of Niall's cup," she said to Rachel. Then: "How bright-eyed and blooming *you* look. Are you always madly vital in the morning, or is it just some temporary kind of bridal glow?"

"She hasn't any degenerating habits — such as smoking too much and living on lettuce," Niall said casually, as Rachel tried to control a vivid flush.

Juliet grimaced. "No lectures before lunch-time, I beg. I have enough of them from Robert already. Robert's a lunatic who wants to marry me," she explained to Rachel. "But, talking of fiancés, how did you two come to plight your troths and so forth? You've been extremely devious, Niall, my lad. I didn't even guess you were in love. Or was it one of those instantaneous things — one look and you both knew you'd had it?"

Rachel waited for Niall's expression to harden, and for Juliet's curiosity to be snubbed.

Instead, he said carelessly, "Oh, I've known Rachel for over six months. We were married in rather a rush because she lost her father recently and would otherwise have had to go to England."

"Oh, I see. I'm so sorry about your father," Juliet said gently to Rachel.

Obviously she thought — as Niall must have intended — that they had had an understanding for some time. "All the same I think you might have given us a hint, Niall," she added chidingly. "And why couldn't you have waited and had the wedding here? You know how much Gran would have enjoyed it."

"Yes, but Rachel's father died only about three weeks ago. She naturally didn't want an elaborate wedding. You can fix some entertainments later on."

"Where did Niall find you?" Juliet asked Rachel.

Again it was Niall who answered her. "She's been living in the Bahamas for several years and, before that, in London. Oh, by the way, she lost most of her things in a hurricane they had down there. If you aren't tied up this morning, perhaps you could take her into town and show her round. She needs pretty well everything — don't you, honey?"

"Yes . . . I suppose I do," Rachel murmured.

"Oh, bliss — a shopping binge! Nothing I like better," Juliet said, brightening.

"Perhaps you could lend her a dress to go out in," Niall added. "She's only got beach gear at the moment."

"Yes, surely," his sister agreed. "Well,

162

if we're going to splash your money around, Niall, I'll whip off and get my face fixed. See you in about half an hour, Rachel — and I'll send Rietta along with a dress for you. She may have to turn up the hem, as I'm such a beanstalk, but that won't take long. 'Bye now."

After she had gone, Rachel said anxiously: "Niall, aren't you going to tell your sister the truth? She probably thinks I've lived like this all my life."

"What I did tell her was not *un*truthful," he said drily. "I don't see any need to go into details. I thought you wanted to pass as an 'ordinary' girl?"

"I doubt if I can," she said forlornly. "There are so many things which are new to me."

"Well, try it for a while, anyway. When you come back from your shopping you can meet my grandmother. She'll be asleep now. She reads half the night, so she doesn't receive visitors till after eleven. Now I must go and dress. I want to see Teaboy."

"Niall . . ."

About to walk back to his room, he turned and waited.

"Niall, you don't have to use that cigarette case now," Rachel said, flushing. "It isn't a very good one, I'm afraid. I expect you have a much better one here."

His eyes narrowed and he looked at her in silence for some moments. Then he said, "I have several, as a matter of fact."

"Well then, why not give mine to Teaboy? I shan't be offended . . . honestly."

"You only gave it to me because it seemed the correct thing to do?" he enquired coolly.

"Oh, no! That is . . . yes, I suppose so. I—I wanted to make some return for your presents to me," she said awkwardly.

"I see," he said coldly, frowning now. "Well, since you don't appear to have grasped it yet, perhaps I had better explain a point. Whatever I give you, or do for you, is free . . . without strings. You understand that? There's no question of your being under any kind of obligation to me."

Before she could answer, he had gone.

Rachel had intended to buy only a few clothes — just whatever was essential to

164

the life she would be leading from now on. But Juliet had other ideas.

"Don't be silly, sweetie," she said, when Rachel averred that two cotton dresses were all she would need for daytime wear. "You aren't eking out your pin-money now, remember. You spend what you like, when you like. Niall won't quibble. He keeps *me* on a fairly strict allowance, but he'll let you get away with murder. Besides, any moment now there'll be a flood of invitations, so you won't need two frocks — you'll need twenty."

So Rachel, unwilling to argue too fiercely in front of the saleswoman, was forced into buying all sorts of things which she would never have considered had she been allowed to go shopping by herself.

According to Juliet, it was not in the least extravagant to have a dozen pairs of gay Bermuda shorts.

"You'll live in them, sweetie," she assured her. "Oh, by the way, nobody wears short shorts here. At least, the tourists sometimes do — but not for long. It's considered madly *infra dig*, and everyone glowers at them."

And the shorts were only a beginning.

165

Indeed, after two hours in department stores and boutiques, Rachel had lost track of exactly what they had or had not bought. And, with Juliet ignoring all price-tags as if they were only put on for the benefit of the salesgirls, she had even less idea how much they had spent. But it must be a staggering amount, she thought uneasily.

"Time for a coffee-break, I think," Juliet said, shortly after eleven. "Let's pop over the road to the *Tea Cosy* — it's rather a nice little English lunch place. Oh, incidentally, this is Front Street, and Herricks' is that big place up ahead."

"Herricks'?" Rachel said blankly.

Juliet laughed. "Ye olde family business, sweetie. You *are* in a dreamy state, aren't you? Are you aching to get back to Niall?"

"Oh, no . . . no, of course not," Rachel said hastily. "I—I wasn't thinking for a moment."

What old family business? she wondered. Were there still more revelations in store for her?

Seated in the café, Juliet began to tick off their purchases on her fingers. "Now you're fixed up with most of the casual stuff. The next thing we must do is get you some cashmeres for the cool days, and a couple of little cocktail suits and evening dresses. We'll get those at Herricks', I think. Oh, hello, Bran — how are you?" — this to a slim young man who had just come into the tea shop.

"I saw you from over the road. May I join you for a few minutes?" he enquired.

Juliet grinned at him. "What you mean, I suppose, is that you caught sight of Rachel and thought 'Aha! A fair stranger — I must meet her'. My being at hand merely simplified the matter."

He was not in the least discomfited. "Now how did you guess that, I wonder?" he said cheerfully.

"Because I know how your mind works, dear boy. Rachel, this is Brandon Hart. Of all the two-footed wolves in Bermuda — and the colony is infested with them, unfortunately — Bran is by far the most cunning. Bran, meet Rachel Herrick."

"How do you do, Miss Herrick," he said smilingly. Then: "Herrick? Does that mean you're related to this slanderer?"

It was Juliet who answered him. "Yes, by marriage — *her* marriage," she said mischievously. "I hate to shatter your hopes, Bran sweetie, but it's 'Mrs.' not 'Miss', I'm afraid. Rachel is Niall's brand-new bride."

His mouth took on a quirk of scepticism. "You're having me on, Juliet. Niall's off on one of his sea-jaunts, isn't he?"

"He came back last night — Rachel's his treasure trove. It's true, I assure you. Isn't it, Rachel?"

"Yes, perfectly true, Mr. Hart," Rachel confirmed, with a smile. Whether Bran really was a "wolf", or whether Juliet was only baiting him — and Rachel was not sure what the term implied, anyway — she had taken an immediate liking to him.

He was not particularly good-looking, but he *was* extremely attractive, especially when he smiled. Of medium height and slim but well-knit build, he had hair almost as fair as her own. But his most striking features were his hazel, slightly slant-set eyes, and his beautifully articulated hands.

"Well, lucky Niall! I'm desolated. Oh, will you have another coffee, Mrs. Herrick?" — this as the waitress came to take his order.

"No time, sweetie," said Juliet. "We're

168

in the middle of a shopping whirl and we must fly. Still, it's just as well you stopped by. It's saved you planning any of your infamous strategies. 'Bye now.'"

He rose to his feet. "Cheerio, Juliet. Good-bye, Mrs. Herrick. I'm still very happy to have met you," he added, smiling at her.

"Thank you . . . well, good-bye." Rachel followed Juliet out of the café.

"I bet he is," Juliet said dryly, when they were walking along the street a few moments later. "Happy to have met you, I mean. Bran's not the type to let a little thing like marriage worry him — not when he's really drawn a bead on someone."

"Is he really such a wolf?" Rachel asked, hoping to find out what this meant without asking for enlightenment point-blank.

"My dear, he's the daddy of the species. All the non-wolfish types simply loathe him. They're terrified he'll suddenly take a fancy to their wives or girl-friends, I suppose. Of course women always adore him, and fall like skittles, poor dears. He has the most satanic charm, when he's operating. Fortunately, I've known him since we were tots and so I seem to be inoculated against him. You're safe too, I should think — although you may not be in five or six years' time. The first transports of love do wear off eventually, you know. And that's usually when Bran hooks his fish."

"Well, I don't think I'm likely to be one of them," Rachel said, rather amused.

"Probably not — I certainly hope not. Falling for Bran must be quite hellish. None of his affairs ever lasts more than six weeks at the most. Then his victims suffer agonies, silly idiots. All the same he's obviously attracted to you — and he isn't an admirer of old Niall. He may try something on just for the devil of it. So if you meet him again, do try not to let him flirt too outrageously. When Niall is really angry, he gets primitive. We don't want an *affaire d'honneur*. Now, enough of Bran, we must concentrate."

Niall was out when they returned to Moongates for lunch. They were halfway through the meal before he joined them. So it was early afternoon when Rachel put on one of her new dresses — a simple white piqué sheath with a narrow green belt and sea-green beads — and went with him to meet his grandmother.

The senior Mrs. Herrick was in her seventies. She lay on a sofa in her sitting-room, a light rug covering her legs and a lacy Shetland shawl over her shoulders. In spite of Bermuda's balmy climate, she almost always felt cold, Niall had said.

Rachel's first impression was of a seamed ivory face and shrewd blue eyes. They were faded now, but once they must have been as deeply blue as Niall's.

"Come and sit down, my child," said old Mrs. Herrick. "Is everyone making you welcome? Are you comfortable?"

"Oh yes, very comfortable, thank you," Rachel said nervously. She found the old lady rather awe-inspiring and wanted to make a good impression on her.

It was soon clear that Mrs. Herrick adored her tall grandson. But if she disapproved of his hasty marriage — and thought Rachel a most unsuitable wife for him — she was too gracious, or too astute, to show this.

When they left her — an hour or so later — Rachel was almost convinced that Niall's grandmother genuinely liked her.

In the fortnight that followed, Rachel saw little of Niall. After that first morning, he did not join her for breakfast again because he normally rose at six, sometimes earlier. Nor did he frequently have lunch at home. Most days he either had a meal in his office at Herricks', or went to his club. It was often only a few minutes before dinner when he came back to Moongates and, while Juliet was out dancing or at a party, he and Rachel would spend most of the evening with Mrs. Herrick. Niall would play chess or bézique with her, while Rachel read a book or watched the game. About eleven o'clock they would say goodnight to the old lady, then go to their separate bedrooms — another day over. But, very often, it was one o'clock in the morning before Niall switched out his light and the balcony lay in darkness. Was he working or reading? Rachel wondered. Or was he lying on the bed, unable to sleep — because he had married one girl and was still desperately in love with another one?

Although, after that first night of arrival, she heard no one make a reference to Nadine, Rachel did learn more about the

Herrick family and about her husband. Most of this information she gleaned from Rietta. The Herricks were among the "F.F.B." — the First Families of Bermuda, Rietta explained. This, Rachel gathered, was a kind of merchant aristocracy — the nameboards on the shops and stores in Hamilton being more or less the Colony's social register. Herricks' was one of the oldest-established businesses, having been founded in 1844 by Niall's great-great-grandfather. Niall still supervised the running of the store, and he was also a member of the parliamentary House of Assembly, and a governor of one of the hospitals.

His trips on the *Dolphin*, it seemed, were in the nature of holidays. They were not only a respite from the stresses of business life, they satisfied an inherent love of sea-faring.

One afternoon, finding Rachel gazing at a picture in the drawing-room — it was a painting of the *Koh-i-Noor*, one of the beautiful clipper-built barques which had been built in Bermuda in the 1850s — Joseph stopped to tell her about it. And then, finding she was interested in the house itself, he took her on a personally conducted tour of it.

The name Moongates, she learned, came from the moon-shaped entrances in the high wall surrounding the grounds. The house, one of the oldest in the colony, had been quarried from part of the garden. Over the years, the cream-coloured coral limestone had become pale grey with age and long weathering. The roof was made of thick limestone shingles over massive cedar beams.

"And you notice how it's terraced, Mis' Herrick. That's to catch all the rain for our water tanks," Joseph explained. "And that's also why we have to give it a lime-wash every year. It's the law, you understand — it makes sure all the drinking water is pure."

With an affection for the house that was as deep as if he owned it himself, he showed her the thick south-east chimneys which bore the brunt of heavy gales. A dome-shaped structure outside, known as "the buttery" and now used as an extra bathroom, had once been the cold store for food. And, most intriguing of all, there was an underground apartment beneath the drawing-room which had originally been a hiding place for contraband.

"Don't let old Joe bore you, sweetie," said Juliet, after coming home from the hairdresser to find the butler showing Rachel a book of old engravings and prints from woodcuts. "He's a terrible rambler once he starts."

"I'm not bored — I'm fascinated," Rachel answered. "Don't you love this house, Juliet? Won't you miss it when you marry and have to leave?"

Juliet shrugged. "Oh, I don't think so. Robert's house is just as nice as this. He's coming back from New York in a few days' time. We must make up a foursome. Would you like a martini, sweetie?"

"Not for me, thanks." Rachel watched her sister-in-law stroll over to the cocktail cabinet and pour herself a generous shot of gin with a small splash of vermouth added to it. She sometimes wondered if Juliet was battling with some secret un-happiness.

Not that there was any real evidence of this. Juliet never *looked* unhappy or worried. In fact, once she had recovered from what she called the "dawn doldrums", she was so unflaggingly vivacious and talkative that it was sometimes slightly wearing. Yet, in spite of her constant slangy chatter — and her frivolous attitude to life in general — Rachel still had this intuitive feeling that her gaiety was partly, if not wholly, assumed.

But what could be troubling her sister-in-law, she had no idea. On the face of it, Juliet had everything a girl could possibly want. And, according to Rietta, she would be even more indulged after she married. Her fiancé, Robert Howard, was even wealthier than Niall, and "one of the nicest, kindest gennelmen you ever done meet, Miss Herrick" — said Rietta.

Maybe that was the trouble, Rachel thought. Perhaps Juliet was missing Robert. Not that his absence on a business trip to the States seemed to curtail her social life at all. Sometimes she would leave the house after breakfast and not return until the small hours of the morning, or only dash back to change her clothes and make-up.

Robert's flight from New York was due in at three in the afternoon, and Juliet went to meet him in a ravishing scarlet linen dress. It was sleeveless and shaped close to her slender body down to mid-thigh level, then it flared out into a swirl of superbly set godets. Her shoes and bag were of the same vivid linen and she wore crisp white gloves and a hat made of red velvet poinsettia blossoms — the lovely flowers which would be at their best at Christmas time, and, in Bermuda, replaced holly for decorations.

"You look gorgeous, Julie," said Rachel. She had been watching her sister-in-law dressing and had never seen her looking more glamorous.

"Thanks, sweetie. I must admit I feel rather dazzling. Let's hope Robby is equally impressed. He may have been on the razzle with some siren in New York."

"Are you sure he will want to go out tonight? Won't he be tired?" Rachel asked.

Having persuaded Niall that it was high time Rachel was launched into the social round, Juliet had booked a table in the Rendezvous Room at the vast Castle Harbour Hotel. But although she was rather looking forward to wearing one of her new evening dresses, Rachel could not help feeling that, after a hectic round of business in New York, her sister-in-law's fiancé would probably prefer to spend a quiet evening alone with her.

"Oh, Robby wants whatever I want," Juliet said carelessly. "He can nap for an hour after tea. 'Bye now."

It was eight o'clock when Robert Howard came round to Moongates for a drink before they set out together. He was brought up to old Mrs. Herrick's sitting-room where the girls had been showing off their dresses. Juliet was svelte and sophisticated in a low-cut second skin of gold lamé. Rachel wore floating white chiffon, with a panel drifting back over one shoulder and a mother-of-pearl filet in her hair. This had been given to her by Niall's grandmother after she had seen the white dress on a hanger. It certainly was the perfect finishing touch.

Juliet had never described Robert to Rachel, but she had expected that he would be something like Niall — somewhere in his thirties, tall and attractive.

But not only was Robert Howard at least fifteen years senior to his prospective brother-in-law; he was not quite as tall as his fianceé and had a round puddingy face and — or so it seemed to Rachel on first meeting him — a most pompous and irritating manner.

However, before she had time to appraise him more closely, they had to say goodnight to Niall's grandmother and start out for the hotel.

They had been shown to their table by the dance floor and the two men were considering the menu, when Rachel noticed that all heads were turning towards the entrance. Looking that way herself, she saw that two people had just come in. The man was having a word with the head waiter, and his companion was surveying the room at large.

Apparently unconcerned at being instantly the cynosure of attention, she stood fingering the jewels at her throat. They were aquamarines, and she was wearing a dress made of yards of silvery poult, shot through with the blue-green lights of the stones. Slipping off her pale bare shoulders was a pastel grey mutation mink stole, and there were several diamond bracelets over the wrists of her long dove-grey kid gloves.

But it was not her clothes that were

making people stare. It was the exquisite contours and colouring of her lovely, rather arrogant face, and the rare, rich auburn of her hair. She was the most beautiful and compelling creature Rachel had ever seen.

Touching Juliet's wrist — her sister-in-law was fiddling with a faulty cigarette lighter — she murmured, "Do look who's just come in, Julie. Have you any idea who she is?"

Juliet followed her glance, and it seemed to Rachel that her nostrils flared slightly and her lips compressed.

"I know her very well," she said coolly. "That's Nadine Fraser — or rather, Lady Oakhill as she is now."

She had raised her voice slightly, as if she wanted the two men to hear the name.

Robert looked up immediately, and swung round to follow her glance. But Niall, although he must have heard what she said, seemed intent on the list of wines. But Rachel, who knew what to look for, saw the tell-tale clenching of his jaw that was always a signal of his displeasure.

CHAPTER FIVE

TO Rachel's relief, Nadine and her escort were shown to a table on the opposite side of the dance-floor and, as this was already quite crowded, they were hidden behind the couples on the floor. Had they been seated close by, she would have felt an overwhelming temptation to stare at them. As it was, she had only to control the impulse during the short breaks between each group of dances.

Although he had turned to look at Nadine and then exchanged an enigmatic glance with Juliet, Robert had made no remark about the other girl. He spent most of the meal telling them about his trip to New York. As he was no *raconteur* — and said he had been far too busy to see any of the current Broadway hits or any interesting exhibitions — his activites made rather boring hearing. And since Niall gave most of his attention to the food and wine, and Juliet's eyes kept straying to the people at the surrounding tables, it was left to Rachel to pay him the courtesy of listening attentively.

It was possible, she supposed, that Robert had many excellent qualities. But, whatever these might be, they were certainly well under the surface. On initial acquaintance he was neither physically attractive nor at all amusing or interesting. What could possibly have attracted Juliet to him was quite beyond Rachel's comprehension.

While they were waiting for coffee, Robert asked his fiancée to dance. He was not a good dancer. Rachel noticed, before they moved out of her view. He held himself too stiffly, moving in a series of jerks like a puppet and pumping Juliet's hand up and down. Not that *that* mattered particularly, she reflected. There must be thousands of delightful men who were hopeless dancers. But somehow, seeing those two on the floor seemed to emphasise their total incongruity. Here they were again — as strikingly ill-assorted as a gracefully swaying sea-anemone and an ungainly and unsightly crab.

"Would you like to dance, Rachel?" Niall asked, startling her out of her abstraction.

Rachel nodded, and they rose and went on to the floor together. But this time it was very different from their wedding evening in Nassau. Niall held her slightly away from him so that it was more difficult to follow his steps. She made several mistakes for which he politely apologised and thus added to her chagrin. She was glad when the music came to an end and they rejoined the others.

The next dance was a cha-cha and Juliet suddenly became much more animated, her eyes brightening, her shoulders moving to the rhythm.

"Come on, Niall. I'll do this with you," she announced, jumping up and seizing her brother's hand.

Robert watched her go off with an oddly wistful expression on his face. Then he recollected his duty.

"May I have the honour, Mrs. Herrick?" he asked formally, beginning to stand up.

But Rachel shook her head. "I'm sorry, Mr. Howard. I can't do whatever this dance is."

He sat down again, looking relieved. "To be frank with you, neither can I," he admitted ruefully. "I do my best, you know — because I know how much Juliet enjoys dancing — but I'm afraid I have two left feet, as the saying goes."

His tone was quite different from the stiff and stuffy manner in which he had been talking earlier on. He sounded shy, even humble. Rachel warmed to him — and was ashamed of her recent critical thoughts. Perhaps he also felt that Juliet was too young and glamorous and gay for him. Perhaps he was terrified of losing her, poor man, and it was his efforts to hide his inward uncertainty that made him appear so pompous and dogmatic.

"I expect you are rather tired, aren't you?" she said gently. "From what you were telling us earlier, New York sounds rather an exhausting place."

"Yes, it is," he agreed. "Even the air is very enervating when one is used to sea breezes, as we are here. I always find these trips extremely wearing. But I hope I don't appear too tired to enjoy this evening?" he added anxiously.

"Oh, no, not at all," Rachel assured him, somewhat untruthfully.

"Well, that's good. I should hate to feel I'd been a drag on you all."

"Perhaps we can leave fairly early," she suggested. "I'm not used to late nights. I expect *I* shall be feeling sleepy soon."

"Do you think so?" he asked, looking surprised. "I always thought you ladies hated to miss anything. I know Juliet does. She has the most fantastic vitality — never seems to flag whatever the hour."

"You should see her first thing in the morning," Rachel thought drily. Aloud, she said, "Yes, but she hasn't any work to do like you have. When you're married and she has a home to run — " She broke off suddenly.

Coming towards them, one hand controlling the sweep of her full skirt as she passed between the tables, was Nadine Oakhill.

At first, Rachel thought that Nadine must have friends at one of the tables beside or just behind them. But it was at their table that the older girl stopped.

"Good-evening, Robert. Good-evening, Mrs. Herrick," she said graciously. "May I join you for a moment or two?"

Robert hastily rose to his feet and held a chair for her. He had flushed and looked embarrassed.

"This is Lady Oakhill, Mrs. Herrick," he explained gruffly.

"Oh, please . . . I want to introduce myself," Nadine said, smiling. "I'm an old friend of Niall and Juliet — and of yours, too, I hope, from now on, Mrs. Herrick. Oh, look, can't we dispense with the formalities? I hate being called Lady Oakhill — it makes me feel like some formidable old dowager — and I can't possibly call *you* Mrs. Herrick when you look so young and unmatronly. May I know your first name? Mine is Nadine."

"It's Rachel."

"Oh, really? How appropriate," Nadine said. Then, when Rachel looked puzzled. "Well 'Rachel' means 'a ewe' in Hebrew, doesn't it?"

"Really, Nadine, I can scarcely see any resemblance between a sheep and Mrs. Herrick," Robert put in, his tone sharp with reproof.

Nadine laughed. "Oh, Robert, you haven't changed a bit, you old fusspot! Of course I didn't mean *that*, silly man. Rachel is not in the least like a sheep — but she does look like someone's ewe-lamb." She turned to look at Rachel again.

"Niall's little white ewe-lamb — that doesn't offer.d you, does it?"

Before Rachel could answer, they were joined by Niall and Juliet. But the music had not stopped. Rachel realised. So they must have come back because they had seen Nadine with her.

"Hello, Niall . . . hello, Juliet. How nice to see you both again. How are you?" Nadine asked warmly.

When Rachel had first seen her near the entrance, she had looked aloof and slightly disdainful. But now, smiling, her cheeks touched with colour, she looked even more beautiful than before.

"Hello, Nadine. We heard you were back. Where have you been hiding yourself?" Juliet enquired. She spoke quite amiably, but certainly not with the pleasure of someone meeting a close friend who had been absent for some years.

"I haven't felt like meeting people lately," Nadine answered quietly. "I didn't really want to come out tonight but" — with a slight shrug — "one has to pick up the threads sooner or later." She looked at Rachel again. "You see my husband died a short time ago. It happened while we were on holiday, and was completely unexpected. He had not been ill or run-down. So since then, I've been feeling . . . rather lost."

"I'm sorry," Rachel said awkwardly. She was remembering how Mrs. Lancaster had referred to Nadine's marriage — as if it had been a source of cynical amusement to everyone — a joke in slightly questionable taste.

Yet, just now, as Nadine had glanced down at the rings on her slender left hand — a magnificent solitaire diamond and a broad band of faceted platinum — she had looked sad and deeply lonely. Not like a woman who, far from mourning her husband, was unmoved, even relieved, by his death.

Nadine made a slight gesture of dismissal, as if it were neither the time nor the place to speak of such things.

"I've just been making myself known to your wife, Niall," she said, her tone light again. "She's charming. I congratulate you most sincerely." Then, as he acknowledged this with an unsmiling inclination of the head, "I suppose you know the whole Colony is dying to have a chance to meet her. Everyone is intrigued." She turned back to Rachel. "It's so romantic — Niall coming back from one of his sea-trips with a bride who is a stranger to us all." She glanced down at the folds of Rachel's skirt, her expression suddenly mischievous. "Do you know what *I* think, Rachel? I'm beginning to suspect that you're a mermaid."

Rachel laughed and lifted the hem of her dress to show two slim brown ankles and *pointelle* slippers. But none of the others seemed to find the remark amusing. And, just as she had warmed to Robert Howard when Juliet had gone off to dance the cha-cha, she found herself being equally sorry for Nadine.

She would have to be very insensitive not to realise that her presence was unwelcome. The others might at least be decently polite to her.

"Of course I quite understand that you don't want to start a whirl of parties while you're still more or less on your honeymoon," Nadine went on, with amirable poise (Rachel knew that she would have been completely tongue-tied if people had treated her with such marked reserve).

"But, as I know that Niall always goes to his club on Fridays, I wondered if you would care to come and lunch with me tomorrow? There would be only the two of us, and pot-luck. It wouldn't be one of these rather frantic hen-parties."

Before Rachel could answer, Niall said smoothly, "I expect my wife would have enjoyed it, Nadine, but I shall not be at the store tomorrow, so we've planned an outing in the *Sea Sprite*. I've been tied up lately, and we haven't had too much time together."

If Nadine guessed that this was the first Rachel had heard of this idea — and she must have caught the flicker of surprise on the younger girl's face — she gave no sign of it.

"Oh, that will be much more fun for you," she said readily. "You can lunch with me some other day, perhaps. Now I see my escort has come back. He'll be wondering where I am." She waved her hand at the man who was standing at her table. "Good-bye," she said pleasantly to the other three. "Good-bye, Rachel, I'm so glad I've met you, and I shall look forward to the next time."

Then she was gone, her ivory-pale shoulders — so striking among all the different tones of sun-tan — held gracefully erect, her red-gold hair gleaming in the subdued lights from the table lamps.

Juliet lit another cigarette from the tip of the one she had just finished, and fitted it into her holder.

"Hm . . . still the same old Nadine, I see," she said, in an odd tone.

"I like her," Rachel said abruptly. The words seemed to come out on their own. She had not meant to say them, and she had sounded rather aggressive, she realised uncomfortably.

Robert coughed and cleared his throat, and Juliet raised her eyebrows.

"Why not, sweetie? Nadine is charm personified. Talking of charmers, I see Bran has just arrived — over there, joining the Mannings." She indicated a table some yards away. "Odd! He hasn't got a partner. Do you suppose he's chasing Betsy Manning? Not that George would worry much if he did. I was watching them earlier on and they looked so bored with each other, poor dears. But that's how it goes after ten years of marriage, I suppose."

"I don't believe it's inevitable," Robert said, frowning. "George and Betsy have never got on from the first. A great many couples *never* become bored with each other — however long they have been married."

Juliet shrugged. "Still, I wouldn't have thought Betsy was Bran's type," she murmured thoughtfully. "She's always so maddeningly skittish . . . and just listen to that corncrake laugh."

Evidently Bran had said something amusing, because the woman to whom Juliet was referring had emitted a high-pitched jarring sound, and was now archly reproving him.

Robert, who obviously disliked the turn the conversation had taken, said, "Ah, a waltz, Mrs. Herrick, Now this is something I can do, and we must have at least one dance together."

"I wish you would call me Rachel, Mr. Howard," she said, when they were moving round the floor.

"I should be delighted to do so — thank you. Perhaps, in that case, you would also use my first name. After all, we shall soon be related to each other."

"I've never asked Juliet when the wedding is to be," Rachel said. "Are you planning to marry fairly soon?"

"Oh, not for a month or two yet. We only became engaged about six weeks ago, you know," he explained. "Frankly, I have a feeling that Juliet is just a little bit worried over taking on the running of a house. Naturally, she has never had any domestic responsibilities before, and I suppose housekeeping must seem somewhat onerous to her."

"I don't see why it should — if you have a staff like the one at Moongates. She won't have to do everything herself, will she?"

"Oh, good lord, no! — of course not," Robert seemed to be quite shocked by such a prospect.

Yet, now that she thought about it, Rachel knew that, as far as she was concerned, she would be a good deal happier if she had to do some work in the house.

As soon as they were established on Anguna, her father had insisted that Octavia should teach her some housewifery — although, of course, on Anguna the art of housekeeping was necessarily a fairly primitive business.

But the other afternoon, when Joseph had shown her the kitchen at Moongates, she had been fascinated by all the modern equipment. The Herricks' chef had been trained in one of the Colony's best hotels, and his cuisine was of the highest standard. Pausing a moment to watch him making cakes for their tea — flaky *millefeuilles*, and *babas au rhum* — Rachel had longed to try her hand at these confections. She would have liked to ask him if he could spare the time to give her an occasional lesson, but was afraid to suggest this in case he was already busy enough with his routine work.

But if only she could cook Niall's meals and wash his clothes, she would not have this dejecting feeling of being utterly useless and unnecessary to him.

Lost in thought, she did not notice Brandon Hart standing at the edge of the dance-floor. So she was as surprised as Robert when he touched the older man's shoulder and said, "May I cut in, Robert? I have been introduced to Mrs. Herrick."

And somehow, before Robert could object, he had skilfully inserted himself between them and begun to steer Rachel away again. It was done so expertly that neither Robert nor Rachel had had time to object to the change-over. But there was no doubt that Robert would have dissented, had he known what was about to happen. His face, as he watched them swing away, was a study of suppressed indignation.

"Another black mark in Bran's book. Are you angry with me, too, Mrs. Herrick?" the young man asked teasingly, tightening his arm round her waist because the floor was very crowded now.

"Is that a rude thing to do — cutting in?" she asked.

"Not rude exactly, but it was natural that Robert should resent my stealing you away from him. For girls, cutting-in can be a life-saver — when they're stuck with a partner they don't like, you know."

"But I *do* like Mr. Howard — very much."

"Oh, certainly — why not?" Bran said negligently. "But you like me just as well, don't you?"

"I don't know you yet."

He smiled at that. "You will," he assured her, in a dry tone.

It was not until they had been dancing for several minutes that Rachel suddenly realised she had been following his lead as easily as if she had danced all her life.

Bran must have noticed this too, because he said, "How come — when you dance so delightfully — you don't know about cutting-in?"

"Oh, it isn't ever done where I come from," she said evasively.

He did not ask where she *did* come from, but it was obviously in his mind, because he went on, "You're something of an enigma to the Colony, you know. Janet Adams — one of the women who was up at Moongates the night you arrived — has told everyone that you and Niall looked as if you'd just crossed the Atlantic on a raft. Allowing for the fact that women invariably exaggerate, you must have looked fairly bedraggled. And, since Niall is back at Herricks', it does seem curious that he slides out of all the invitations to you both."

"What invitations?" Rachel asked, puzzled.

"So you're in the dark too, are you?" Bran looked even more intrigued. "Well, you see, since most of the people here are either related by marriage or have known each other all their lives, anyone new to the Colony is a welcome relief from the monotony. One can't count the tourists, because they're just transients. Naturally, when the news got around that you'd arrived, all the local hostesses began vying with each other to lay on the most lavish welcome-to-the-bride party. They're all furious because Niall isn't biting." He smiled at her, a smile which gave his puckish and slightly dissipated face a sudden look of schoolboy mischievousness. "Personally, I think he's behaving very naturally. If you were my wife I should want to keep you to myself, too."

It was at this moment that, glancing over his shoulder, Rachel saw Niall signalling to her.

"Oh, look, Niall's beckoning. I'm afraid you'll have to excuse me," she said.

"It can't be anything urgent. We can finish this dance, can't we?" he said easily.

"No, please — I'd rather go and see what he wants."

Bran steered her out of the flow of

dancers and, his hand under her forearm, escorted her back to her husband.

"Hello, Julie . . . Niall," he said pleasantly. Then, to Rachel, "Thank you, Mrs. Herrick. That was most enjoyable. Perhaps you will spare me another dance later on?"

"I'm afraid not. Juliet has a headache, so we're leaving now," Niall said coldly. He took the little beaded velvet cape from the back of Rachel's chair and put it round her.

"I am sorry to hear that," Bran said gravely. "One of your unfortunate bouts of migraine, is it, Julie? What a pity it had to happen tonight. I hope you feel better in the morning. Well, good-night, everyone. Good-night, Mrs. Herrick."

Before Rachel realised what he intended, he was bowing over her hand, his lips lightly brushing her knuckles. Then he left them.

"Young bounder!" Robert muttered furiously.

Five minutes later they were driving out of the hotel grounds.

Nobody spoke until they reached Moongates. Then Robert helped the two girls out of the car and Niall drove it away to the garage.

"I think, if you don't mind, I won't come in again," Robert said. "Will you lunch with me tomorrow, Juliet? I thought we might meet at La Caravelle about one?"

Juliet nodded and he kissed her lightly on the cheek, said good-night to Rachel and climbed into his own car.

"I'm sorry about your headache, Juliet. Is it very bad?" Rachel asked, as they went into the house and up the stairs.

Her sister-in-law laughed. "Oh, what an engaging innocent you are, sweetie! I haven't a headache. That was just Niall's spur-of-the-moment excuse for getting you out of Bran's clutches."

"But Mr. Hart said something about your having migraines —" Rachel began.

"Apart from all the usual sordid children's diseases the only thing I've ever suffered from is a racking hangover. Bran knew it was just an excuse, and he was letting Niall know that he knew. That's why he kissed your hand with such a flourish — to make poor old Niall furious. Oh, God, What an abominable evening! I think I'll have an early night for once."

In her bedroom, Rachel took off the white chiffon dress and hung it carefully in the long built-in wardrobe. Then she got out of her underclothes and stockings, and put on a short white cotton nightdress splashed with sprays of mimosa and a plain white quilted nylon dressing-gown. She had unpinned her hair and was about to plait it when she heard Niall go into the next-door bedroom. For some moments she fiddled with her comb, frowning slightly, her underlip caught between her teeth. Then, making up her mind, she flung the comb back on the dressing-table and marched firmly to the dressing-room door.

It opened into a small narrow apartment with wardrobes along one side and built-in drawers and cupboards along the other. The far door was already ajar and she could hear the clink of china and the sound of liquid being poured out.

She tapped on the panel. "May I come in a moment, Niall?"

"Rachel? Yes, of course," he said, looking surprised.

He was standing by a table near the window, a coffee-pot in one hand and a sandwich in the other. He had already taken off his white dinner jacket and black tie.

"Are you hungry? Would you like some of this?" he asked, gesturing at the tray he had brought up.

The sandwiches must have been ready in the kitchen, Rachel thought. If Niall had cut them himself the bread would have been thicker and in whole slices, not in neat triangles, each garnished with a sprig of parsley or a tiny posy of cress.

"I wouldn't mind some coffee," she said.

"I didn't bring any milk up. I'll go and get some, and another cup."

While he was away, Rachel looked round his room. It was smaller than hers and much more plainly furnished in various tones of brown and yellow ochre. The carpet was a very dark teak shade, the curtains ochre linen, the covers on the chairs of mid-brown repp. The bed was a single one, with an oiled teak headboard extending into cabinets on either side. One of these bore a telephone, lamp and large glass ashtray. The other held books and a small leather travelling clock.

Niall's dressing-table was bare of anything but a brush and comb, a clothes-

201

brush and a leather stud-box. But a desk by the window was littered with papers and files, and a row of large reference books. There was one painting — of a galleon foundering on a reef — above the bed, and a model of the *Dolphin* on a bracket on another wall.

She was sitting on one of the two armchairs which flanked the low coffee table when Niall came back. He poured a cup of coffee for her, helped himself to another sandwich and sat down. Then his glance fell on her feet.

"Didn't you buy any bedroom slippers? You ought to have something on your feet," he said.

"Yes, I bought some. But as I've gone bare-footed half my life, and not on thick carpets either, I don't see why I need wear them."

His eyebrows rose at her tone. "Have you come in here to quarrel with me?" he asked coolly.

This had not been her intention. But now that he had made the suggestion, she felt that it might be a good idea. Nothing could be worse than going on as they were at the moment.

"I want to know why you were so rude to Mr. Hart this evening," she said, equally cool.

Niall lit a cigarette, and crossed his long legs. "I don't recall being rude to him."

"Not by your standards perhaps. *I* think it was very rude to lie about Juliet having a headache. What harm was he doing — just dancing with me?"

"Were you enjoying it so much?" His tone was clipped.

"Yes, I was, as it happens — very much. I think he's a very pleasant person."

"Which is precisely why I thought it best to leave," Niall said coldly. " 'Pleasant' as he may appear to you, Brandon Hart is a most unsuitable person for you to cultivate, Rachel."

"Is that why you prevented me from lunching with Lady Oakhill tomorrow? Is she also an unsuitable person?"

Niall didn't answer, but she knew he was annoyed by the hardening of his jaw muscles, and the way he stared fixedly at the tip of his cigarette.

And, suddenly, she had a keen desire to make him even more annoyed — to make him so furiously, blazingly angry with her that, finally, he had to unleash all control. Then, once he really lost his temper, she might at last learn some truths about their marriage.

"Well, *was* it?" she persisted.

"Yes, it was," he said icily, after a pause. "I know why I mustn't 'cultivate' Mr. Hart because Juliet has already explained that. But I don't see why I can't be friends with Lady Oakhill."

Niall got to his feet and swung away from her. "Because I say so," he said curtly, looking out into the darkness of the garden.

"You mean you keep me, so you have the right to dictate to me?"

He did not move. "Go to bed, Rachel. It's late, and you're tired and overwrought. We can discuss this tomorrow if you still want to."

Rachel also sprang up, but not to leave. "I *won't* go to bed! Why should I? You treat me as . . . as if I were your daughter."

At that he turned round his eyes narrowing. "Don't spit fire at me, Rachel. I'm not in the mood for it."

"I don't care a jot what mood you're in. I'm sick of always doing what I'm told.

Why should I take orders 'because you say so'? It just isn't good enough, Niall."

"If you aren't out of here in five seconds, you'll wish to God you'd never come in." He spoke through set teeth, his eyes steely.

This was what she had wanted, Rachel saw. He was within a hairsbreadth of being too furious to care what he said. If she flung one more barbed defiance at him . . .

For an instant her courage ebbed away. Then, shaking and sick with apprehension, but determined to finish what she had begun, she thrust out her chin and said boldly, "I don't think you're likely to actually beat me, are you? So why shouldn't I say what *I* think for a change? I don't care if you do pay for my clothes and everything else. You aren't going to dictate my entire life for me. If I want to see more of Brian and Nadine — " She broke off, gasping, as he grabbed her.

"I warned you . . ." Niall was gripping her by the shoulders, looking merciless. In that moment she was genuinely and helplessly afraid of him. This was a stranger, a man she had never even glimpsed before.

Then, roughly, he flung her away from him. Snatching his car keys from the top of a tallboy, he slammed out on to the landing and left her.

"You look as if you'd had a rotten night. Why didn't you spend the morning in bed?" said Juliet. It was a little after eleven the following day, and she had just found Rachel wandering round the garden.

"I didn't sleep too well," Rachel admitted, since it would be futile to deny that there were heavy shadows under her wide dark-amber eyes. "Perhaps I had too much to eat — I — I was dreaming all night."

"Didn't Niall tell you to stay in bed?" Juliet asked.

Pretending to be examining a flowering shrub, Rachel turned away to hide her flush. "He had gone before I woke up." Had Juliet heard their raised voices and the slam of Niall's door followed, some minutes later, by the car going off? Was she trying to find out what had happened?

"You haven't been sick or anything, have you?" her sister-in-law enquired.

"Oh, no — I'm never sick. It was just indigestion, I suppose."

Juliet lit a cigarette. "Sorry: I didn't mean to pry, sweetie. Only . . . well, Gran has been pretty dickey lately, and it would make her terribly happy to know that another generation was on the way."

Rachel looked blank for some seconds. Then as she grasped what Juliet was talking about, her flush became a deep suffusion of colour.

"Personally, I find the whole prospect too ghastly," Juliet went on, with a yawn. "But I gather that if you are going to have lots of babies, the best plan is to have them in rapid succession. Then, after three or four years of plodding around like a barrel, you can let a good Nanny take over and get back to normal again. I have a depressing feeling that Robert will want at least six," she added, grimacing. "I shall probably be in purdah for years."

Since her sister-in-law did not seem to have noticed her embarrassment, Rachel managed to give a strained little laugh. "Why do you always pretend to be so unfeeling, Julie? I'm sure you'll be an awfully good mother."

"Not me — I loathe the little blighters. What's more they seem to sense I don't dote on 'em. On the rare occasions when I've been forced to pick one up, it's immediately started bellowing or wetting me."

"Oh, it's different with one's own, I expect."

"It will be for you, no doubt. You're the type to adore rocking a cradle. You'll probably look even prettier when you're pregnant, and your infants will all be fat cherubs. Whereas I shall look utterly hideous and feel like death, only to produce some hideous, squalling skinless sausage brat. Ugh! What a spine-chilling prospect!"

"Oh, Juliet, that's nonsense and you know it," Rachel said, laughing at her gloom.

"What's nonsense?" His shoes making no sound on the thick turf, Niall had come up behind them. He was looking at his sister, not at Rachel.

"Rachel has just been trying to convince me what a splendid mama I shall be," Juliet said, grinning. "Let's rest our feet, shall we?" She moved to some nearby garden chairs under a fringed red beach umbrella. "By the way, I asked Joe to bring us some coffee . . . oh, here he comes now."

While the butler was setting out the coffee cups, Rachel glanced covertly at

Niall. It had been almost three o'clock when she had finally fallen asleep, and he had not then returned to the house. But however little rest he had had, unlike herself, he did not look visibly fatigued. He was not wearing a lounge suit this morning, but was dressed in sailcloth slacks and a blue beach shirt.

"Is Robert so anxious to ensure the family line that he's made you put the wedding date forward?" Niall asked his sister, when Joseph had returned to the house.

"Oh, if he'd had his way, we'd have been married five minutes after our engagement," Juliet said, shrugging. "No, the subject of babies came up because Rachel was looking slightly wan this morning and I, being a natural nosey-parker, thought there might be a little stranger in the offing." She turned to Rachel. "Don't you abhor people who use all those whimsy-mimsy expressions like 'little stranger' and 'happy event' and so on?"

But Rachel was bending down to fiddle with the strap of her sandal and seemed not to have heard her.

Mercifully, Juliet suddenly remembered

that she was lunching with Robert at La Caravelle, and had a fitting for a cocktail dress before that.

"If you're ready, we may as well start," said Niall, after his sister had rushed away.

"Start?"

"Our trip in the *Sea-Sprite* — remember? Cook has packed us a lunch box and I thought we'd run up the coast to Surf Bay. We can always move on if it's too crowded."

"Oh . . . I didn't think you really meant to go," she said awkwardly.

"Certainly I meant it. Now that I've caught up with various business backlogs, I'll be able to spend more time with you. Tomorrow afternoon I may take you to see Crystal Cave, or we could go over to St. George, the old capital."

"Niall . . . about last night — " she began. "I'm sorry I said all those things. I — I didn't really mean them."

"Let's forget last night, shall we?" He held out his hand to pull her up.

But as she went indoors to fetch her bathing suit, Rachel knew that such a bitter scene between them could not be forgotten so easily.

Accustomed to the Angunans' small fishing boats, she was soon at home in *Sea-Sprite*, a graceful fifteen-foot "Snipe".

After sailing some way up the coast — past rugged stretches of rock-face, deep gorges and little sandy coves — they came to a large, crescent bay between two rugged headlands. There was no one about but some men collecting seaweed for fertiliser, and Niall decided to make this their picnic place.

After the men had gone — a plump grey pony hauling their ramshackle weed cart up the steep track between the bay grape trees — they had the place entirely to themselves. And it was an idyllic spot for a picnic, with a fringe of foam-edged wavelets washing gently on the foreshore, a company of graceful white-winged bosun birds gliding and circling overhead, and the wind making a strange plaintive music in the branches of an ancient twisted cedar.

They swam in the translucent turquoise water, and then put on old canvas shoes and clambered about the tidepools near the headland, finding chitins and limpets and black mussels. And there were moments — as when Rachel slipped and grazed her knee and Niall fetched a plaster and put it on for her, or when they bent together over a stranded jelly-fish — when they seemed to have recaptured some of the easy companionship of those first days on board the *Dolphin*.

But there were other moments, too — times when Niall appeared to have forgotten that Rachel was with him.

Once, when they were lazing after lunch, she said, "Oh, Niall, how is Teaboy getting on now?"

But he did not answer her. He was staring out at the reef, so lost in his thoughts that he had even forgotten the cigarette which dwingled to ash between his long slim fingers. And when, after she had twice repeated her enquiry, he finally roused from his abstraction, she had the deflating impression that he had expected to find someone else with him. Someone with tawny eyes flecked with green, and hair like copper in firelight, she thought wretchedly.

A few days later, perhaps sensing that Rachel would be glad of something useful to do instead of always being at leisure, old

Mrs. Herrick asked her to fetch some books from a shop in Hamilton.

"I did ask Niall to collect them for me, but he might forget and I have nothing to read in bed tonight," his grandmother explained. "So would you mind fetching them for me, dear?"

"I'd be glad to," Rachel said readily.

For the first time in her life she was beginning to suffer from long spells of stultifying boredom. She had always loved reading and swimming, but these were recreations, and it was not recreation she needed. What she did need, desperately, was work — some form of really hard physical work which would leave no time for brooding and make her sleep properly. For the past two nights she had only been able to get to sleep after slipping down to the private beach and swimming for an hour. And she knew that if Niall ever caught her, he would probably forbid such a practice.

After she had found her way to the bookshop and picked up the old lady's order, she wandered aimlessly about the streets for half an hour, looking in shop windows or watching the tourists.

She was just thinking that it would pass another half hour to have a milk shake somewhere, when someone called her name.

For a moment, the "Hello, Mrs. Herrick" did not register. Then she turned and saw Nadine Oakhill stepping out of a taxi close by.

"I was just going home, but now that we've run into each other, let's have tea together, shall we ?" Nadine suggested.

And before Rachel could reply, she had bent to speak to the driver, telling him where to take several parcels which were piled on the back seat.

"Now, where shall we go ?" she asked, when the cab had driven off. "Over there ?" — indicating an expensive-looking restaurant across the street.

"Yes, if you like," Rachel agreed.

A few minutes later, when they were seated at a table overlooking the street and after she had ordered Russian tea for herself and a lime squash for Rachel, Nadine asked, "Well, what do you think of Bermuda now that you've had time to get your bearings ?"

"It's . . . very beautiful," Rachel said,

stating the obvious but unable to think of any more original comment.

Nadine made a slight moue. Today she was wearing a casual little suit of rough cotton tweed, the colour of clotted cream, and a finely pleated caramel silk over-blouse. A large gold and coral brooch was pinned close to the collar of her jacket, and she wore an enormous domed ring of coral and turquoise on her right hand.

"Yes, the islands are heavenly," she conceded. "It's the people who spoil them from being perfect — the women particularly. Oh, the gossip and the rivalries that go on — you wait till you've been here longer. The trouble is that most of them have so little to occupy them, and so they have to cook up various petty intrigues to make life interesting. At the moment, of course, they're all chattering their heads off about us."

"Us ?" Rachel said enquiringly.

Nadine laughed. "Well, mostly you, I expect. Where Niall met you . . . whether you get on with his grandmother . . . all that kind of thing. But I certainly provide an excellent topic for the ones who prefer a spice of scandal. Some of the old dears are just like vultures — they live by pecking away at other people's reputations."

"Are they really as bad as all that?" Rachel asked doubtfully.

"Oh, yes, I'm not exaggerating, my dear. There was a girl I used to know, several years ago, who tried to kill herself because of gossip. She didn't manage it, fortunately, but it was a near thing. She overheard rumours — quite unfounded — that her husband was carrying on with someone else. Instead of ignoring it, or telling him about it, she swallowed a bottle of aspirins. But I don't suppose the women who had spread the tale were very bothered. They were probably too busy condemning her for what she'd done."

"How terrible," Rachel said soberly.

"I'm sorry — I didn't mean to depress you," Nadine said gently. "I just wanted to warn you not to believe everything you'll hear — or have heard so far." She smiled. "For instance, I'm sure you must have already heard something about 'that awful Nadine Oakhill', haven't you?"

Rachel was about to deny this, when she remembered Mrs. Lancaster in Nassau.

Her momentary hesitation made Nadine

say lightly, "Yes, obviously you have — it was inevitable. I suppose they told you all the 'facts' about my marriage? Or did they first dig up the really ancient history?"

"Someone mentioned your marriage, but nothing else," Rachel said uncomfortably.

"Don't worry — they will," Nadine assured her. "Whenever they run short of fresh material, they dig out our engagement again."

"Your engagement?" Rachel said, not understanding.

Nadine frowned slightly. "Niall has told you about it, hasn't he?" she asked, looking puzzled. "Oh, surely he *must* have?"

"About what?"

"About our being engaged . . . and my breaking it off at the last moment. Oh, heavens — no, obviously he hasn't. I'm most terribly sorry, my dear. I naturally assumed that you knew. Oh, how stupid of him not to mention it. He must have known someone would refer to it sooner or later, and crow over the fact that you didn't know."

"Well, I know now," Rachel said, trying to sound casual.

"And, after all, it only confirms what I already suspected," she thought heavily.

"Does it put you off me — the fact that Niall once wanted to marry me?" Nadine asked her anxiously. She was obviously very much distressed at having made such an embarrassing *faux pas*.

"No . . . of course not," Rachel said awkwardly. "What happened exactly? What . . . went wrong?"

Nadine hesitated a moment, twisting her big studded ring.

"I suppose it's better for me to tell you than for you to hear some highly embroidered version," she said reluctantly. "We were engaged for about six months. It was after Niall came out of the Navy, and we were both very young and rather foolish. About three weeks before the wedding, we had a furious row about something. I can't even remember what it was now. Anyway, we both lost our tempers and said the usual wounding things to each other."

She paused to glance abstractedly out of the window, her mouth curved into a little rueful smile.

"One has so much pride at that age. *I* wasn't going to be the first to say I was

218

sorry — and neither was Niall, of course. Then — after about a week of waiting for him to crawl back to me — I returned his ring and all his presents. I thought he would rush round to our house in a panic. No one else knew we had quarrelled, you see. All the wedding arrangements were still going on."

"But he didn't come?" Rachel prompted quietly, after Nadine had been silent again for several minutes.

"No, he didn't come," Nadine said huskily. She reached for her bag and took out a gold cigarette case. After she had lit a cigarette, she said, more briskly, "That was really the end of it — although I couldn't believe it was then. After the wedding had been cancelled, I went to Europe with some friends of ours. I didn't want to go, but my parents more or less made me. Niall was in New York at the time. Anyway, for several months after that, I went on expecting him to write, to beg me to come back to him. I — I was still in love with him, you see."

"Why didn't *you* write to him?" Rachel asked.

"I was going to — I was desperate,"

Nadine said wryly. "Then someone mentioned in a letter that he seemed very involved with an American girl, and my idiotic pride flared up again. The next thing I heard was that Niall had gone off to the Pacific, and was expected to be away for a couple of years. So then I couldn't have written if I'd wanted to. Even his family didn't know where he was." She relapsed into silence again.

The waitress came across to their table. "Would you care for anything else, madam?"

The way Nadine looked at the girl was the way Niall had looked at her the other afternoon on the beach, Rachel realised. It was the blank, lost look of someone for whom the past has more reality than the present.

Since they wanted nothing else, the waitress wrote out their bill and Nadine took it and sat fingering it.

"I've forgotten what I was saying," she said, after a moment.

"Niall had gone to the Pacific," Rachel reminded her.

"Oh, yes . . . Niall had gone to the Pacific," Nadine repeated slowly. "Well —

eventually — I got over it," she went on. "About a year or so later, I met James and he asked me to marry him and I accepted. So, you see, as I said, it's ancient history."

"Yes, I see. Thank you for telling me."

Nadine stubbed out her cigarette, searched for a tip and smoothed her glove. "I expect the truth is that Niall has practically forgotten it," she said lightly. "We were so young, and it was such a long time ago." She glanced at her little gold wrist watch. "Oh, heavens, look at the time! I do hope I haven't made you late for anything. Let's share a taxi. I can drop you off at Moongates on my way home."

"Thanks, but I have to go to . . . to the chemist," Rachel said quickly. She did not want to go home yet. Juliet would be back now and would want to chat. Then Niall would arrive and it would be dinner time.

"Will you forgive me if I fly?" Nadine pulled on her gloves and eased the fingers. "And you will still have lunch with me — in spite of this? Oh, good. Then I'll ring you in a day or two."

They parted outside the restaurant doors, Nadine to hurry away to the taxi-rank, and Rachel to walk for a while to collect herself.

She had wanted to know the truth, and now she did know. But it was not the relief she had anticipated: it was agony. Because now, as well as sensing that Niall still loved Nadine, it was clear that Nadine also loved him. Oh, she had dismissed it as an episode far in the past — but she had lied when she said she had got over it.

"She still loves him — as much as I do," Rachel thought achingly.

She was halfway back to Moongates when a car drew up alongside her.

"Hello, Mrs. Herrick. May I give you a lift?" Brandon Hart reached over to open the door for her.

CHAPTER SIX

"AND how is our Mystery Girl today?" he asked when, after a momentary hesitation, she had climbed in beside him. "Here, let me put that parcel in the back for you."

"I'm very well, thank you. How are you?" Rachel said politely, when he had relieved her of the books and the car was moving again.

"Oh, black sheep always flourish," he said cheerfully. "But, from the back, you looked as if you might be feeling blue — or was it merely that your parcel was getting heavy?"

"The pavements make me tired. I'm not used to them," she said unguardedly. It was true. She had noticed that walking in the city made her feet ache.

Bran shot a glance at her. "No cutting-in at dances, no pavements — the mystery thickens by the minute," he remarked quizzically.

"If you must know, Mr. Hart, I've been living on an out island in the Bahamas for some years," Rachel told him, on impulse. "So you see there isn't any mystery. I'm just rather out of touch with city life."

"You disappoint me, Mrs. Herrick. I've been working on some much more interesting theories. So you come from the Bahamas? Whereabouts?"

"Oh, one of the small southern islands — I doubt if you'd know it," she said casually.

"You mean the fleshpots of Nassau are more my style? The de luxe hotels, the plushy night-spots . . . the *dolce far niente*, as the Italians say."

"What does that mean?" Rachel asked.

"Well, literally, a life of 'sweet idleness'. But some people translate it as wasting time."

"And *is* that your style, Mr. Hart — doing nothing but enjoying yourself?"

He grinned at her. "But it's the dedicated sybarites, like myself, who provide a living for the workers of the world. So we are a very important section of society."

"Doesn't it bore you — nothing but leisure? It bores me terribly," she added, without thinking.

"Ah, that's probably because you've been brought up to believe that 'the Devil makes work for idle hands',", he told her flippantly. "Now I was never harrowed by all that dismal Nanny-lore. My conscience just didn't develop. One isn't born with one, you know. It has to be nurtured in childhood. All very misguided, in my view. People are so much happier without one."

"He sounds like Juliet — when she wants to be shocking," Rachel thought. Recently, she had begun to realise that "city folk" — as Octavia had always termed them — were quite different from people who lived in quiet backwaters. They lacked simplicity and candour. What they said was not always what they meant, because they so often hid themselves behind false attitudes. They reminded her of hermit crabs. Their poses and affectations were like the crabs' borrowed shells, without which they had no defence against lurking predators. Though why human beings should feel that natural, spontaneous behaviour made them vulnerable — or to what — was something she had not yet fathomed.

Aloud, she said, "I don't think you mean that, Mr. Hart. You're just trying to live up to your reputation."

"Which you don't take very seriously, I gather."

"I think it's better to judge people for one's self — especially in a place like Bermuda." She was remembering what Nadine had said about the colony being rife with scandalous gossip.

"Yes, but judgement calls for experience," he replied, rather abruptly. "Somehow I don't think you have much experience, Mrs. Herrick. Not of people like myself, that's to say."

That was what Niall had warned her. How surprised he would be if he knew that his views were supported by the very person against whom he had been cautioning her.

"Perhaps not," she said quietly. "But, have *you* much experience of people like me, Mr. Hart?"

He laughed. "No, I daresay I haven't, now you mention it. I'm not exactly popular with matchmaking mothers, and the young married set don't welcome me either. So, as you suggest, my acquaintance with 'nice' girls is rather limited."

They had reached the main entrance to Moongates, but he did not turn into the drive.

"I'll drop you here, I think," he said. "Unfortunately the Herricks don't share your belief in giving people the benefit of the doubt. They accept the general opinion of my character, so it will save you from being catechised if they don't see us together. Good-bye, Mrs. Herrick."

After he had gone, Rachel walked slowly up the driveway. Somehow those few minutes with Bran Hart had lightened her misery a little. He was such an insouciant person himself that it was impossible to feel completely despondent while one was in his company.

That night, when they had finished dinner, Niall asked Rachel to go to the study for a few minutes.

"I have something to show you," he said, as they rose from the table.

The study was a small book-lined room, not often used. Rachel had only been in it once before, when Joseph had showed her over the whole house. There was a large roll-topped desk against one wall and, selecting the key from his ring, Niall unlocked it and pushed up the slatted lid.

"You remember I asked you if you would mind waiting for an engagement ring?" he said, over his shoulder. "That was because there was a ring here which I thought you would like."

Inside the desk were three large oblong-shaped parcels, neatly wrapped in stiff white paper and sealed with blobs of red wax. As he stripped off the wrappings, Rachel saw that each parcel contained a leather case.

"All this jewellery belonged to my mother — and now to you," Niall explained. "I've had some of it re-set in more modern designs — the pieces you can wear in the daytime. The more elaborate sets for evening wear will have to be kept at the bank and taken out when you need them. Personally I like them as they are, but they can also be modernised if you would prefer it."

He opened all three boxes, one after the other, and stood back for her to see their contents.

Although old Mrs. Herrick wore several fine rings on her thin fingers, and Juliet had put on a beautiful ruby pendant for their dinner party at the Rendezvous Rooms, Rachel had never imagined such magnificent jewellery as that which now sparkled in the lamplight.

"These pearls and the jade ear-rings and brooch you can wear when you like," said Niall. "The jade was brought back from China by my great-grandfather. The Chinese believe that, as well as being ornamental, the stone brings the wearer good luck. This is the family engagement ring. It was first worn by my great-great-grandmother."

He opened a small leather box and showed her a single perfect pearl surrounded by diamonds. Taking her left hand in his, he slipped it into place above her wedding ring. "Do you like it?" he asked. "There are several other rings if you don't care for it."

"Oh, Niall, it's beautiful," she said, in a shaken voice. "But it must be very valuable. If I wear it all the time, it may be damaged."

"I shouldn't think so. If you like, you can wear it only in the evenings."

"It isn't that I don't want to wear it. I just don't want to harm it, or lose it."

The evening jewels he had mentioned were two matching sets of necklaces, bracelets and ear-rings. One was of emeralds, the other of sapphires and diamonds. Niall showed her how the sapphire necklace could also be worn as a diadem on very grand occasions, and how a large topaz brooch divided into two smaller clips.

"May I try them on?" Rachel asked diffidently, when he had emptied all the little inner boxes and chamois rolls, and the whole glittering collection lay spread on the desk.

"Of course — I've told you, they're yours now."

So Rachel tried everything on, moving back and forth between the desk and the looking glass on the opposite wall so that she could see how each piece looked on her. The sapphire and diamond necklace she left until the last of all, but it had an intricate safety clasp and she had to ask Niall to help her with it.

When he had fastened it, and she had screwed the long shimmering pendant ear-rings to her lobes, she moved closer to the glass with a slight drawing in of breath. It was as if the jewels, so beautiful in themselves, had a magical effect on their wearer. Somehow — and of course it was only an illusion — the necklace made her neck seem quite swanlike, the poise of her head more graceful. Even her eyes seemed to have an added sparkle, and her hair a silkier gloss than usual. And as she studied her reflection, moving her head a little to see the sapphires flash and gleam with deep blue fire, she felt a curious upsurge of exaltation.

The image in the glass was not that of someone gauche and troubled and un-happy, like the reflection she saw in the bathroom every morning. This face was calm and confident, and beginning to smile. Not the face of a girl who could never belong to this house, but of someone **who** could take her place anywhere. It **was** like looking at a portrait of herself which was not just an accurate likeness, but a picture of how she would like to be.

And then, behind her, Niall moved, so that his face was reflected above her own.

"Turn round for a moment. Let me see," he said quietly.

She turned to him, holding her breath. There had been an expression on his face that she had not seen before, and it was still there now, as they faced each other.

He put up a hand and touched the exquisite necklace, and then her throat. "You look lovely in them," he said softly.

Then the telephone rang in the hall, and he frowned, and after a moment went to answer it. Rachel kept very still. Perhaps if she stayed where she was . . . and if Niall came back . . . and if that look on his face was still there . . .

Niall did come back — but he was still frowning and spoke briskly.

"There's been a robbery at the store, Rachel. Our watchman has been injured. The police want me down there immediately. Look, put all this stuff back in the boxes and ask Joseph to look after them for tonight, will you?"

"How long will you be, Niall? Shall I come with you?"

"No, this may take some time — you'd better stay here. But don't mention it to Gran. It might upset her." He seemed about to say something else, but changed his mind.

Checking that he had his car keys on him, he turned back into the hall and left the house.

After she had heard the car leave, Rachel leaned against the door jamb and sighed.

She felt as if something very important had been roughly snatched away from her. She was not even sure what she had lost . . . only that she might never be so close to it again.

Having rung for Joseph and asked him to take care of the jewel cases, she went up to see Niall's grandmother. Fortunately the old lady accepted her casual remark that Niall had gone out for an hour or so without asking any awkward questions. But this was because she already had something else on her mind.

"Tell me, Rachel, what do you think of this marriage between Juliet and Robert Howard?" she asked bluntly.

Rachel hesitated. "How do you mean, Mrs. Herrick?"

"I mean do you think it is likely to be a success?"

Rachel hesitated. "I like Robert very much — and I'm sure he is devoted to Juliet," she said cautiously.

"Yes, yes, child — but that's not what I'm asking you," the old lady said, a shade testily. "Do you think Juliet will be happy with him? Does she seem happy *now*, if it comes to that?"

"No, I don't think she does, to be

honest," Rachel said, after a moment. "Robert told me that he thought she was worried about having a household to manage, but I don't see how it *can* be that really. She — she couldn't possibly be in love with someone else, could she, Mrs. Herrick?"

"How should I know? I'm tied to this room all the time — I have no idea what is going on," the old lady answered tartly. "All I do know is Juliet is *not* behaving like a girl at one of the happiest periods of her life. She smokes too much, I suspect that she drinks too many cocktails, and she never seems to relax for a second. It is all most disquieting."

"Oh, please, don't distress yourself, Mrs. Herrick," Rachel said anxiously, worried by her agitated tone. She regretted now that she had disclosed her opinion on the matter, but she had thought the old lady too shrewd to be fobbed off with any feeble evasions of the truth. "It may be that Juliet is just keyed-up with excitement. I expect most girls have some last-minute doubts about committing themselves," she said lightly.

"Did you?" Mrs. Herrick asked keenly.

Rachel flushed. "I didn't have much time to think about it, but — yes, I was very nervous."

"May I ask why?" Mrs. Herrick enquired. She had relaxed against her cushions again, and was not twisting her rings quite so rapidly — always a sign that she was irritated or disturbed by something.

Rachel thought for a moment — she had to be careful how she answered. Then, remembering that Mrs. Herrick was not aware that she had been completely in the dark about Niall's real background when she married him, she said, "I wasn't sure that I could fit in with all this — Moongates and Herricks' and . . . and the social life here. My own background was so utterly different." She paused and, in a low voice, added, "I still don't really feel that I belong here. Mrs. Herrick . . . were you very disappointed when — when you saw what sort of person I was?"

The old lady was pouring herself a glass of some sweet cordial, and did not reply until she had sipped it. "Did I give you that impression?" she asked drily.

"Oh, no — you've always been most kind to me. But it must have been a great shock to you . . . and perhaps not a very agreeable one."

"Quite the contrary, my child," said Mrs. Herrick. "My reaction — after Niall had brought you to see me that first day — was one of complete approval and relief."

"You were glad?" Rachel asked, disbelievingly.

Mrs. Herrick smiled slightly. "You have one serious fault, Rachel, my dear. You are far too prone to underrate yourself. Too much diffidence is as much to be deplored as over-confidence, you know. Your lack of assurance is something you must try to overcome."

She paused for a moment to select a *marron glacé* from the large box which Niall brought home for her each week. She did not offer them to Rachel as she knew that the girl did not care for them.

"There were only two qualities which I hoped to find in the girl whom Niall chose for his wife," she went on, unwrapping the silver paper and dissecting the candied chestnut with a small pearl-handled fruit fork. "One was that she should be a kind girl — and, by that, I mean sensitive to other people's feelings and considerate of them. The second and equally important qualification was that she should have married my grandson for himself — not because of Herricks' or Moongates or the superficial pleasures of life in Bermuda. Since it was immediately clear to me that you fulfilled both those requirements, I was not in the least upset at being presented with a *fait accompli*, as it were. I am only sorry that I have apparently failed to demonstrate my approval."

There could be no doubting her sincerity, and Rachel was so surprised and moved that she had to swallow a lump in her throat.

"Thank you," she said huskily. "I will try to have more confidence in myself. It — it will be easier now that I know you're not disappointed in me."

Then, because it seemed an ideal moment to unburden herself on another matter, she told Niall's grandmother how much she disliked being idle, and about her unexpressed longing to learn some more advanced cookery.

"Why, of course you can, child. Why ever not?" Mrs. Herrick seemed amazed that she should have hesitated to mention her wish. "You know, Rachel, you must not feel that because Niall allows me to live here, you lack the authority of other wives. I have supervised the running of the house since Niall's mother died because Juliet has never shown any inclination to take over the reins, and because we are fortunate in having people like Joseph to serve us. But I should much prefer to be relieved of all domestic concerns. In fact I shall tell Joseph tomorrow that, from now on, you will deal with everything. Naturally I shall be pleased to advise you, if you need it. But I am sure it will not take you long to master the management of the house, and you will probably make a great many improvements."

They talked for about another half an hour, and then Rachel said good-night and went to her room. But although she changed into her night things, she did not go to bed. She wanted to wait up for Niall.

It was past eleven o'clock when she heard a car coming. But when she ran downstairs, she found it was Juliet who had returned from an evening out with Robert. For once, her sister-in-law seemed disinclined to chat till all hours. After she had gone upstairs, Rachel told Joseph not to wait up any longer as she would stay downstairs until Niall came back.

It was nearing midnight when he came. Rachel had been in the kitchen, finding out how the electric cooker worked and investigating the big glossy white refrigerator and the air-cooled pantry. Niall saw her standing in the kitchen doorway as he pulled down the garage door.

"You needn't have waited up for me, Rachel." He looked tired and rather drawn.

"I thought you might be hungry. Can't I get you something to eat? There's some cocoa in the store. I could make it like we had it on the *Dolphin* — and scramble some eggs with buttered toast."

"Bless you! I could do with something hot," he admitted. "I've been over at the hospital most of the time."

"Why the hospital? Oh, with the watchman who was injured. I'd forgotten that. Is he very badly hurt?"

Niall sat down on a chair by the kitchen table. "He died half an hour ago," he said heavily.

"*Oh, no!*" Rachel whispered. "Oh, how

terrible!" Instinctively, she moved round the table to where he sat and put her hands on his shoulders to comfort him. "Poor man! Was he married? Is there someone who will look after his wife tonight?"

"He was an old man, a widower," Niall said. "He lived with his daughter and her husband. They were at the hospital with me. Perhaps you could go and call on her tomorrow. I think she'd appreciate that. Her father had worked for Herricks' all his life. He used to drive the delivery carriage in the days before cars were allowed here." He put up his right hand and gripped Rachel's left one. "I don't suppose they meant to kill him — whoever broke into the place. He must have caught them trying the safe, and they panicked and coshed him too heavily. He never regained consciousness."

"Will they catch the man who did it, do you think?"

"Oh, yes — within hours, I should think. We don't have a high crime rate here. It was probably someone the police have their eye on already. It won't be easy for him to hide with a capital charge against him."

Rachel gently freed her hand. "I'll

get the food ready," she said quietly.

After he had eaten the scrambled eggs, Niall smoked a cigarette while Rachel washed his plate and scoured the pan. As she was putting these away, he said suddenly, "It was nice of you to stay up for me, Rachel. Thank you."

A glow of pleasure spread through her, and she felt that somehow in the past few hours their relationship had undergone a subtle and hopeful change. This afternoon, after her meeting with Nadine Oakhill, she had been in a mood of such profound despair that she had even considered methods of leaving Bermuda without Niall knowing. But now — because of the way he had looked at her in the library, and after her talk with his grandmother and this present domestic interlude in the otherwise silent, unlighted house — she felt a surge of new optimism and resolution. Perhaps she had been wrong about Niall's feelings for Nadine. Perhaps what he felt for the other girl was not true love at all, but only a powerful physical attraction which, when he was younger, he had mistaken for something deeper. Perhaps he would always be secretly haunted by the memory of Nadine's beauty — just as he hungered for the freedom of the sea — but that did not mean he wanted her for his wife.

They switched out the kitchen lights, and Niall, who knew the house too well to need lights to find his way, guided Rachel across the dark hall and up the wide graceful staircase. Outside the door of her room, he turned her to face him. There was just enough moonlight from the window at the far end of the corridor to outline his head and shoulders, but his expression was hidden from her. She felt his fingers moving lightly on the thick soft quilting of her dressing-gown, then tightening to grip her shoulders. She closed her eyes, hardly daring to breathe. If only he would kiss her, hold her close . . .

He did kiss her. But it was a kiss of quiet affection, not passion. A gentle, grateful kiss for a very young girl — to say goodnight. Not a kiss that demanded a response, and would lead to other, closer, wilder embraces.

"Sleep well," Niall said quietly. Then he opened her bedroom door and moved past her to his own door along the shadowy corridor.

A week later, Rachel was lying on the Herricks' private beach after her customary afternoon bathe, when a man waded out of the water. It was not until he pushed up his diving goggles that she recognised Brandon Hart.

"Hello there. May I come ashore?" he asked, grinning.

"What are you doing here?" Rachel asked in astonishment, when he had sat down on the sand beside her and was raking back his thick fair hair.

"I'm your neighbour from over the water — didn't you know?" He indicated the sprawling pink-washed house which stood on the wooded slope on the far side of the inlet.

"I could see you sunbathing from my terrace, so I thought I'd swim over for half an hour," he went on. "But perhaps you're not 'At Home' today? Shall I go again?"

Rachel hesitated. She was torn between reluctance to flout Niall's expressed wishes, and her own instinctive liking for this man. It was not as if she had invited him over, she thought. Now that he was here it would be churlish to insist on his leaving immediately, or to make some thin excuse for her own retreat.

Avoiding a direct answer, she said, "I had no idea you lived in the pink house. What is it called?"

Bran eased himself on to his elbow and produced a cigarette pack from a waterproof pocket in his swimming trunks. "It hasn't got a name. It's known as 'the Hart place'," he said.

"How many Harts are there?"

"Only me."

"You live there all alone?" she asked. It looked as large a house as Moongates — much too large for one man on his own.

He shook his head. "No, the house is shut up now. I rent a cottage in the Cambridge Beeches colony. I only come over here occasionally, just to see that the place isn't falling apart, or sometimes" — with that disarming schoolboy grin — "to dally in the moonlight with some girl."

"But you'll live there again when you marry, won't you?"

Rachel hated to think of a house in such beautiful surroundings being shuttered against the sun, and growing musty and mildewed from disuse.

"Perhaps — *if* I marry, which isn't at all likely."

"You don't want to get married?" she asked curiously. It did not occur to her that this was a most personal question to put to someone she had met only three times.

"I've never had to consider it," Bran said carelessly. "The usual inducements to marriage have not applied to me so far."

"What are the usual inducements?"

He shrugged. "Needing someone to wash your shirts . . . seeing a short cut to a directorship via the chairman's daughter . . . forgetting that girls who look knockouts by candlelight may be hags the morning after without their war-paint." His tone was not caustic, merely matter-of-fact. "Does such cynicism shock you, Mrs. Herrick? — or may I call you Rachel now?"

"Yes, do," she said absently.

She was not so much shocked by his cynicism as curious to know what lay behind it. He might not sound bitter, but it must have been some bitterly harrowing experience which had led to such extreme disenchantment.

"Well, if those are the reasons men marry, I wonder which one of them was Niall's," she said lightly. *That* ought to test his smooth tongue, she thought, with amusement.

But Bran did not hesitate. "I guess Niall fell in love," he said evenly.

"You *believe* in that old-fashioned idea?" she enquired sceptically.

Bran drew on his cigarette and blew a smoke ring. Watching it widen and dissolve, he said slowly, "Let's say I believe there are some women with whom familiarity does not breed contempt. I think you're one of them. Niall's lucky."

He sounded so sincere that Rachel was taken aback.

"Well . . . thank you, Bran," she said, uncertainly.

He studied her for a moment. "Tell me something . . . what would you do if I lived up to my reputation and kissed you?"

Rachel coloured, but she did not look away. "I don't think you would," she answered quietly. "But if you did, I should be sorry and disappointed."

He smiled, but it was not his usual teasing grin. "Don't worry: I won't blot my copybook. To be credited with principles is a novel experience for me. I find it rather agreeable."

Soon after that he said good-bye and swam away. But he returned at the same time the following day, and the day after that. When, on the fourth day, he did not come, Rachel was surprised to find how much she missed their time together.

In the following fortnight, Bran swam over to Moongates almost every afternoon, apart from the week-ends. Rachel knew that Niall would be furious if he knew, and that she ought to discourage Bran. But, although she suffered twinges of guilt over the meetings, she could not bring herself to give up a perfectly innocent and harmless friendship just because Bran was generally thought to be a blackguard. If she could have relied on Niall believing that Bran always behaved impeccably towards her, she would have told him without hesitation. But she knew that he would not believe it, and that he disliked Bran so much that he was quite capable of blacking his eye for even setting foot on Herrick sand, let alone having a daily rendezvous with his wife.

One afternoon, after she and Bran had been discussing a book he had lent her — bringing it across the inlet with him in a sealed rubber bag a few days earlier — he said "We shall be meeting in public again next week. I take it you're all going to the Malcolm girl's wedding?"

"What? Oh . . . yes, I believe we are," Rachel said abstractedly.

Bran smiled at her. "What's the matter, Rachel? You seem very preoccupied this afternoon. Is anything wrong?"

She hesitated. "We're having some people to dinner and it's partly because I'm a little on edge about coping with them."

"I'm sure you'll cope charmingly. What's the other part?"

"Oh, Bran, I don't know how to say this without sounding rude and unkind," she began unhappily.

"Then I'll say it for you — you'd rather I didn't come over any more."

"But how did you know?" she exclaimed, startled.

"I guessed that was it half an hour ago. You were obviously nerving yourself to say something embarrassing to you. What

248

else could it be? Don't worry: you haven't hurt my feelings. I know how you feel."

"Do you?" she asked him anxiously. "Do you really, Bran?"

He reached out and held her hand in a light friendly clasp for a moment. Then, after giving it a little shake, he released it again. "I understand perfectly, young Rachel. You know Niall doesn't approve of me, so you haven't mentioned these afternoon sunbathing sessions. But since you're an exceptionally punctilious creature, the slightest disloyalty to him worries you. You're perfectly right. I ought never to have come over in the first place. I realise that now."

"All the same, I'm very glad you did," she said candidly. "I like you so much, Bran. I do wish you and Niall were friends."

He helped her to her feet and watched her roll up her thick red beach towel.

"You're terribly in love with that husband of yours, aren't you, Rachel?" he said, in a strange tone.

"Yes, I am," she answered simply.

Bran nodded. Then, without saying good-bye, he turned away and walked back into the clear green water. As soon as it was up to his armpits he flung himself forward and began swimming towards the landing-stage below his house.

After watching him till he was halfway there, Rachel stepped into her beach-mules and climbed up the rough rock steps on to the lawn. Why had Bran looked at her so strangely before he left? Did he know about Nadine? Did he pity her for being in love with a husband whose heart was generally acknowledged to belong to some-one else? Sighing, she quickened her pace. In three hours' time, she would be hostess at her first dinner-party. Several of Niall's friends were coming to dinner, and Robert was bringing an American business asso-ciate and his wife. It was important that she should make a good impression on them. She must concentrate on the evening ahead of her.

But as she lay in a warm scented bath and later, when she sat at her dressing-table, watching Rietta's skilful dark fingers pin-ning up her hair, Rachel could not help letting her thoughts wander.

Since the night of the robbery at Her-ricks', Niall had been much more attentive to her. They had had breakfast together on the balcony every morning, and he had come home for lunch each day. One evening he had taken her to the cinema, another day they had driven over to Fort St. Catherine and joined a party of tourists to see the dioramas of notable events in Bermuda's history, and walked through a maze of galleries and tunnels to the powder magazine which lay deep under the keep of the fortress. As well as devoting more of his time to her, Niall had given her a number of small presents which, because they were small and quite cheap, had seemed far more personal than some expensive luxury from the store's gift department.

But Rachel's pleasure in one of these gifts — a little seashell-decorated box in which to keep her hair-pins — had been spoilt by Juliet saying teasingly, "You'll have to watch him, Rachel sweetie. When husbands start loading wives with presents, it's generally because they've got a guilty conscience."

Even before Niall had rounded on his sister, saying curtly that he did not care for that cheap brand of humour, Rachel had recognised that Juliet's thoughtless quip was probably all too true. Indeed, the sharpness of Niall's reproof seemed to confirm that it had been.

But, whatever the true reason for Niall's sudden excess of attentiveness might be, it was impossible for Rachel not to derive some pleasure and encouragement from it. Just as he could ruin her whole day with one aloof glance or sardonic remark, so he could exalt her to a new peak of happiness with an unexpected smile or some small intimacy that most wives — even brides — would have taken for granted. He had only to pinch her cheek or to use the most commonplace of endearments to give her a sharp pang of pleasure.

When she was dressed — in a simple pale rose silk frock with the triple string of milky heirloom pearls around her neck — Rachel went downstairs to inspect the dining-room. Earlier in the day she had arranged the flowers for the centre-piece, and it was she who had chosen the menu and decided what table linen and china should be used. At first, when old Mrs. Herrick had insisted on her making these decisions, she had been horrified. But, in spite of her pleas for advice, Niall's grandmother had refused to have any say in the arrangements.

"And I have told Joseph not to influence you either," she had said. "Every young wife suffers a certain amount of agony with her first dinner-party, my dear. You must cope with this on your own. At least you will not have to cook the meal and serve it. Now that is a real test of strength."

So, with both Joseph and the cook forbidden to help her out, Rachel had gone to a book shop in Hamilton, bought several volumes on the art of entertaining, and spent almost the whole of one night poring over them.

Niall was late coming home. He went straight upstairs to shower and change, coming down again only ten minutes before the guests were due to arrive. He found Rachel waiting anxiously on the terrace where, except during exceptionally cool spells, the Herricks always had their main meals.

"That's a very spectacular piece of floristry, Joe. Did Hunts send it up?" he asked the butler, when Joseph brought them both drinks.

"No, sir — those Mis' Herrick's

flowers," the old man said gravely. "Mis' Herrick arranged everything tonight 'cept the wines, Mister Niall."

Niall's eyebrows went up. "You have unsuspected talents, Rachel. Those flowers look most professional."

"I do hope I haven't made any mistakes, Niall," she said worriedly. "Your grandmother insisted that I should decide everything by myself?"

"What are we having to eat?" he enquired.

"Well, we're starting with iced cucumber soup, and then we're having a French *quiche* which will be hot. It's a pastry tart with a cheese filling," she added, in case the dish should be new to him. "The main course is stuffed baked lobsters with an avocado and pineapple salad, and the pudding is chestnut mousse with some things called *cenci*. They're sort of brandy biscuits, and Cook let me make them this morning. Does that sound all right to you, Niall?"

"It sounds a great deal more appetising than the Chicken Maryland and soggy sponge trifle which seem to be the standard fare in a lot of other houses," he said approvingly. "Oh, by the way, I know you like wearing your father's watch in the daytime, but I thought this might be more appropriate with your evening things."

Slipping a hand into his inside jacket pocket, he brought out a folded envelope which contained a narrow gold clasp bracelet with a concealed watch face under the engraved central section.

He slipped it on her wrist, but before she could thank him, there were voices in the hall and Joseph announced the first of their guests. Robert and his American friends were the last to arrive and, just before they came, Niall went upstairs to fetch his grandmother. He had to carry her in his arms because she was forbidden to walk even a few steps. Joseph had a wheelchair waiting for her at the foot of the stairs and, standing beside him, Rachel found something curiously moving in the sight of her tall, powerful husband bearing the old lady's slight form as easily as if she were a child.

As they settled her comfortably in the chair, Mrs. Herrick gripped Rachel's fingers for an instant.

"Niall tells me the table looks perfectly

delightful, my dear. I believe we shall **be** very proud of you," she murmured in **an** encouraging aside.

Perhaps it was because Niall's friends were both most likeable and unaffected couples, and the Americans were also a very homely, friendly pair, but within minutes of them all taking their places at the table, Rachel's apprehension melted away and she began genuinely to enjoy her new role.

All the women remarked how unusual and artistic her flowers were, and her choice of dishes seemed to be equally successful. One of the things which had worried her most was that she might not be able to keep the conversation flowing. But as the middle-aged American on her right was keenly interested in folk music, he was eager to learn everything she knew about Bahamian goombay. The rather younger man on her left was a doctor with a passion for skin-diving. He wanted to know how the reef-life round Bermuda differed from the reefs with which Rachel was so familiar.

But what pleased Rachel most was that whenever she had an opportunity to glance down the table at Niall, he seemed to sense that she was watching him and would return her look with a smile that had a far more heady effect than the wine in the tall crystal goblets. Once, he even raised his glass to her in a silent toast. When, a moment later, her American guest spoke to her, she gave him such a radiant smile that he forgot what he had been about to say.

Soon after ten o'clock, old Mrs. Herrick said good-night and Niall took her back to her room. Rachel went into the hall with them as the old lady had indicated that she wished to speak to her for a moment.

"There, you see, child? It has not been such an ordeal for you, has it?" she asked teasingly, looking up from her wheelchair with a twinkle. "You had planned everything carefully beforehand, and you looked perfectly at ease and behaved delightfully. You couldn't possibly have managed the evening better. Which is exactly what I expected. Now, give me a kiss, dear, and go back to your guests. I am sure they are in no hurry to leave."

Rachel bent and kissed the old lady's soft cheek. And then, as she flashed a smile at Niall and turned to go back into the drawing-room, he caught hold of her arm. With his grandmother watching them affectionately, he drew Rachel to him, bent his head and brushed a light, swift kiss on her mouth. Then he let her go and turned to lift Mrs. Herrick from the chair.

Rachel was so astonished that she still had not moved when they were halfway up the staircase. Then, as they passed out of sight on the landing, she made a strong effort to collect herself. Her heart was hammering wildly against her ribs and her legs felt as if the bones had suddenly melted.

A few moments after she had returned to the drawing-room, Joseph came in with an envelope in his hand.

"This letter come for Mister Niall, Mis' Herrick. I think maybe it's urgent."

"He's just gone upstairs with his grandmother. I'll give it to him as soon as he's back, Joseph," said Rachel.

When Niall reappeared, she was talking to the American's plump jolly wife about the superb Scottish cashmeres in the shops.

"Oh, excuse me, Mrs. Spockman. Niall, this note arrived a few minutes ago." Looking up at him and handing over the envelope, Rachel felt a fiery blush suffusing her face and throat.

Niall took the letter but held her glance for a second before attending to it. There was a glint of gentle mockery in his eyes, as if he knew that she could still feel the imprint of his lips on hers, and that her heart was still beating much too fast.

"Where did this come from, Joseph?" he asked, as the butler passed behind him to get someone another drink.

"I couldn't say, sir. It was delivered by a boy. I gave him a shilling and he ran off."

"Are you sure it's for me?" It isn't addressed."

"Oh, it's certainly for you, Mister Niall. The boy said 'for the Master' most particular."

Niall shrugged. "Will you excuse me for a moment, Mrs. Spockman?" He slit open the envelope.

"Are you looking for cashmeres for yourself or for presents, Mrs. Spockman?" Rachel asked.

"Oh, I guess I'll pick a couple for myself, but my daughters back home are just crazy for them. If I don't take back at least — " Mrs. Spockman stopped short.

She had just glanced up at Niall, and now she said, "Is anything wrong, Mr. Herrick? You haven't had bad news, I hope?"

But whatever expression had made her jump to this conclusion had been swiftly erased from Niall's face.

"No, it's nothing important," he said smoothly, tearing the note into pieces and dropping them in a waste basket beside the couch where the two women were sitting. "Let me get you another Vodkatini, Mrs. Spockman. A daiquiri for you, isn't it, Rachel?"

"What a very striking man your husband is, my dear," said Mrs. Spockman, when he had moved across to the cocktail cupboard. "And you've been married only a short time, I understand?"

"Yes . . . yes, just a few weeks," Rachel said, smiling. "To be honest, I was dreadfully nervous earlier. This is my first experience of giving a party and I was afraid I might seem very gauche to everyone." "And now I'm dying for you all to go so that I can be alone with Niall," she thought, with a tremor.

But as the evening went on, and their guests showed no signs of leaving early, it seemed to Rachel that Niall was avoiding speaking to her. He did not even look at her again and — although it must be her fancy, she thought uneasily — his geniality seemed curiously forced.

It was after midnight when the party finally broke up and she and Niall and Juliet went out on to the drive to wave good-bye.

"Well, that was a raging success if ever there was one," Juliet said, patting Rachel on the back as they went indoors again. "You made a great hit with everyone, sweetie. Do you know what? . . . I'm hungry. Let's go into the kitchen and gorge the left-overs. To blazes with my waistline for once. I'm sick of counting calories all the time. Anyway I must have had at least two thousand already this evening, so another few hundred won't matter. I can always starve tomorrow."

Niall had bolted the front door, and was switching off the lights. He had sent Joseph to bed earlier on.

"You two can sit up till dawn, if you like. I'm tired," he said flatly. "You did very well, Rachel. Congratulations." Moving past them, he went swiftly up the stairs.

"Wow! What's the matter with him?" Julie asked blankly, when he was out of earshot. "He sounded rather snarly, I thought."

"He's tired. He's had a heavy day at Herricks'. Do you really want something to eat, Julie?"

"Yes, I'm ravenous. Come on, let's have a feast on our own. Or must you dash off and soothe your lord and master?"

Rachel shook her head. "I'm hungry too, and Niall will be asleep in five minutes," she said lightly.

But, inwardly, she was stupefied. "What has gone wrong?" Why is he angry? Is it my fault?" she thought bewilderedly.

Juliet, a naturally nocturnal creature, would have chatted until two if Rachel had been willing. But after making her sister-in-law some fresh coffee and watching her eat the remains of the mousse and *cenci* and some wafers and cheese, Rachel said they must go to bed or they would be wrecks the next day.

In the hall, she said, "You go on up, Julie. I just want to make sure no one has left a cigarette burning in the drawing-room."

But Juliet said she would wait and, after a few moments, Rachel rejoined her and they went upstairs and said good-night on the landing.

In her room, Rachel closed the door and stood listening for some seconds. But there was no sound from Niall's room, and no light shining out on to the balcony.

Shivering a little, although the bedroom was as warm as the rest of the house, she sat down on the dressing stool and fumbled in her pockets for the torn scraps of paper which she had retrieved from the waste basket downstairs. All the time Juliet had been eating her supper, she had felt more and more convinced that the note in the grubby unaddressed envelope had been the cause of Niall's strange *volte-face*.

It was not difficult to reconstruct the note, as there seemed to be only one line of typescript covering five or six scraps. The rest of the fragments were blank. Fitting the words together like a jig-saw puzzle, Rachel read the message. It was in the form of a question. There was no signature.

"*Did you know your wife spends the after-noons with Brandon Hart?*" someone had written.

CHAPTER SEVEN

WHO? Whose sharp, spiteful eyes had spied on them all this past fortnight? Whose hands had tapped out the neat black typescript? Who hated her so much that they had not shrunk from using this most loathsome and vicious of all weapons — the treacherous stab in the back of an anonymous letter? Who . . . who . . . *who*?

A sudden breath of wind from the open window fluttered among the ragged shreds of paper, blowing one of them on to her lap and then to the floor. Rachel recoiled from it, shuddering. She was so appalled that anyone could do such a vile thing that she felt even the paper itself was contaminated, foul. A wave of real physical nausea swept her, as if she had been assailed by some foetid effluence. When, after some moments, the sickness passed, and she raised her head and looked dazedly at her reflection in the mirror, there was a sheen of moisture on her forehead and upper lip. *Oh, God,* she thought, with anguish — *and*

Niall read this horrible thing with all those people round him.

Five seconds later, she was on the other side of the bedroom, wrenching at the door of the dressing-room.

"Niall . . . oh, Niall darling . . . you *can't* believe that — "

But, after bursting into his darkened, curtained room, she stopped short, her voice dying away. Even before she had found the panel of light switches, she knew that the room was empty.

The jacket of his lounge suit had been flung over a chair, and his olive silk tie lay in a twist on the end of the bed, like an uncoiling snake. There was an unlit cigarette, broken in half, on the ochre rug. But his poplin pyjamas lay immaculately folded on the pillow above the turned-down bedclothes, and his black leather slippers were still placed neatly together against the box-pleated valance.

Where had he gone? she thought, in terror. To find Bran? To accuse him of seducing her? To punish him . . . perhaps to half kill him?

A billow of curtain belled out from the balcony doors. Rachel rushed to pull it back. Yes, the doors were unlatched and slightly ajar. Niall must have left the house by way of the balcony. There was a staircase at the other end of the house which led down on to the spider lily path. But if he had gone after Bran, he must have taken the car. She and Juliet would have heard the garage door going up while they were in the kitchen. If not the door, then certainly the starting of the motor. *Dear God, what shall I do?* she thought feverishly.

Beyond the lawn, where the placid water of the inlet shimmered faintly in the starlight — there was a cloud over the moon so that the gardens lay in darkness — there was a sudden flicker of light. It lasted barely three seconds, but long enough for Rachel to recognise it as the tiny spurting flame of a cigarette lighter. There was someone on the beach. It had to be Niall.

Trembling with the force of her relief, she hurried along the balcony, past the chinks of light that showed between the curtains of Juliet's room, to the head of the wrought-iron spiral staircase. The treads were patterned like lace and she had almost reached the bottom when one of the high tapering heels of her ottoman evening shoes caught fast in a hole. Losing her slack grasp of the handrail, her foot held fast by the shoe's beaded instep strap, she lurched painfully against the central column and fell heavily down on to the flagstones. Some-body screamed . . . there was a kaleidos-copic splintering of light . . . then darkness, and depths of nothingness.

Coming up from her dive, and dimly wondering why the ascent took so long and why all the fishes had suddenly disappeared — did that mean there was a barracuda about ? — Rachel saw Juliet's face above her. Why wasn't she wearing her bathing-cap ? And what was she doing in the sea in her emerald kimono ?

"You've had a fall, Rachel. Don't talk. Just lie still until the doctor comes," Juliet said soothingly, bending over her.

Then Rachel discovered she was not in the water, but on her bed. "My head hurts," she murmured, wishing Juliet would not sway about like that.

"You hit it as you fell. Try closing your eyes," Juliet said, rocking backwards and forwards so that one moment her face was far away and, the next, very close.

Rachel did as she suggested, but it was not much help because there seemed to be a tight band round her forehead, and something sharp jabbing into her crown.

"Can't you undo it?" she muttered fretfully. "This thing round my head — it hurts."

"Yes, we will, dear. Just as soon as the doctor comes," Juliet promised.

After that everything was confused. There was a man there and Juliet kept calling him "Doctor", but they did not take away whatever was cutting into her forehead and she could only hear them talking when it slackened a little and hurt less.

The man said something about a severe sprain and any loss of consciousness needing to be taken seriously. Then she heard Niall's voice asking about an X-ray, and she had a muddled feeling that there was something vitally important which she must tell him at once. But she could not remember what it was and, when she tried to struggle up on her elbow, the pain was so bad it made her groan, and she was glad when they pressed her gently down again and said she must lie very still and not worry.

But although her head ached so badly and there were other but less acute pains in the region of her left foot, she continued to feel vaguely uneasy about whatever Niall ought to have been told. And in the hours after they had turned out all the lights — long dragging night hours in which she never seemed to sleep for more than a few minutes before her throbbing head roused her again — there were periods when she was fretted by a sense of some impending disaster which she was powerless to avert. Or had something terrible already happened? Or had she only dreamed it, and was dreaming still?

Suddenly — or so it seemed to Rachel — it was daylight again.

Then she realised that she must have been asleep for several hours because the last time she had opened her eyes the room had been dark, and now it was filled with pale gold light. Outside the closed curtains, the sun must be flooding the balcony and drying out the dew on the lawn.

Her second discovery was that the pain in her left ankle was now much worse than her headache. This had subsided to a persistent but bearable throb somewhere behind her right ear. But at the least movement, her ankle felt as if it had been lanced by a hundred sea-urchins' barbs.

She was bracing herself for the torture that would result from an attempt to sit up, when Juliet came into the room.

"Oh, you're awake, poor pet. How do you feel this morning? You know what happened, I suppose? You caught your heel on the balcony stairs and pitched down head first. Fortunately I had just got back from the bathroom, so I heard you yell and rushed out. Then Niall came pelting up from the cove and carried you up here. My lord! — you nearly gave us heart failure, sweetie. We thought you'd broken your neck."

"I'm sorry. How stupid of me to — " Rachel stopped short. Julie's reference to Niall having been on the beach when the accident occurred had brought everything back to her. The dinner-party . . . the delivery of the note . . . her own horrified discovery of its contents . . . her terror of how Niall might react.

She must have made some stifled sound that could have been a moan of pain, because Juliet took her hand. "What is it? Your poor head? I'll give you one of the pills the doctor left for you."

"No, no, it isn't my head. That's much better now. Juliet . . . I left some paper on the dressing table last night. Where is it? Has someone thrown it away?"

"What sort of paper, sweetie? I didn't notice anything. Was it something important?"

"Yes — no! It — it was a bill I'd torn up by mistake. See if it's in the waste basket, will you?"

"There's nothing here but a lipstick tissue," Juliet said, after she had looked in the lacquered waste box. Then, obviously perplexed by Rachel's anxiety, "Does it matter particularly? What was it a bill for?"

Rachel bit her lip. "Oh, I suppose it isn't really important," she said, more calmly. "Never mind — forget it, Julie. What time is it?"

"Just gone eight. Could you drink a cup of tea, do you think?"

"Yes, but I'll have it after I've bathed. I feel so sticky and messy at the moment. Could you give me a hand out of bed? My ankle feels as if I'd broken the wretched thing."

"You were lucky you didn't break it, and it's very badly sprained. You can't possibly get up for several days," Juliet informed her. "Apart from your ankle, you knocked yourself out for five minutes, so you've got to take life easy for a while. Doctor Harris will be here in half an hour. We had him in last night, but I think you were too woozy to take in much."

"No, I remember you talking to him. Julie . . . was Niall in here then, or had he gone?"

"Well, of course he was in here. You don't think he'd breeze off while you were laid out, do you? You don't seem to appreciate what a devoted spouse he is, my pet — even if he was a bit grouchy after the party last night. He even insisted on sitting up with you all night. He wouldn't trust me to stay awake." She glanced at her watch. "He's having a nap now, but he was glued to your bedside until about an hour ago."

Niall had been with her all night? Rachel thought, astounded. Then it had not been only a dream that someone had given her a sip of water, and held her hand during one of the worst attacks of headache. Well, it showed how groggy she must have been. She had thought it was part of her dream of being in hospital.

Presently, Doctor Harris arrived. He was a quiet grey-haired man with twinkling brown eyes.

"I think perhaps you'd better have an X-ray, just to make sure there's no fracture there, Mrs. Herrick," he said, after gently examining her scalp. "I'm pretty sure that you have nothing worse than an extremely sore head, but I know it would relieve your husband's mind. I'll arrange for him to bring you down to the hospital this afternoon. I'm afraid you'll have that headache for a while, but I'll give you some more tablets to relieve it. Your ankle just needs to be kept up for three or four days with the compresses changed fairly frequently. Oh, and you might be as well to keep to a liquid diet for the next thirty-six hours, with some bread and butter if you're really hungry."

When Rietta brought her lunch — an egg whipped up in milk flavoured with honey — Rachel asked the maid if she had removed the scraps of paper from the dressing-table. But Rietta said she had not been in the bedroom since she had turned down the bed the previous evening.

"There ain't been no one in here 'cept Marse Niall, an' Miss Julie an' that Doctor Harris, Mis' Herrick," she said.

So it must have been Niall who had seen and removed the torn-up note, Rachel realised miserably. What had he thought when he saw it there on her dressing-table? What would anyone think in the circumstances? That a wife who not only had secret assignations with another man but who also pried into her husband's private correspondence must be a pretty despicable sort of person. It would not be a very convincing defence to plead that she had never intended to pry, but had acted on impulse, having an instinctive conviction that the note endangered her marriage.

No, you did that yourself. If you hadn't met Bran on the sly, the note could never have been written, whispered her conscience. *Why should Niall listen to your excuses? You deceived him, and now you must pay for it. His contempt is only what you deserve.*

"But if he despises me, why did he look after me last night?" she thought, twisting the sheet between her fingers. "And surely he can't believe that, within a few weeks of marrying him, I would let another man make love to me?"

By two o'clock, when Juliet came to get her ready for the trip to the hospital, Rachel was so distraught at the thought of facing Niall that the pain of moving her ankle, which, normally, she would have borne with gritted teeth, brought tears welling up in her eyes.

"I'm sorry to be so feeble," she muttered, ashamed.

"Oh, rubbish, sweetie. If I were as black and blue as you are, my yells would lift the roof," Juliet assured her cheerfully.

After helping her to dress, and insisting on her wearing a warm wool coat over her blouse and skirt, Juliet went off to tell Niall they were ready to go down, and then to see if her grandmother wanted any errands run. A few moments later, Niall came through the dressing-room door.

"Hello, Rachel. How are you feeling now?" he asked. "I'm sorry I couldn't get in to see you earlier, but I slept till ten and then I had to go to a committee meeting."

His manner was so normal and friendly that Rachel was completely taken aback.

"Oh . . . did you?" she said blankly.

"Juliet tells me your head is better, but that your ankle is giving you hell now. I'll do my best not to jog it, but it's bound to give you a jab when I lift you. Ready?"

Rachel nodded, tensing. Was it possible that he had not seen the note last night? she wondered. But, if so, what *had* happened to it?

Niall slid one arm under her knees and the other behind her waist. Then, very slowly and carefully, he lifted her out of the chair.

"Put your right arm round my neck, will you? There: are you fairly comfortable?"

By the time he had settled her in the car, Juliet had joined them. It was she who did most of the talking during the drive to the hospital. Niall answered her from time to time. Rachel said nothing at all.

It was not until the return journey when he dropped his sister in Hamilton that Rachel was alone with him again.

"I expect you'll be glad to get back into bed, won't you? You must feel pretty shaken up," he said, as they halted at a junction.

"Yes . . . yes, I do," she agreed, in a low voice. "But not only because of my fall, Niall. Please . . . there's something I must explain to you."

He was waiting for a break in the cross traffic. "Not yet, Rachel. Wait till we get home, will you?" Now, for the first time, there was an edge of coldness in his voice.

She did not attempt to speak to him again and, when they reached the house, he called Rietta to help her into bed.

"I'll come back and have some tea with you presently," he said, after he had lowered her into the chair once more.

In fact it was more than half an hour after Rietta had brought the tea before he did come back. And every second of the waiting time put an extra strain on Rachel's nerves. In the last ten minutes before he finally tapped at the door, she had begun to wonder if he was deliberately tormenting her.

But having ascribed his delay to a telephone call, Niall placed a straight-backed chair to face the bed and asked her permission to smoke.

"Now," he said evenly, "what is it you want to discuss with me so urgently?"

Rachel forced herself to meet his level glance. "You may already know," she said, in a shaking voice. "I—I read that note which was sent to you, Niall. I took the bits out of the basket and put them together and read them. They — they were there on my dressing-table when I fell down the balcony stairs."

"Yes, I know. I saw them and destroyed them. Is there an ash-tray in here?"

"There's one on the mantelpiece." How could he sit there so calmly, concerned about the trifling detail of an ash-tray, when she had just admitted doing something he must find contemptible?

"Oh, Niall, I know what you must think of me — but won't you even try to understand?" she began again.

"By all means — although I doubt if you do know what I think of you," he said drily. "But I shan't listen to anything if you're going to distress yourself."

"*Distress myself!*" Rachel exclaimed, a note of hysteria in her voice. "How could I *not* be distressed? Whatever you may think of me, I'm not so shabby that I — "

But he cut her short. "I wish you were not so convinced of your ability to read my thoughts, Rachel. If, as you insist, you already know my opinion of you — and feel you are unlikely to improve it — then there's not very much point in going on. No, listen to me now, please," — as she opened her mouth to protest.

Then, surprising her even more, he came and sat beside her on the bed, and took possession of her hot restless hands.

"I blame myself entirely for what happened last night," he said quietly. "I should have burnt that filthy letter as soon as I'd read it. If you hadn't seen it, you wouldn't have been upset and fallen. Now let's try to forget it ever came."

"But it was true, Niall. Don't you understand . . . it was true. I have been seeing Bran in the afternoons."

"Yes, I know — but not for the purpose implied in that note."

"You knew? How could you possibly know?"

He shrugged. "I came home the other afternoon and saw you together. I had intended to take you sailing, but you seemed to be enjoying yourself, so I came up to my room and caught up with some paper work."

"Why didn't you say something? Weren't you angry?"

His mouth twisted in a smile, but his eyes remained cold. "My dear Rachel, we're not in the Middle Ages. I can't forbid you to know people — however much I may dislike them myself. Naturally I expected you to mention that Hart had swum over. When you didn't — well, I guessed you thought I would raise hell and you funked it."

He released her hands and stood up, moving over to the window where he lit another cigarette. "Do you feel better now?" he asked casually.

Rachel fiddled with the tail of her braid. "A little," she said slowly. "But, Niall — that note. Who could have written it? Who hates me — or you — enough to send such a horrible thing?"

"I don't know — but if they try it a second time, they'll have the police on their tail," he said grimly. "Personally I can't believe it was aimed at you at all — I think that was incidental."

"But it must have been meant to injure

me. It more or less accused me of . . . of betraying you," she said, flushing.

"No, I think not," Niall said, his eyes narrowed. "I fancy it was either a particularly nasty piece of mischief-making designed to take the wind out of my sails, or else it was intended to ricochet on Hart."

"How do you mean?" she asked, puzzled.

His glance was sardonic. "Despite *your* high opinion of him, there are a great many people who have considerable justification for wanting to see Hart come a cropper. It could be that whoever wrote that note was counting on me to beat the daylights out of him."

"That was what I thought you might do when I found you weren't in your room last night," she admitted. "Then I saw you were down in the cove. I was never so relieved in my life."

"Were you?" he said, in an odd tone. "Was your relief for me or for Bran, Rachel?"

"Why, for you of course — for you, Niall."

"Was it?" His tone was sceptical. After glancing at his watch, he said, "I must go now, and you must get some sleep. I'll send Juliet up to give you your medicine." Then he left her.

Rachel's ankle was still rather tender when, at the end of the following week, she accompanied Niall and Juliet to the fashionable wedding of two popular members of the Colony's younger set.

As far as she could recall, Rachel had never been to a wedding before and, when the bride came up the aisle on her father's arm, she could not help feeling a pang of regret that she had missed most of, if not all, "the trappings" as Niall had once called them. The reception was held at the home of the bride's parents, which was a very modern house, built almost entirely of glass and surrounded by a shallow moat filled with flowering water lilies and stone plinths on which some very odd examples of modern sculpture were displayed. Juliet had told Rachel that the house had been designed by a famous American architect, and was one of the showplaces of Bermuda. But Rachel thought it looked like an enormous fish-tank and was one of the ugliest places she had ever seen.

Having studied the section on wedding

breakfasts in her book on festive catering, Rachel had expected to see a tall iced cake in the centre of the long buffet table. But instead, there were two cakes — one covered in silver leaf for the groom, and the other in gold leaf for the bride. Juliet told her that, before the terrible blight which had ravaged so many of the islands' cedar trees, these unusual Bermudan wedding cakes had always been decorated with cedar seedlings to be planted after the reception.

So many people had been invited that it was not until the bride had disappeared to change into her going-away clothes that Rachel saw Bran among the crowd. He was standing quite close to her, talking to a sophisticated blonde in an almost backless white dress and a hat made of huge black silk cabbage roses. But, while the blonde was all smiles and fluttering eyelashes, Bran looked faintly bored. Today even Rachel, who still lacked the ability to categorise people at first sight, would have recognised him as a young man with too much money and too much time on his hands. The imprints of dissolute living were clearly marked on his face.

He must have sensed someone staring at him because he turned and caught her eye and, for a moment, she thought he would come over and speak to her. But he only bowed, as if they were barely acquainted with each other, and then said something to his companion and shepherded her away towards the buffet tables.

Nadine Oakhill was also present, but Rachel caught only occasional glimpses of her. She was wearing a superbly draped dress of vivid tangerine chiffon which made all the women in pastels look insipid, just as the simplicity of her hat — a broadbrimmed Breton of white organza — made all flowery hats look fussy and hackneyed.

And there was another, older woman there whom Rachel had never met, but who seemed to be watching her with more than the casual interest of one woman appraising another's clothes. Rachel had seen her before in shops in Hamilton and had felt then that she was being scrutinised with unusual attention.

"Julie, who is that woman — the one in dark blue lace with the hideous grey fur?" she asked her sister-in-law.

Juliet giggled in a way which made

Rachel suspect that she had had too many glasses of champagne.

"That 'hideous grey fur' happens to be chinchilla, sweetie. Though why these old dears have to cocoon themselves in fur when the temperature is in the seventies is beyond me."

"Yes, but do you know who she is?" Rachel persisted.

"Haven't a clue, pet. I've seen her about fairly often, but she doesn't live here. She's probably a regular visitor. There are dozens of rich old girls who come to broil their ageing flesh in the sun twice a year."

"She seems to be watching me all the time . . . as if she knew me," Rachel said perplexedly.

"I expect she's envying your schoolgirl complexion. *She's* obviously wearing out her third or fourth face-lift," Juliet said cruelly. "Haven't you noticed how these poor old ducks have nary a wrinkle — but their eyes are too pathetically ancient."

"Oh, Julie, that's unkind. People can't help getting older."

Her sister-in-law shrugged. "I wish I was old sometimes." Then her mouth began to quiver and, to Rachel's consternation, her eyes were suddenly brilliant with unshed tears.

"In fact I wish I were dead," she said vehemently, and turned and hurried into the house.

Rachel started to follow her, then changed her mind and looked anxiously about for Niall. If Juliet was on the verge of a *vin triste*, they must somehow get her away before she attracted attention.

Niall was not to be found in the main part of the garden and, thinking he might have become bored with all the social chit-chat and slipped off to have a quiet smoke somewhere, Rachel edged through the crush and strolled at a discreet pace towards the series of sloping terraces which led down to her hosts' private beach.

She had reached the lowest terrace when the sound of a muted altercation made her stop short.

"You're mad! How can you even suggest such a thing?" a woman said. She was trying to keep her voice down, but she was obviously under the stress of some strong emotion and the words were quite distinct.

"Why not?" a man's voice asked levelly. "You must have known I'd sense the truth

sooner or later. I know you rather well . . .
have you forgotten that? I haven't forgotten anything."

As if she were hypnotised, Rachel moved
towards the balustrade and looked over.
Immediately below her, standing close to
the foot of the storm wall, were Niall and
Nadine. They were both much too absorbed
to sense her presence. Indeed she was just
in time to see Niall catch hold of Nadine's
wrists and draw her towards him.

"Admit it!" he demanded, in a tone
which Rachel would not have recognised,
it was so vibrant with passion.

Nadine tried to break away, but he
would not release her and, with a tormented
whimper, she swayed towards him.

Stepping quickly back from the balustrade, Rachel shut her eyes. For a moment
the shock of what she had seen and heard
made her feel physically sick. Then, in a
cold terror of hearing any more, she turned
and stumbled dazedly up the slope.

There was a stone bench set in a recess
on the topmost terrace. With a long shuddering breath she sank on to it and tried to
pull herself together.

So it had happened at last, she thought

dully. Even Niall — iron-willed, inflexible Niall — was not so super-human that he could go on honouring their travesty of a marriage when the woman he really loved had come back into his life, and still loved him.

Had he asked her to go away with him? Was that why Nadine had sounded so appalled just now?

He loves her so much that he would even give up Moongates for her, Rachel thought achingly. Oh, God, how can I bear it? What shall I do?

But she had to bear it, and there was nothing to be done but yield to the inevitable. And when, a few minutes later, she returned to the upper garden, she was pale but composed, her head held high. No one would have guessed that, inwardly, she was racked by a misery which was no easier to suffer because she had been expecting it for weeks.

About ten minutes after Rachel had rejoined the other guests — she had completely forgotten her original concern for Juliet — Nadine appeared.

There had been a drift to the front of the house as it was nearly time for the bridal couple to leave for the airport. But, ignoring someone who spoke to her as she passed, Nadine walked swiftly across the grass and disappeared through an archway leading to a side road where many of the guests had parked their cars.

Rachel hovered on the lawn, waiting for Niall to come up. But after five minutes there was still no sign of him and she was obliged to follow the others round to the driveway.

The bride and groom were spending their honeymoon in Europe. After they had gone, and the blizzard of flower petals and carnival streamers had settled, Rachel saw Juliet again. Her sister-in-law had her arm linked with Robert's, and was laughingly dusting some confetti off his shoulders. She appeared to have completely recovered from her earlier mood, and called Rachel to join them.

"We're going on a club-crawl, sweetie," she said gaily. "Will you and Niall join us? Where is Niall? I haven't seen him for ages."

"Oh, he's somewhere about," Rachel said vaguely, a bright smile fixed on her face like a mask.

"Ah, there he is," Juliet said, beckoning to her brother who had just come out of the house with one of the ushers.

"Robert and I are going on a binge, Niall," she explained, as he came to join them. "How about making up a foursome? It will be so flat to spend the evening at home."

"Would you like to go out tonight, Rachel?" Niall asked.

She could not look at him. "I — I don't mind. Whatever you want."

"I would rather dine quietly at home," he said.

"You would, you old spoilsport!" Juliet made a face at him. "Never mind: you and Rachel go off and have a cosy domestic evening together. We'll live it up a little. Let's see if Bob and Joyce are keener, Robert. These two old married people are too staid for the likes of us." With a wink and a grin at Rachel, she led Robert away.

"Do you want to hang on here — or have you had enough? Let's go home, shall we? I could do with a shower and a glass of beer," Niall said, deciding the matter before she had time to answer.

Driving back to Moongates, Rachel

thought of Juliet's phrase "a cosy domestic evening together" and felt an urge to break into peals of hysterical laughter. But she managed to keep a grip on herself.

Presently, stealing a glance at Niall's profile, she marvelled that he could look so normal after what had happened down on the beach. At this very moment, when all his attention seemed to be on the road, he was probably rehearsing what he was going to tell her as soon as they reached the house.

How little people knew of each other's private thoughts and secret agonies, she thought wearily. Perhaps she and Niall were not the only ones who had attended the wedding with serene cheerful faces while, inwardly, they were torn by some deep emotional conflict. Perhaps half the people there had been enduring some painful personal dilemma which no one else would ever know about, unless — as Juliet had done — they let down their guard for a moment.

You could live with someone, watch them, study them, and still be deceived by a false manner, Rachel realised. People were like icebergs. There was more lying hidden under the surface than one would ever guess from the little they revealed of themselves.

When they reached home, she expected Niall to say, "Rachel, I must talk to you."

Instead, he asked Joseph to take some iced beer up to old Mrs. Herrick's sitting-room. "I expect Gran is anxious to hear all the details. I'll join you as soon as I've changed and had a shower," he told Rachel.

As the evening passed — they had dinner upstairs with the old lady — and Niall failed to suggest that they should stroll in the garden, or to make some other excuse to be alone with her, Rachel began to wonder if he was funking what he had to tell her. But she could not believe he was suffering from moral cowardice. He was not that kind of man. If he had something unpleasant to do, he would tackle it at once, get it over.

About half past nine, Mrs. Herrick said, "You look tired, Rachel. Why not go to bed early, dear?"

"Yes, I think I will, if you don't mind." Rachel bent to kiss the old lady good-night, and when she straightened she saw Niall was also on his feet.

"Good-night, Gran. Sleep well." He,

too, bent to kiss Mrs. Herrick, then moved across the room to open the door for his wife.

Walking past him into the corridor, Rachel braced herself. Now, at last, he was going to tell her about Nadine.

But after he had shut the door behind him, Niall said quietly, "Yes, you do **look** tired tonight. Have a bath. It will help **you** get to sleep quickly. I'll ask Rietta to bring you up a hot drink. Good-night, Rachel."

But when Juliet came home, some time after midnight, Rachel was still awake. After hours of thought, it seemed to her that there could only be one reason why Niall had not taken the irrevocable step of telling her he loved another woman. Somehow, in spite of the way she felt about him, Nadine must have steeled herself to resist him.

"*Admit it!*" he had said, down there on the beach. Remembering that fierce, passionate demand, Rachel trembled. Even a stranger, overhearing him then, would have known what he was asking, she thought bleakly. *Admit you still love me . . . admit we belong together . . . admit we can't live without each other.*

Yet, although the answer must have been in Nadine's eyes as she looked up at him, somehow she must have had the enormous strength of will not to yield.

Perhaps she could not face being involved in another scandal. Perhaps, in spite of what people said about her, she had too much conscience to break up a marriage — even an unhappy marriage. Perhaps it was simply that she thought it was too late . . . that she and Niall had had their chance of happiness together, but it was something which could not be recaptured.

But whatever her reasons, she had obviously withstood his appeal. She must have done. What other explanation could there be?

Deciding that she ought to learn to sew, Rachel had bought some cheap cotton and a paper pattern for a blouse. One afternoon, a few days after the wedding, she carefully followed the instructions on cutting out, and then took the pieces of material into the garden to tack them together.

She had thought that Juliet was out shopping, but her sister-in-law was lying on a

294

lounger under the umbrella, the inevitable cigarette dangling between her fingers, a banana daiquiri on the table beside her. She was wearing smoked glasses, and it was not until Rachel sat down that she realized the older girl was crying quietly.

"Juliet darling, what is it? What's wrong?" she exclaimed compassionately.

Juliet took off the dark glasses, wiped her brimming eyes with an already soaked handkerchief and drew in a long shuddering breath.

"I was hoping you'd come out," she said huskily. "I just can't go on pretending — I must talk to someone. Oh God, if you knew how miserable I am, Rachel. What am I going to do? What *can* I do?" She began to cry again, turning so that her face was hidden in the cushions, her shoulders heaving with sobs.

Rachel did not try to comfort her for some minutes. Then, when the outburst of weeping had slackened slightly, she put her own dry handkerchief into Juliet's hand and said quietly, "If you tell me what's the matter, perhaps I can help."

"No, you can't! No one can help. It's too late now. I had my chance . . . and I lost it."

"Your chance of what, Juliet darling?"

"Of . . . of being happy like you are."

Rachel's mouth twisted, but she said calmly, "You don't want to marry Robert, do you? It was a mistake, but you're afraid to tell him so. But you will have to tell him, dear. You must. You can't marry a man you don't love."

"I must marry someone. If it can't be Michael, I don't much care who it is," Juliet said dully.

"Who is Michael?"

Juliet gulped down some of the daiquiri and lit another cigarette. Her cheeks were streaked with mascara, her lipstick was smeared. She looked both physically and emotionally exhausted.

"Michael's a pilot for B.O.A.C.," she said wearily. "I met him when I flew to London last year."

"And you fell in love with him?"

Juliet nodded. "We both fell . . . too fast and too far."

"What went wrong? Was he married already?"

The older girl finished her drink. It was a very sweet concoction, Rachel knew.

But Juliet looked as if it had tasted as bitter as aloes.

"No, he wasn't actually married — but he might just as well have been. He has a widowed sister and three nephews to support. That leaves him about as much money as I spend on cosmetics."

"Yes, but you're very extravagant with make-up," Rachel said, smiling faintly. She was beginning to comprehend the situation.

"Oh, Rachel, you could never understand," Juliet said, suddenly fierce. "You don't care about clothes and things, not like I do. You would have married Niall if he had been a . . . a penniless shipping clerk. You think love solves every problem — but it doesn't!"

"Perhaps not — but neither does money, Juliet," said Rachel, with a touch of asperity in her voice. "Did Michael actually ask you to marry him? Or did you decide against him before it got to that point?"

"Yes, he asked me — and I told him the truth. He obviously thought exactly what you are thinking — that I'm shallow and mercenary and thoroughly despicable. But it's not my fault that I've been brought up with servants to wait on me, and to spend money freely and to have expensive clothes and . . . and everything. I can't suddenly change my whole outlook. I — I just wouldn't fit in with Michael's background. Oh, Rachel, be honest — can you see me living in a hideous little semi-detached villa in some ghastly London suburb, and doing all my own housework? And, apart from all the drudgery, I should be so lonely. Michael would be away half the time and I wouldn't be able to mix with the people I know in London now. Oh, surely you must see it would be hopeless? I'd be right out of my element . . . utterly miserable."

"You're utterly miserable now, aren't you?" Rachel asked gravely.

Juliet bit her lower lip. "Yes . . . I am," she admitted huskily. "But at least I'm miserable in comfort. Besides, it may not be so grim after a while. They say time heals everything, don't they?"

"Time may change the way you feel about Michael, but it won't alter your feelings for Robert. You don't love him now. You never will."

"I'm quite fond of him," Juliet said

bleakly. "Lots of couples aren't madly in love with each other, but they get on all right. So will we."

"Do they?" Rachel asked sceptically. "They may seem to in public — but I wonder? Oh, Juliet, you mustn't marry Robert. It isn't enough to be 'fond' of him — not nearly enough, believe me. However kind Robert might be to you, however considerate . . . it could never be a truly happy marriage. You'd feel guilty all the time, and he would be bound to sense it and feel . . . cheated. You think you couldn't feel more wretched than you do now — but a marriage without love would be sheer purgatory."

Juliet had been plucking at a loose thread on the lounger cover, her eyebrows contracted into a scowl, her mouth mutinous.

"Robert *knows* I'm not crazy about him. He accepts — " She stopped short. "Niall! How long have you been listening in?" Rachel whirled round. Niall was standing a few paces behind her chair. For one tense moment he looked down into her startled upturned face. Then, without a word, he moved on towards the steps to the beach.

"Oh, damn him!" Juliet said savagely. She sprang up from the lounger and marched back towards the house.

When they had both disappeared, Rachel let out a long quivering breath. Then she lay back in her chair and closed her eyes. It was futile to go on deceiving herself, she thought listlessly.

It was no wonder Niall had looked so grim just now. If he had heard what she had been saying to his sister — as he obviously had — every word must have cut him to the bone. It was he who should have told Juliet just what hell a loveless marriage could be. For it was wretchedly clear that he had not and never would succeed in stamping out his longing for Nadine Oakhill.

The following morning Rachel received a letter which puzzled and intrigued her. It was written on the thick die-stamped writing paper of one of the Colony's biggest and best hotels, and was signed "C. E. Devon". Without giving any reason for the request, the writer asked her to call on him — or her — at any time between two and four o'clock that afternoon.

Was "C. E. Devon" some unknown relation of hers? she wondered, with mounting excitement. But, if so, how had they learnt her maiden name? Soon she was in such a fever of curiosity that the hours until lunch time seemed interminable. Juliet — who had spent the previous evening shut in her room — had gone out very early, and Niall had also left word that he would not be home for lunch. So Rachel asked for an early meal on a tray, and then changed for her mysterious appointment.

Arriving at the hotel, she told the reception clerk that she was expected in Suite 16 and, after confirming this on the house telephone, he summoned a bellboy to show her the way. The door of the suite was opened by a prim-looking middle-aged woman in a severely plain blouse and skirt. She showed Rachel into a luxuriously appointed sitting-room, and said that "Madam" would join her in a moment. Presumably she was a maid or companion to "Madam".

It was nearly ten minutes before the door of the adjoining bedroom opened and C. E. Devon revealed herself. But she was not entirely a stranger. She was the woman who had worn blue lace and a chinchilla cape at Jennifer Malcolm's wedding — the woman whom Rachel had felt was watching her.

"Good afternoon, Mrs. Herrick. How very good of you to accept my suggestion that we should meet," she said smilingly. "May I offer you a cigarette? No? Then a glass of sherry, perhaps?"

Watching her lift one of several cut glass decanters ranged on a side table, Rachel wondered if she had met this woman during her childhood. Now that she was seeing her at close range, there seemed to be something familiar about her.

Having poured out two glasses of sherry and lighted a cigarette for herself, Mrs. Devon settled herself in a chair. "Now I will spare you any further suspense, and come straight to the point of this meeting," she said, more briskly. "As you may already have guessed, we are distantly related, Mrs. Herrick. I recognised you by your extraordinary likeness to your mother, when she was very young. At first I thought it must be a coincidence, but I enquired about your maiden name and discovered that it was not."

"I wondered why you seemed to be watching me. I never dreamed that you might be a relative. How exactly are we related?" Rachel asked.

"Oh, it is only a very slight connection by marriage," the older woman told her. "In fact, to be frank, I did not originally intend to make myself known to you. However certain circumstances changed my mind. I am told you have only been married a short time, and did not live in Bermuda before your marriage. Tell me, have you met a girl called Nadine Oakhill yet?"

Rachel stiffened slightly. "Yes, I have met her," she said warily.

"And you know that, some years ago, she was engaged to your husband?"

Rachel nodded. What was the point of these questions? she wondered uneasily.

Mrs. Devon sipped her sherry for a moment, as if choosing her next words with great care. "But I wonder if you realise that Nadine Oakhill is determined to wreck your marriage?" she said, at length. "No, please — hear me out, Mrs. Herrick" — as Rachel went very pale, and would have risen. "I can guess what you are thinking,

303

my dear. You are wondering whether I am slightly deranged, or if I am merely a malicious scandal-monger. I am neither. I am warning you against Nadine because I know what she is really like — and I doubt if you have any idea. So please, for your own sake, do listen to me. I am not being melodramatic when I say that your future happiness may depend on it."

For some moments Rachel was too dumbfounded to know what to think. Finally she gave a slight nod to indicate that she would listen to whatever Mrs. Devon had to say.

"I have known Nadine for some years," the older woman went on. "I would not describe us as friends, but we move in the same circles and see a good deal of each other. We are sufficiently intimate for Nadine to have revealed her true colours to me. They are very different from those she assumes in public, I may say. I think she is probably one of the most ruthless egoists I have ever encountered, and at the moment she is fanatically intent on re-kindling your husband's passion for her and somehow discrediting you. She is quite capable of doing both — unless you have some defence against her. It would not be the first marriage she has broken. Men are such fools! Her looks seem to completely befuddle them."

Rachel sat staring down at her tightly locked hands for some moments. She was thinking of the anonymous letter. Was it possible that Nadine had written it?

"What do you suggest I should do?" she said, at last.

"I don't know, my dear. I wish I did. But you are aware of her intentions now. No marriage is invulnerable, and a wife who recognises that fact — however unwillingly — is in a very much stronger position than one who does not. It may be that your husband is no longer susceptible to Nadine's wiles. But at least you will no longer be deluded by that deceptive charm of hers. Now I can see that this has come as a great shock to you, so we will have some tea while you collect yourself."

After she had telephoned an order to the hotel's room service, Mrs. Devin fitted another cigarette into her slender gold holder and said, "I am very curious to know what has been happening to you in the years since your father took you away.

305

Where is Charles living? In America?"

"No . . . Father is dead now," Rachel said quietly. And she told the older woman all that she remembered of their travels on the way to Anguna, and of her life from that time until the present.

"So you know nothing of the reasons why he left England? He never mentioned your mother to you?" Mrs. Devon asked, when Rachel had finished and after their tea had been brought in by a waiter.

"No . . . never. Is she dead, too, now?"

"No, she is alive." Mrs. Devon handed her a cup of China tea and indicated that she should help herself to the selection of sandwiches and cakes.

But Rachel had never felt less hungry. "I wish you would tell me what happened. I've wondred about it so often," she said.

Mrs. Devon leaned back in her chair and crossed her slim, pretty legs. In spite of Juliet's scathing remark about face-lifts, Rachel did not think she could be more than forty-five, perhaps not that. As a girl, she must have been a great beauty. But now, although her skin was still firm and her throat smooth, there were deep lines incised from her nose to the sides of her mouth. And her heavy, stylised make-up and bleached blonde hair did not counterfeit the lost glow of youth. They only emphasised that it had faded, and made her look much older than she was.

"Very well, I will tell you the whole story. But it is not a pleasant one," she said wryly.

Since Rachel had often suspected that her father had been some kind of doctor, it was not a great surprise to hear that he had actually been an eminent neuro-surgeon.

"He was completely absorbed in his work, and everyone thought he was a confirmed bachelor, I believe," said Mrs. Devon. "Then, when he was in his early forties, he met a girl called Celia Marsden — the daughter of one of his patients. He fell desperately in love with her, poor wretch."

It had been a marriage doomed to failure, Rachel learned. Within a few weeks after the wedding, her father had discovered that his twenty-year-old wife — while breath-takingly lovely to look at — was shallow, vain and utterly self-centred.

"Not unlike Nadine Oakhill, in fact," Mrs. Devon commented dryly.

Celia — once the novelty of being able to indulge her extravagant tastes had worn off — was equally disappointed in her husband. All her clothes and furs and jewels were wasted, she felt, because Charles had neither the time nor inclination for a gay social life. When Rachel was born, she had proved to be another bone of contention. Charles adored her. Her mother thought children a bore.

"When you were six, she went off with another man," Mrs. Devon said, frowning slightly. "Your father wrote and begged her to return to him — it must have humiliated him terribly — but she did not even answer his letters. Then, about six months later, he was involved in a serious motor accident. His right hand was damaged and it was thought he would not be able to operate again."

"I never knew that," Rachel said, in surprise. "I do remember him being away in hospital, now that you've recalled it. But his hand must have healed perfectly. It was scarred, but he could use it quite normally."

"Yes, but perhaps not well enough for surgery," said Mrs. Devon. "However, as I was about to say, while he was convalescent, his wife came back and visited him. She had finally begun to realise what a fine man he was, you see. But it was too late. She had lost her power over him. She pleaded with him to forgive her, but now it was he who would not listen. As soon as he was fit enough to travel, he sold up the house in London, and took you on that cruise to South America. Although she did not deserve it, he did make your mother a very generous settlement. Then he disappeared. Nobody heard of him again — although, every so often, the gossip columnists still speculate on his whereabouts. An old scandal is better than no scandal at all."

"And my mother — what became of her?"

Mrs. Devon shrugged. "She grew older and less captivating." She gave Rachel a searching glance. "Don't you despise her, now you know what she was like — and how little affection she had for you?"

Rachel sat silent for some moments. "No . . . I think I pity her," she said slowly. "She missed all the best things in life. Where is she now, Mrs. Devon? Do you still see her sometimes?"

"Frequently. She lives in London most

of the year. But I think it would be a great mistake for you to try to get in touch with her, you know. She is not the type of person of whom your husband and his family would approve. I should put her out of your mind now. It is never wise to rake up dead ashes, my dear."

"No, I suppose not," Rachel said uncertainly. "Although, now I know the whole story, I can't help being curious about her. Before . . . she was never quite real to me. I didn't often think about her. Now . . . now I don't know *what* I feel. It's very odd to have a mother whom I would not even recognise if I saw her."

The older woman glanced at her watch, then rose. "Yes, it must feel rather strange, I suppose — but it's better so," she said briskly, her manner intimating that she had said all she wished to say, and had no desire to dwell on the subject.

Rachel took the hint. She wanted to be alone, to think over all she had learned.

"Well, thank you for telling me all this," she said, as they moved towards the door. "Are you staying in Bermuda long?"

"I'm not sure. I'm booked here until the end of the month, but I may change my plans and leave earlier," Mrs. Devon said vaguely. She held out her hand. "Good-bye, Mrs. Herrick. Thank you for coming to see me . . . and you will take me seriously, I hope — about Nadine Oakhill, I mean?"

Rachel nodded. "Yes, I will," she answered gravely. "Good-bye."

A few moments later, alone in the corridor, she drew on her gloves and smoothed each finger into place. There was a staircase at the end of the passage, and she walked slowly towards it and down three thickly carpeted flights to the entrance lounge.

Suddenly, turning in the direction of the main doors, she stopped dead. Near the archway into the cocktail bar, there was an alcove with an illuminated fountain playing over a marble basin. Transfixed by the thought which had just struck her, Rachel stood very still, her eyes on the sparkling jet of water, her mind grappling with an idea which made her draw in her breath and hold it.

Suppose Nadine *had* written that horrible anonymous note to Niall . . . could it be that he had suspected her of it, and that she, Rachel, had been wildly, utterly wrong in her interpretation of the scene she had overheard between them on the day of the wedding? What if the admission he had wanted had not been for Nadine to say she loved him — but to confess that she had written the note?

Hardly daring to believe that the truth of the matter might be exactly the reverse of what she had thought, Rachel closed her eyes for a minute. "Oh, let me be right . . . *please* let me be right," she prayed silently.

"Rachel, aren't you well?"

She opened her eyes to find Bran Hart standing beside her.

"I saw you from the cocktail bar. What is it? Do you feel faint?" he asked anxiously.

"Oh, hello, Bran. No, I'm not ill. I — I've just had a bit of a shock, that's all."

"Come into the bar and have a brandy," he urged, taking her arm as if he expected her to collapse at any moment.

"No, I'd rather not, thanks," she said hastily. "I'm all right — truly I am."

"Are you alone?"

She nodded. "I . . . I've been calling on a friend."

Still holding her arm, he gave her a searching glance. "Well then, I'll run you home. I was just leaving anyway," he said firmly.

The entrance to the hotel was flanked by broad awning-shaded terraces where the residents could relax in gay cane chairs, order drinks, and watch the comings and goings. Both terraces were fairly crowded, and a coach from the airport had just arrived, when Bran steered Rachel down the double flight of stone steps.

At the foot of the steps, she felt his fingers tighten on her arm. He was looking towards the car park and, following his glance, she saw that Niall and an elderly man were coming towards them across the gravel. Her husband did not see her until he and his companion were almost abreast of them. Then he halted so abruptly that the other man gave him a startled, interrogative glance.

"Henley, I hope you don't mind, but I'll have to leave you now. I've just remembered some rather pressing business," Niall said to him.

"That's all right, old chap. See you later, then? Thanks very much for meeting me."

The man called Henley clapped Niall on the shoulder and went on up the steps, past Bran and Rachel.

Niall looked at his wife with eyes like flints. "And what in hell's name are you doing here?" he enquired softly.

It was Bran who answered him. "Rachel isn't feeling too good," he said. "I met her in the hotel just now and offered to drive her home."

"Oh, yes?" Niall's voice was still dangerously quiet. "Well, you can save your gallantry for someone else's wife, Hart. The next time I find you with mine, you're going to regret it. Is that clear?"

"Damn it all, Herrick, I was only — "

But, before Bran could finish his protest, Niall had grasped Rachel's wrist and was marching her back to his car. His expression was demoniacal.

CHAPTER EIGHT

AFTER bundling Rachel into the passenger seat, Niall strode round the bonnet, slid behind the wheel and slammed his door. They shot away from the parking rank like competitors in a motor rally, and Rachel had only a fleeting glimpse of Bran's worried face as they roared past the steps and down the drive.

But, although he looked as if he would like to stamp on the throttle and touch ninety, once they were on the main road Niall kept scrupulously within the colony's low speed limit. Ten minutes later they were back at Moongates.

As Niall brought the car to a halt under the portico, Joseph came out of the house and helped Rachel alight. He told Niall that his secretary at Herricks' had just rung up and, hearing the car coming, he had asked her to hold the line.

"Say I'll ring back, Joe," Niall said curtly. He gripped Rachel's elbow and steered her indoors, towards the staircase.

"I reckon it's a matter of some importance, Mister Niall," the butler said, following them in.

With one foot on the stairs, Niall hesitated. "Oh, very well — I'll speak to her," he said impatiently. Then, to Rachel, "Go up to your room. I'll be with you in a few minutes."

Reaching her bedroom, Rachel left the door open, cast her bag and gloves on a chair and kicked off her high-heeled shoes. Then she sank wearily on to her dressing stool and waited for Niall to come up. Strangely, instead of being alarmed or indignant, she was curious to find out how he planned to deal with her.

It was five or six minutes before she heard him coming up the stairs and, instinctively, she stood up and straightened her shoulders.

Niall came into the bedroom, closed the door and turned the key in the lock. The distraction of the telephone call did not appear to have cooled his temper. His mouth was set hard, his eyes glittered. Moving across to the fireplace, he put the key on the high stone mantelpiece and stood with his back to her for some seconds.

Then, swinging to face her, he said softly: "Come here."

Rachel moved a few steps towards him, then halted. But he beckoned her closer, and closer still, until she was only a yard or so away from him.

"Well, what have you got to say for yourself?" he enquired silkily, his hands in his trouser pockets.

"Whatever I say, you won't believe me, Niall," she answered steadily.

But it was not easy to remain composed now that she was within an arm's length of him, and forced to look up to meet his eyes. She wished she had kept her shoes on.

"Probably not — but I'll hear you out," he said unpleasantly.

The way he was looking at her made Rachel's colour rise. "Then I may as well save my breath," she said, in a low tone. "You've insulted Bran — what are you going to do to me?"

Niall's eyes narrowed. "To you?" he said reflectively. "Oh, merely something I should have done some time ago." He took his hands out of his pockets, caught her by the waist and pulled her roughly against him.

317

"Oh, Niall — no!" she exclaimed, trying to free herself.

"Why not? You're my wife," he told her harshly. His left arm enclosed her like a vice, his right hand came up to caress her throat. "Try closing your eyes and imagining that it's Hart who is making love to you," he suggested cruelly.

Rachel did close her eyes — because she could not bear to see the savage mockery in his. Her mouth quivered as his fingers traced the outline of her lips, and hot tears stung her tightly closed lids.

Niall searched for the little ivory combs which held her chignon and pulled them out. Then, gripping the long loosed coil of hair and forcing her head back, he began to kiss her slim brown neck.

When his lips reached the curve of her chin, Rachel moaned and tried to struggle free again.

"Let me go, Niall . . . *please* . . . I beg you . . ."

But her entreaty was stifled by the swift and pitiless pressure of his mouth on hers. There was a knock at the door. Not Rietta's soft tap, but a loud insistent tattoo.

"Rachel? Rachel, are you there? Can I

come in?" It was Juliet's voice pitched high with excitement and urgency.

Niall raised his head, glared at the door and smothered a single harsh expletive. Then, so suddenly she almost fell, he thrust Rachel away, turned, and slammed out through the dressing-room.

She stood there, swaying, one hand up to her bruised and smarting lips. She was shivering, and her heart was pounding as wildly as a goombay drum.

"Rachel? Do let me in. I want to talk to you." Juliet rattled the door knob impatiently.

"Wait a minute . . . I — I'm coming," Rachel called out hoarsely.

Where had Niall put the key? Oh, yes . . . on the mantelpiece.

Her hands were so unsteady she had difficulty in fitting it into the keyhole. Mustering the remnants of her self-control, she opened the door.

"Were you resting? Did I wake you up?" Juliet whirled into the room and flung herself down on the sofa as if she had run all the way home from Hamilton. "Well, I've done it!" she announced dramatically.

"Done it?" Rachel repeated blankly.

Her sister-in-law fluttered the fingers of her left hand.

"No ring, sweetie. I'm back on the shelf again."

"You mean . . . you've broken it off with Robert?" Rachel moved across to the dressing table and sank down on the stool before her legs gave under her.

Juliet nodded. "About half an hour ago, after a ghastly dull lunch at the Marrisons'. Oh, sweetie, what a relief to be free again — you can't imagine."

Rachel picked up a hand mirror and studied her reflection. Mercifully, she had blotted her lipstick carefully before going out, so there were no betraying smudges round her mouth . . . no evidence at all of what had happened a few minutes earlier. Yet, invisible though it might be to other eyes, she could still feel the imprint of that fierce punishing kiss.

"How did Robert take it?" she asked, putting the mirror down and starting to comb her hair as a pretext for keeping her face averted. "Was he very upset?"

"Not terribly. I think he had begun to have second thoughts himself. I've led him rather a dance these last few weeks, I suppose. Anyway he accepted it in the best stiff-upper-lip tradition," Juliet said lightly, but with an under-note of contrition.

"What made you change your mind? Yesterday you seemed quite set on going ahead."

"I wasn't — not really. My feet have been getting colder and colder every day. I guessed it was your homily yesterday which finally clinched the thing. You made me feel so horribly spoilt and self-centred —which I am, of course," Juliet added, with a wry grin.

"What about Michael? Will you get in touch with him again now?"

"Perhaps . . . I don't know yet," Juliet said soberly. "I shall have to think about it. Do you honestly believe I could make a go of it, Rachel? . . . being hard up and hard-worked, I mean?"

I am the oracle . . . I am the girl whose marriage is so brilliantly successful, so idyllic, that I must know all the answers. Oh, Juliet, if you only knew — if you had any idea . . .

But the bitter satire of Rachel's thoughts did not show in her face as she said slowly,

"I should think so — if you love Michael enough. But that's something only you can answer. You know how strongly you feel about him."

Juliet rose from the sofa and moved restlessly about the bedroom.

"Sometimes I've missed him so desperately I've wanted to rush to the airport and catch the first flight to London," she said in a low voice, stopping beside the dressing table and picking up one of Rachel's scent sprays.

For some moments she balanced the little crystal container on her palm, her dark wing-shaped eyebrows contracted in a frown of indecision.

"Oh, why is love supposed to be such heaven?" she said, with a flash of irritation. "I think it's the very devil. You were lucky, Rachel. You had none of the problems which seem to harry most people."

Rachel stood up so abruptly that she knocked a trinket box over the edge of the dressing table. It fell on the rug, spilling beads and ear-clips over the thick cream sheepskin.

Stooping to retrieve them, she said unsteadily, "I must have a shower and change."

Juliet did not notice the tremor in her voice. "Yes, it is sticky today," she agreed. "I think I'll cool off, too. Maybe there's a storm blowing up. See you later, sweetie. Sorry I spoiled your nap, but I was bursting to tell my news. I'll tell Gran and Niall after dinner." She strolled back to the sofa to pick up her bag and sun-glasses.

"Juliet . . ." Rachel stopped short, biting her lip.

"Yes?" Her hand on the door, her sister-in-law turned to look at her.

Rachel started to unbutton her dress. She had been going to say, "Does our marriage really seem so flawless to you?" — but she changed her mind.

"Oh . . . nothing. See you downstairs."

A few minutes after Juliet had gone, she was tucking her hair into a shower cap when the telephone rang. Picking up the white and gold receiver, her voice husky, she said, "Hello?"

"Rachel? This is Bran. Are you alone?"

She shot a nervous glance towards the dressing-room. Was Niall still in his bedroom? Had he heard the bell and picked up his own extension? Was he listening in?

"What is it? What do you want?" she asked tensely.

There was a pause before Bran said, "Did you manage to make Niall see reason? Did you explain what really happened?"

"Yes . . . yes, of course I did," she answered quickly and untruthfully. "It's all right now, Bran — don't worry. I'm sorry there was . . . some unpleasantness."

"Unpleasantness!" He gave a short hollow laugh. "What a masterpiece of understatement! I thought I was going to get my teeth knocked in." Then, his voice low and urgent, "Look, Rachel, I must see you again. I can't explain why over the phone, but it's very important to me. I'll be up at the house all tomorrow. If you can possibly get an hour to yourself, will you swim over and meet me there? In the circumstances, I can't come to you."

He must be mad, she thought. "Oh, Bran, I can't. In fact I don't think we should meet again — ever."

"We must — just this once. Please, Rachel."

"No, I . . . there's someone at the door.

324

I must go. Good-bye, Bran." Before he could protest, she had replaced the receiver on its rest.

It was Rietta at the door this time. She had a pile of clean underwear to put away. For once Rachel did not encourage her to chatter.

After the maid had left, Rachel waited for five minutes, expecting Niall to storm in — even angrier than before at what he had heard on the extension. But he did not come, and when she tiptoed into the dressing-room and listened, there was no sound from his room. With mixed feelings of relief and anti-climax, she decided that he must have gone out.

After she had had a shower, she drew the curtains and, wrapped in a thin silk robe, lay down on the bed. She had never felt so exhausted. Today had drained her last reserves of strength. She was too spent even to cry. All she wanted was to lie in the diffused gold gloom and feel nothing . . . not despair, not misery, nothing.

She must have fallen asleep. When she opened her eyes the room had grown dimmer and Rietta was bending over her.

"I's sorry to wake you, Mis' Herrick,

but Mister Niall he want you to go down to the lib'ry and speak with him."

Rachel struggled up on to her elbows. "Now?" she asked, blinking.

"Yes, ma'am. I told him you was restin', but he say he wish to see you most particular."

"Very well, I'll be down in a few minutes," Rachel told her.

"What now?" she thought, as she dressed and brushed her tangled hair. She did not bother to pin it up but tied it back with a length of yellow ribbon.

The door of the library was ajar when she crossed the hall. Pushing it open, she saw Niall standing by the desk with his back to her. He was putting documents into a briefcase, and there was a leather wardrobe case on the floor nearby. Earlier he had been wearing a shirt and slacks. Now he was dressed in a light grey lounge suit.

"You wanted to see me?" she said quietly, closing the door and moving forward into the room, her hands in the pockets of her skirt.

Niall swung round and, as their eyes met, a slow flush crept up from Rachel's throat as she thought of what had happened upstairs.

"I'm catching the evening plane to New York. It leaves in just under an hour," Niall said, in a clipped voice. He turned away again and fastened the straps on the briefcase. "I was going next week but, in the circumstances, I've decided to go at once. I shall be back on Saturday," he added, speaking over his shoulder.

Rachel stared at his broad straight back. "The circumstances?" she said flatly.

"I've told Teaboy to have the *Dolphin* ready for sailing on Sunday morning. We'll run over to Florida — or back to the Out Islands, if you prefer it." He paused for a moment, then said, "It was a mistake to bring you back here so soon. We should have stayed at sea longer."

"It was a mistake to marry me, wasn't it?" she said coldly. "What's the use of pretending any longer?"

Niall took his cigarette case — the one she had given him on their wedding day — from his inside pocket. He moved across the room to fill it from the silver box on the coffee table.

"There's no time to discuss anything

327

now," he said briskly. "We'll talk when I come back."

Rachel had heard people use that tone to children. "Not now, dear — I'm busy," they said, or "Run along and play, there's a good girl." Children, being children, had to accept it.

But she was not a child and, suddenly, from the depths of what she had thought was a bottomless void of resignation, there rose a boiling spring of anger and bitter resentment.

"*If* I'm still here then," she burst out recklessly.

Niall did not even look up from the business of fitting a neat row of cigarettes into each side of the case. "What is that supposed to mean?" he enquired evenly.

It was then — when he failed to show the slightest sign of being disturbed by her retort — that she at last made up her mind to take action.

There was no "if" about it — she would *not* be here when he came back.

"Good-bye, Niall," she said stiffly, and turned and walked out of the room.

A few minutes later she heard him leave the house.

Early next morning, Rachel went back to the hotel where Mrs. Devon was staying. It was impossible to get away from Bermuda without money, and she had only two or three pounds in her purse — not even enough to buy a passage to the Bahamas on a cargo boat.

During the night, she had tried to think of some feasible pretext for borrowing some money from her sister-in-law. But although Niall gave his sister a fixed quarterly allowance — whereas Rachel was permitted to spend as much as she pleased and have her purchases charged to his account — it was more than likely that Juliet had already spent most of this quarter's pin-money.

"Sorry, sweetie — I'm broke. Ask Gran. She'll lend you what you need," she might say. And then, "What is it you want to buy? Why not charge it?"

Rachel did not doubt that old Mrs. Herrick would advance whatever she asked for without question. But she could not bring herself to deceive the old lady into innocently abetting her flight. The distress which her departure would inflict on Niall's grandmother lay heavily on her conscience.

Reaching the hotel, she was stunned to learn from the reception clerk that Mrs. Devon had left the place late last night.

"Are you Mrs. Herrick?" the man asked. "Oh, then this letter is for you, madam. Mrs. Devon left instructions for us to hold it in case you called back in the next few days. If not, we were to post it on to you."

Rachel took the envelope, thanked him, and turned perplexedly away. There was a taxi in the hotel driveway. She asked the driver to take her back to Moongates, settled in the back seat, and opened the letter.

Dear Rachel, (she read)

I lied to you today. I thought it was the best way. Now I feel it was wrong — that you will eventually guess the whole truth and wonder why I wanted to hide it from you.

You see, I am not a distant connection. I am your mother.

I am telling you this because I do not want you to think of me (as I could see you did this afternoon) as a mysterious and rather tragic person — with whom, in spite of everything, you have a bond.

In the circumstances, I have decided to leave Bermuda at once. I hope that everything goes well for you, and that you find all the happiness I forfeited. Women like N. and myself are more to be pitied than despised. In the end, we pay bitterly for our selfishness.
Celia Devon.

When the taxi stopped under the portico at Moongates, Rachel was still feeling stunned. It was not until Joseph came out to open the door for her that she thrust the letter into her bag and fumbled for money to pay the fare.

At lunch, Juliet said, "You look rather doleful today. Are you pining for your lord and master? Why didn't he take you with him? The shops in New York are heaven."

"Oh, Niall is only there for such a short time it didn't seem worth my while going too," Rachel said casually.

Suddenly she remembered Bran's telephone call, and that he had said he would be at the house over the water all afternoon. Would he help her?

Fortunately Juliet had an appointment with her hairdresser that afternoon. She suggested that they should meet for tea and shopping later on, but accepted Rachel's excuse that she wanted to spend the afternoon on the beach.

Bran was waiting on the landing stage with a towelling beach coat when Rachel reached the other side of the inlet about half an hour later. They climbed the stone steps up to the house and he offered her a martini from the large vacuum flask he had with him.

"I didn't think you would come," he said, sitting beside her on a faded and creaking swing couch.

"I had to come. Bran, will you do me a very great favour?" she asked bluntly.

"You must know I will. What is it?" he asked curiously.

"I want to borrow enough money to get to England. I'll pay you back eventually ...I promise. You see, I—I'm leaving Niall. I must. I just can't go on."

"Not because of what happened yesterday?" he asked sharply. "Oh God, what a damned silly mess. Look, I'll see Niall myself. This is crazy. He can't throw you out because — "

"He isn't throwing me out. He's in New York. He won't know I've left till he comes

332

back — or until Juliet sends for him. This isn't anything to do with you, Bran. It was inevitable before I ever met you."

"But you've only been married a few weeks," he said blankly. "You can't be on the rocks as soon as this."

Rachel's mouth twisted. "We were 'on the rocks', as you put, it about six hours after our wedding," she said wryly. And, in a low strained voice, she told him the truth about her marriage.

Bran heard her out in silence, his eyebrows contracted. When she had finished, he said, "What are you going to do when you get to England?"

"Oh . . . find a job somewhere. Start afresh. I'm young and healthy. I'll manage."

He lit a cigarette and studied the pattern on his lighter as if he had never noticed it before. After a pause, he said, "Have you any idea why I wanted to see you today, Rachel?"

She shook her head. "I'd forgotten you'd asked me to come over, I'm afraid. I've been so absorbed in my own affairs. I remembered you had said you would be here — so I came for help."

"I'm going away too," he told her slowly. "I wanted to see you today to say good-bye." He stopped, turned his head to look at her, and added: "You see, I'm in love with you, young Rachel."

She stared at him, aghast. "Oh, Bran, you don't mean that . . . you can't!"

He reached out to take her hand in his. "I didn't intend to tell you, and I wouldn't have done. But now that you're leaving Niall, it changes the situation. You can't go off to England on your own, honey. Why not let me take care of you? I'm planning to spend the next few months in Paris. You'd like Paris, darling. Say you'll come with me."

"Oh, no, Bran — no! I couldn't possibly." She tried to free her hand, but he held it fast.

"Look, you don't think I'm suggesting a casual *affaire*, do you?" he asked, frowning. "I want to spend the rest of my life with you — I swear it. Oh, I know you don't care for me as you do for Niall — damn him! But you can't live on dreams for ever, my dear. The only way to forget him is to concentrate on someone else, you'll find. You like me. Why can't it be me?"

"Oh, Bran — *dear* Bran — if you had ever lived with someone who didn't love you, you would never suggest it," she said gently. "Believe me, it's agony — absolute hell."

"Hell with you would be better than the hell of being without you," he persisted.

"Yes, that's what I thought, once. But it isn't true. Do you think I *want* to leave Niall? Never to see him again . . . never to hear his voice. No, of course I don't. I go cold at the very thought of it. But nothing could possibly be worse than being with him, and knowing he doesn't love me and never will. That's a torture I wouldn't wish on anyone." Her voice broke, and she had to set her teeth to stop herself crying.

Bran waited until she was calmer. "Maybe you're right," he said, with a sigh. "But I'll give you my address in Paris — just in case you ever change your mind, honey. I can't honestly pretend that, if I can't have you, I'm never going to look at another woman. But *if* I had you — well, that would be different. Can you believe that, Rachel?"

"Yes, I can believe it, Bran dear. I've

always believed the best of you," she said warmly.

"And if you're ever in any kind of trouble, you will promise to let me know and help you?"

"I promise."

"Perhaps when he finds you've gone, Niall may come to his senses about you," he said thoughtfully. "Are you certain he still has a yen for Nadine Oakhill? I wasn't here when their engagement blew up, but I've heard all the details, of course. Frankly, she doesn't strike me as being any great loss. A girl who marries a man old enough to be her grandfather . . ." He gave an expressive shrug.

"I don't know about Nadine . . . I'm not sure of anything any more. I only know he doesn't love me," Rachel said flatly.

"When is he coming back from New York?" Bran asked.

"On Saturday."

Bran grimaced. "I think you've had it, honey," he said, shaking his head.

"What do you mean?"

He spread out his hands. "Ships and planes aren't like buses — one can't hop aboard at a moment's notice. I'm afraid your chances of getting away before Saturday are pretty thin — unless there's a last-minute cancellation."

"But I must get away," she exclaimed. "I must! If I don't . . ." She stopped short.

After Saturday it would be too late. Niall would force her to go with him on the *Dolphin* and . . . her mind shied from the implication of another voyage alone with him.

"Well, I'll see what I can do," Bran said dubiously. "I'll go into Hamilton now. Will you wait for me here — I may be away some time — or shall I ring you at Moongates later?"

"I'll wait here. I won't be missed before six. I—I wish I didn't have to ask you to help me, Bran."

"Don't be silly," he said briskly. "I'll be as quick as I can, but if you're not here when I get back, I'll phone during the evening."

After he had gone, Rachel wandered restlessly about the terrace. Some of the flags had cracked and weeds were pushing up through the crevices. The paint on the shutters screening the windows had long since blistered in the sun and was flaking

337

from the warped slats. The whole place —
once, no doubt, as well kept as Moongates —
had a forlorn, forsaken atmosphere. She
wondered why Bran did not rent it to
tourists. It seemed criminal to let it fall into
decay.

Bran had been gone about an hour, and
she was sitting on the couch trying not to
think of anything in particular, when she
heard a car approaching. But it stopped
some distance away — perhaps at the house
with a flat roof further along the ridge —
and she relaxed again, feeling a strange
sense of unreality as if she were dreaming.
This time next week she would have left
Bermuda for ever, and be starting a whole
new life, alone. It was a frightening
prospect and one which it was better not to
dwell upon. If she let herself think about it
too closely, her courage might fail her.

Slow footsteps — a man's — coming
round the side of the house made her catch
in her breath. She was briefly and appre-
hensively conscious of how isolated the
place was, and instinctively she rose from
the couch and moved swiftly closer to the
staircase leading down to the landing stage.

The couch, free of her weight, swung

gently to and fro, the rusty chains creaking.

"*Niall!*" Rachel froze, her eyes dilating.

For several moments her husband stood very still at the far end of the terrace. Then, slowly, he came towards her. When he was about six feet away, he stopped again.

"Hello, Rachel," he said quietly.

"W-what are you doing here?" she whispered. "You said — "

"I said everything but the right thing, it seems." His voice was oddly husky, and she had never seen him looking so haggard, not even after that storm had struck the *Dolphin*. "So you meant what you said about not being here when I came back?" he said, in a flat tone.

"Yes, I meant it."

His eyes blazed suddenly, and he crossed the space between them in two swift paces, catching her by the shoulders, gripping, hurting.

"I love you," he said fiercely. "You can't go — I won't let you. You belong to me."

For a moment she did not react at all. Then, with a little choked sound, she began to laugh and to cry.

"Oh, Niall . . . oh, Niall . . ."

He pulled her close, pressing her face

339

into his shoulder and patting her back. "Don't cry, darling . . . please, Rachel, don't cry."

"I'm not crying. Not really — " There was a handkerchief in his breast pocket and she pulled it out and dried her cheeks with the soft white linen. "Oh, Niall," she said for the third time, "do you really mean it?"

"That I love you?" He took her face between his hands and made her look at him. "Yes, I mean it. After I got on that plane I was suddenly so scared of losing you that I spent all night at the airport, waiting for the next flight back here. Oh, God, if you'd gone — "

He kissed her and, this time, she clung to him. She had dreamed of a moment like this, of Niall holding her as if he would never let her go, and of her own willing surrender. Now, miraculously, her dreams had become a reality. Niall loved her. How could she doubt it when his lips were so tender and his heart was thudding against the palm of her hand?

It was some time before he raised his head and smiled down at her. "I must have been off my head. If you felt like that about me, couldn't you have given a subtle hint?" he asked, with a quizzical gleam.

He slackened his hold slightly and she drew back a little, feeling a tremor of delight when his arms instantly tightened.

"Don't joke, Niall," she said softly. "If you knew how miserable I've been!"

"I know," he said, with feeling. "I've been going through a few hoops myself. Say it, Rachel — say you love me."

Her shyness of him, her paralysing sense of inadequacy, seemed to have melted like a mist in the morning sun. Slipping her arms round his neck, she locked her fingers at the back of his head.

"I love you. I've always loved you . . . since that first time you came to Anguna. Oh, darling Niall, couldn't you see it — didn't you guess?"

His voice thickened. "You never looked at me like this before. I thought you couldn't bear me to touch you."

She drew his head down until she could press her mouth against his lean brown cheek. "I wanted you to hold me like this more than anything in the world," she murmured softly.

There was an even longer interval before they drew apart again and Niall said rapidly, "Let's go home. I want a shower and a long cold drink and to be alone with you. I've a taxi waiting outside the gates." With an arm round her shoulders, he steered her towards the path round the house.

"Niall, how did you know where to find me?" she asked, when they were walking down the overgrown drive.

He gave her a swift veiled glance and his arm dropped from her shoulders. For an instant, she was afraid she had lost him again. But then he took her hand and gave it a quick reassuring squeeze.

"I seem to have been a fool in several directions," he said wryly. "I was driving home from the airport when I saw Hart going into town. Five minutes later he was on my tail to Moongates. Before I could get a word in, he'd told me that you had asked him to help you get away and that I was every kind of a blackguard to have made life such hell for you. He wouldn't tell me where you were until I . . . . well, until I made it clear that I'd had a taste of hell too."

"Weren't you very angry?" she asked warily.

"Yes, I was," he admitted. "But when he told me why you had been so unhappy I forgot about everything else. I can't say I like needing Hart's help to straighten my marriage out — but it's straight now, thank God. That's the main thing. Maybe I've judged him too harshly. I have an idea he's in love with you, poor devil. Did he tell you?"

She nodded. "Yes, this afternoon. But I've never thought of him as anything but a friend, Niall. You do believe that now, don't you?"

"I never really doubted it, my love. But lately, when things seemed to be going from bad to worse between us, I've been as jealous as hell of everyone who looked at you."

They had reached the last bend of the drive. Ahead, beyond the tall iron gates, the taxi waited. In the shade of the fringed sun canopy which replaced a hard roof on most Bermudan taxis, the coloured driver appeared to be taking a nap. He would not mind how long he had to wait as long as he was paid for his time.

Rachel stopped walking so that Niall also had to halt. Before they left "the Hart place" she wanted to feel that the last shadow of misunderstanding had been safely dispelled.

"I was jealous too," she said quietly. "I thought you still loved Nadine Oakhill. Are you sure you've really got over her, Niall? Are you certain?"

They were facing each other now. He touched her cheek with his forefinger, and his eyes held infinite tenderness.

"Yes, Hart mentioned Nadine," he said ruefully. "He more or less accused me of carrying on with her under your nose — though God knows how either of you could think that. I 'got over' Nadine years ago. It was a short-lived infatuation, and it ended with my detesting the very sight of her."

"But I don't understand — " Rachel began, and she told him about meeting Nadine in Hamilton and how the older woman had described their youthful love affair.

"Which you believed — ye gods!" he exclaimed violently. "Listen, I'll tell you the truth — the whole truth. Nadine is rotten, utterly rotten. She has no heart, no scruples, and no morals. But she deceives almost everyone." He paused for a moment, as if trying to recall the details of an episode which had long since become blurred and half forgotten.

"When we were first engaged, I thought I was the luckiest man in Bermuda," he went on, after some seconds. "I never dreamed I was really a prize dupe. Then, one night when I was supposed to be away on a fishing trip, I came back unexpectedly. I found her down at her parents' beach house — with some tourist she had picked up. The next day she came rushing round to Moongates in a panic and tried to convince me that the fellow had got her tight and she hadn't been responsible for her actions. When I wouldn't believe her, she lost her temper and flung the truth at me. She had never cared a rap for me personally — but she had fancied being mistress of Moongates and splashing my money around. She even boasted of all her other . . . adventures. And you thought I loved her!"

"Oh, Niall — how appalling," Rachel whispered.

He shrugged. "It was a narrow escape. I was lucky. Tell me, what on earth made you think I was still carrying that burnt-out torch?"

"Don't you remember our meeting that horrid Lancaster person on our wedding night? She mentioned Nadine, and you were so angry you didn't say a word all the way home."

"I was furious at the way she had looked you over. I can't stand that type of woman. It had nothing to do with Nadine." His mouth hardened. "It was Nadine who wrote that filthy note about you and Hart. I suspected as much at the time, and later I made her admit it."

"I know — at the wedding. I overheard you talking on the beach. I—I thought you were trying to make her confess she still loved you," Rachel said, very low.

He caught her in his arms. "You thought — oh, my God! Nadine hates me. I know what she's really like. She was trying to strike back at me," he said contemptuously.

"But, Niall, if you married me for . . . for love, why didn't you tell me?" Rachel asked softly.

He sighed, his lips close to her temple.

"I should have done, shouldn't I?" he said ruefully. "But you were so terribly young and inexperienced, sweetheart. My original idea was to bring you back to Moongates and wait for you to grow up a bit. Then, in Nassau, I saw how men looked at you, and I was afraid to play a waiting game. I imagined you losing your heart to some slick young wastrel, so I asked you to marry me at once."

"But couldn't you *see* I loved you?" she protested.

"I'm afraid I didn't think you were capable of love — calf love, perhaps, but not love in an adult context. Then when we got back to the *Dolphin* on our wedding night, you seemed so tense and nervous that I concluded you had only married me because you were even more scared of being alone in the world."

"Oh, Niall . . . and all the time I was simply longing for you to make love to me," she murmured shyly.

"You certainly never gave that impression. You seemed to flinch if I so much as glanced at you."

She raised her face to look up at him. "Must you go to New York again now?

Was your business there very important?"

Niall grinned. "Nothing is as important as our honeymoon. If Teaboy has things organised, we'll leave in the morning. I want you all to myself for a while."

Their hands linked, they walked down to the road. As Niall closed the creaking iron gates behind them, Rachel decided to tell about her meeting with her mother another time. She thought fleetingly of Bran . . . to whom she owed everything, but whom she would probably never see again. She thought even more briefly of Nadine . . . beautiful, vicious Nadine whom she need never have feared at all.

Then Niall turned from the gates and took her hand again, and she knew that a few weeks of doubt and despair were a small price to pay for the lifetime of happiness which lay ahead of them.

THE END

ROMANCE TITLES IN THE ULVERSCROFT LARGE PRINT SERIES

OCTAVO SIZE

Hospital Circles	*Lucilla Andrews*
A Hospital Summer	*Lucilla Andrews*
My Friend the Professor	*Lucilla Andrews*
Carpet of Dreams	*Susan Barrie*
Be My Guest	*Elizabeth Cadell*
Violetta	*Anne Duffield*
The Scent of Water	*Elizabeth Goudge*
The Herb of Grace	*Elizabeth Goudge*
The Middle Window	*Elizabeth Goudge*
The Bird in the Tree	*Elizabeth Goudge*
Doctor in Exile	*Maysie Greig*
The Generous Heart	*Dorothy Quentin*
In Trust to Fiona	*Renée Shann*
Anna and Her Daughters	*D. E. Stevenson*
Charlotte Fairlie	*D. E. Stevenson*
Katherine Wentworth	*D. E. Stevenson*
Celia's House	*D. E. Stevenson*
Winter and Rough Weather	*D. E. Stevenson*
South to Forget	*Essie Summers*
The Lark in the Meadow	*Essie Summers*

OTHER ROMANCE TITLES IN THE ORIGINAL ULVERSCROFT LARGE PRINT SERIES

QUARTO SIZE

Flowers from the Doctor	*Lucilla Andrews*
City of Forever	*Barbara Blackburn*
Stormy Haven	*Rosalind Brett*
Hotel Mirador	*Rosalind Brett*
Here I Belong	*Mary Burchell*
The Rhythm of Flamenco	*Isabel Chace*
The English Boss	*Joyce Dingwell*
The Green Popinjays	*Eleanor Fairburn*
The Golden Peaks	*Eleanor Farnes*
Desert Doorway	*Pamela Kent*
Lover Come Lonely	*Marsh Manning*
The Rebel Bride	*Eva McDonald*
Bring Back the Singing	*Stella Morton*
The House on the Hill	*Mairi O'Nair*
The Healing Tide	*Dorothy Quentin*
The Secret Heart	*Fay Ramsay*
Dear Dragon	*Sara Seale*
That Golden Summer	*Renée Shann*
Where No Roads Go	*Essie Summers*
Woman, Lovely Woman	*Guy Trent*
Piper's Gate	*Audrie Manley-Tucker*
The Honey is Bitter	*Violet Winspear*

FICTION TITLES IN THE ULVERSCROFT LARGE PRINT SERIES

OCTAVO SIZE

Flowers for Mrs. Harris and
Mrs. Harris goes to New York

Paul Gallico

Sandals for my Feet   *Phyllis Hastings*
Beauvallet   *Georgette Heyer*
The Convenient Marriage

Georgette Heyer

Faro's Daughter   *Georgette Heyer*
Devil's Cub   *Georgette Heyer*
The Corinthian   *Georgette Heyer*
The Toll-Gate   *Georgette Heyer*
Bride of Pendorric   *Victoria Holt*
Mistress of Mellyn   *Victoria Holt*
Menfreya   *Victoria Holt*
King of the Castle   *Victoria Holt*
Kirkland Revels   *Victoria Holt*
The Shivering Sands   *Victoria Holt*
Atlantic Fury   *Hammond Innes*
The Land God gave to Cain

Hammond Innes

Levkas Man   *Hammond Innes*
The Strode Venturer   *Hammond Innes*
The Wreck of the Mary Deare

Hammond Innes

The Lonely Skier   *Hammond Innes*
The River of Diamonds   *Geoffrey Jenkins*
The Safe Bridge   *Frances Parkinson Keyes*
The Brittle Glass   *Norah Lofts*

OTHER FICTION TITLES IN THE ORIGINAL ULVERSCROFT LARGE PRINT SERIES

QUARTO SIZE

Miss Bagshot goes to Tibet *Anne Telscombe*
The Courageous Exploits of Doctor Syn
R. Thorndike
Black Lobster *Donald Weir*

MYSTERY TITLES IN THE ULVERSCROFT LARGE PRINT SERIES

OCTAVO SIZE

Police at the Funeral — *Margery Allingham*
Death of a Ghost — *Margery Allingham*
A Kind of Anger — *Eric Ambler*
The Night They Killed Joss Varran — *George Bellairs*
The Sad Variety — *Nicholas Blake*
The Thirty-Nine Steps — *John Buchan*
In Spite of Thunder — *J. Dickson Carr*
The Saint on Guard — *Leslie Charteris*
The Saint Around the World — *Leslie Charteris*
The Mirror Crack'd from Side to Side — *Agatha Christie*
Ordeal by Innocence — *Agatha Christie*
Cards on the Table — *Agatha Christie*
Death on the Nile — *Agatha Christie*
Endless Night — *Agatha Christie*
Towards Zero — *Agatha Christie*
The Murder of Roger Ackroyd — *Agatha Christie*
Dumb Witness — *Agatha Christie*
Murder in Mesopotamia — *Agatha Christie*

The Clocks	*Agatha Christie*
The Moving Finger	*Agatha Christie*
Sad Cypress	*Agatha Christie*
The Mists of Fear	*John Creasey*
A Gun for Inspector West	*John Creasey*
Send Superintendent West	*John Creasey*
Nothing is the Number When You Die	
	Joan Fleming
The Long Short Cut	*Andrew Garve*
The Laughing Grave	*Victor Gunn*
The Next One to Die	*Victor Gunn*
The Unfinished Clue	*Georgette Heyer*
Death on Doomsday	*Elizabeth Lemarchand*
Gideon's Day	*J. J. Marric*
Gideon's Week	*J. J. Marric*
The Eye of a Serpent	*Geoffrey Peters*
The Dog Man	*Maurice Procter*
Devil's Due	*Maurice Procter*
If Death Ever Slept	*Rex Stout*
The Mystery of Swordfish Reef	
	Arthur Upfield

OTHER MYSTERY TITLES IN THE ORIGINAL ULVERSCROFT LARGE PRINT SERIES

QUARTO SIZE